SHERRY CRACKER GETS NORMAL

D.J. Connell was born in New Zealand and has lived and worked in various countries, first as a writer for a newspaper then for a non-profit organisation and later in advertising. Her first novel *Julian Corkle is a Filthy Liar* was published by Blue Door in 2010. D.J. Connell is a British national.

Also by D.J. Connell

Julian Corkle is a Filthy Liar

D.J. CONNELL

Sherry Cracker
Gets Normal

blue door

Blue Door
An imprint of HarperCollins*Publishers*
77–85 Fulham Palace Road
Hammersmith, London W6 8JB
www.harpercollins.co.uk

First published by Blue Door in 2011

A catalogue record for this book
is available from the British Library

ISBN 978-0-00-733219-9

Typeset in Minion by Palimpsest Book Production Limited,
Falkirk, Stirlingshire

Printed and bound in Great Britain by
Clays Ltd, St Ives plc

Mixed Sources
Product group from well-managed
forests and other controlled sources
www.fsc.org Cert no. SW-COC-001806
© 1996 Forest Stewardship Council
FSC

FSC is a non-profit international organisation established to promote the responsible
management of the world's forests. Products carrying the FSC label are independently
certified to assure consumers that they come from forests that are managed to meet the
social, economic and ecological needs of present or future generations.

Find out more about HarperCollins and the environment at
www.harpercollins.co.uk/green

To my funny, remarkable mother Marion and her accomplice, my excellent sister Jocelyn.

1

I can now safely say that nothing in life is random. Everything that occurs is connected to whatever has gone on before. If I had not visited Industry Drive I would not have seen the sign and taken an interest in the mayoral campaign. The cardboard square had been stapled to a wooden stake: 'Visit the site of Roger Bottle's proposed factory. Globcom – providing safe, efficient cleanup solutions.' I did not follow the arrow because this would have taken me back the way I had come and that was the last thing I wanted to do. The sign had aroused my curiosity and I made a mental note to follow it up.

I did not always understand the non-random principle. I had to learn it the hard way through a process called the Learning Curve. Apparently, the Learning Curve is a normal part of human experience. This is a comforting fact because, at least in this, I am like other people.

When I apply the non-random principle to the events of my life, I see them as a linear series of theatre scenes connected by an orange electrical cable that charges the dramatic incidents with confusion and opportunity. To get to the present day, the current has to run through all the earlier scenes, which means the decisions my mother made for me as a child still affect the way things work now.

It was my mother who chose our family dentist and it was the dentist who put me off power tools for life. The dentist must have been careless because as a young man he lost three fingers to a whirling chainsaw. I do not know how many times I have imagined this accident. I am thinking of it again right now. It happens very fast. The dentist attempts to pick up the power tool by its chain. There is a soft, dirty sound as his fingers fly off. The chainsaw slows and its motor stops. Then there is silence. The dentist looks at what is left of his hand and is very surprised.

The strange thing about the Learning Curve is that negative events seem to have the most impact. A cup of tea makes me smile but a bump on the head will make me think. That is what I have been doing a lot of lately, thinking. I think something big is going to happen soon. Julius Caesar probably felt the same way before he got a knife in the kidneys. Something is going on in the town. People are disgruntled and restless. There are signs and messages.

I found another message this morning on my way to work. I was an hour early and had stopped at the Kenneth Williams Memorial Rose Gardens to pass the time. I often go to the gardens before work because my employer does not arrive at the office until nine sharp and I do not have a key. He is very particular about office security and finances and does not believe in giving employees keys or paying overtime. If he finds me waiting in front of the office before nine, he calls me the 'early cuckoo bird'. It is his habit to repeat this several times as he unlocks the first door's three German locks while shaking his head. It is not my place to complain or answer back or even to make suggestions. My place is to do as I am told with maximum efficiency and minimum discussion. I understand the necessity of office efficiency but I find the non-discussion rule quite challenging at times.

My employer's name is Mr Chin and he was not born in Great Britain. He came here from Hong Kong after the territory was given back to the Chinese government and he has been very disappointed ever since. He says the chicken chow mein you find in this country is slop and that the so-called Chinese responsible for producing it should have their shirts removed in public and be beaten with green bamboo. 'No mercy is best policy,' he says. 'Must beat on backbone many time or fool never learn.'

That is how he talks. He has strong opinions and is very direct about voicing them. I appreciate this frank manner of speech and respect Mr Chin because he never promises anything he cannot deliver. Neither does he contradict himself. He likes to say that his word is gold and, as I have learned, there is truth to this.

On my first day at work, he told me that I would be employed on a project basis for a limited period of time. I signed no contract but according to my calculations there will be enough work to see me through an Open University degree in Criminology and Psychological Studies. I have chosen this course of study because criminology is a vocation with a future. Crime is on the increase in Britain and job security is high on my agenda. I have already paid the course fees and am looking forward to commencing studies at the end of summer.

This morning I found another person in the rose gardens when I arrived, a grey-haired man in a long fuchsia trench coat. It was the coat that caught my eye. Fuchsia is an unusual colour on a man. I watched him circle the memorial walk with a small yellow dog. He did a lot of shuffling and spent a long time examining the floral clock. Its hands are planted in a white succulent and are impressive against the blue forget-me-nots of the clock face.

I turned to watch him leave and noticed a new message scrawled in pink on the brick wall near the entrance. I did not know who had left the graffiti but it must have been someone with a civic conscience because it had been written in chalk: 'THE TIME HAS COMETH FOR ALL THE GOOD MEN.' Each capital letter had been written in a very firm hand and the choice of 'COMETH' was unusual. The author was clearly a passionate, even biblically–minded person.

This was the second message I had found in the rose gardens within two days. The first was a piece of paper with a single word, 'Beefeater', written in curly handwriting and attached to the mesh fence outside the urinal. The paper had been pleated lengthways and neatly tied to the wire with a single, flattened knot. It is a custom in Japan to leave such paper messages outside Buddhist temples. This is done to invite good fortune or ward off bad luck. The Japanese are a very pragmatic people but they are also highly superstitious. This is called a paradox and cannot be easily explained.

Another person might not have noticed the messages in the rose gardens but the written word has uncommon appeal for me. When I enter a building, I read 'Push' on the door handle out loud in my mind. I have seen people idly step over a crisp bag on the pavement while I pause to read 'Enjoy the tongue-curling pleasure of tangy salt and vinegar.'

I have a file for FOUND WORDS in a subsection of my OBSERVATIONS ring binder. This binder is organised in chronological order and begins with an entry on December sixth of last year: 'Mr Chin changed the locks today. The newsagent put up a new window display of birthday cards decorated with pressed flowers. No one knew it was my birthday.'

My mother would have described a window display of birthday cards on someone's birthday as a coincidence. I have stopped using that word because it implies chance events in a random existence and, as I have already noted, life does not follow a random or even logical course.

The author B. Sigmund Pappenheimer believes that the meaning of life is to find the meaning of life, which is one of those ideas like infinity that I find difficult to grasp. If I think about it too long I get an empty feeling behind my sternum, which is the long flat bone located in the centre of the chest. You should avoid being punched on the sternum because the bone can shatter and puncture the lungs. Professional boxers take this risk every time they enter the ring. Boxing is a dangerous activity, like riding a motorcycle without a helmet. It is not something I plan to take up in the future. I think punching does more harm than good.

I am a big fan of B.S. Pappenheimer's series 'Nuggets of Life', and own all eight of his books. These I bought by mail order from a PO box address. The books have a small paragraph inside the back cover, which explains that B.S. Pappenheimer is a Troubadour Philosopher with a PhD in Philosophology from an American university. It also says that he is a recluse and lives at an unknown location. It is unfortunate that B.S. Pappenheimer does not have a real address. I would like to meet him or at least write to him and discuss his theories. His ideas are challenging for someone without training in philosophology but his writing is very compelling.

Here is a quote from his latest book, *Wheels Within Wheels*: 'Seen from above, the world is a swirling ball of dust. Its inhabitants, a wriggling swamp of DNA curls.' His writing is very poignant and I would not be surprised if he won a Nobel Prize one day. He certainly makes me put on my thinking cap and that has to be a good thing.

The world was a lot more confusing for me before I created my OBSERVATIONS ring binder and began organising my thoughts. At least now I recognise certain patterns in human behaviour. But recognising is not the same as understanding or engaging, as well I know. For as long as I can remember, I have felt suspended over human society in a Perspex pod. This is quite an isolated position, and while my separateness poses no obstacle to observation and information-gathering, I still have a long way to go in terms of understanding human nature.

I have now compiled substantial character profiles of nearly everyone I know and it makes me aware of just how unusual people can be. I have learned that everyone has at least one tic that would be considered unusual if you read about it in an encyclopaedia. For example, Mr Chin likes to clean his ears with a paper clip. He does this at least once a day with his eyes closed and his lips pursed into a point. I have seen the paper clip he uses. It is always the same one and it has been half unbent to allow deeper penetration. This may sound like a strange if not dangerous habit but Mr Chin is a successful businessman and is not the least bit self-conscious about cleaning his ears this way.

One of my mother's tics was to take on a completely different personality when she visited Mr Da Silva's butcher's shop. As she entered, her top lip would stop moving and she would use only the bottom half of her mouth to talk. This made her sound like Marlon Brando's Don Corleone but she never did anything violent or illegal like the cinematic character. When she was in the butcher's shop, she would act in a very respectful manner and give the various meats the same attention that a nun would give the Bible.

I have not heard from my mother for over half a year since she left to marry a sheep farmer in New Zealand called Barry Bunker. They met through a dating service for bachelor farmers and enjoyed a whirlwind romance over the telephone. Pastoral life has its advantages but it can be a lonely and isolated existence. Mr Bunker sent photos of his farm to my mother who was impressed with its acreage and sheep population. The farm was located in hill country and a one-hour tractor ride from its closest neighbour.

My life has been a lot simpler since my mother left. She was a fierce woman and believed she knew best about raising a child despite having never received formal training or supervision. When I was five years old, she launched a campaign to stop me biting my nails. Her method involved creeping up behind me and slapping my hand away from my mouth. This approach did not stop my nail biting but it did prompt a twitch to develop on one side of my face. The twitch went away once she lost interest and ceased her campaign.

Nail biting has always given me genuine pleasure but like all good things, you can take it too far. It was Mr Chin who pointed out that the habit had gone on long enough.

'This chew, chew, chew get on my nerve,' he said.

'It's a nervous habit,' I said. 'From childhood.'

'Rolling of drawer not from childhood. Rolly, rolly, rolly always and constantly get on my nerve.'

He was referring to my habit of opening and shutting my large file drawer at least one hundred times a day. I knew it was one hundred times because I kept a written tally. Again, this was something that gave me pleasure. The metal drawer was heavy but extremely well-designed. Its small plastic wheels made a delightful whir as they moved quickly along their metal guide rails, never catching or jamming.

'Sorry.'

'Sorry not enough.' Mr Chin shook his head and handed me a copy of the town's free newspaper, the *Cockerel*. 'You need a kind of hurdy-gurdy man with pendulum that swing. Best quality gurdy man from Hong Kong. But beggar not chooser.'

On the back page, he had circled an advertisement in the Classifieds: 'Harrison Tanderhill, Registered Hypnotherapist and Master Chakraologist Imperial Grade A. Put yourself in the hands of an expert. Will cure addictions, perversions and overeating.'

I was interested in the addictions part.

2

I must have had expectations because I was disappointed when I arrived at the address. Mr Tanderhill lived on a service road running parallel to Industry Drive. This was not a very attractive setting for a professional therapist. His brick bungalow looked rundown and lonely beside all the warehouses, car-sales yards and showrooms.

In the days when Britain used to produce things, Industry Drive was the pride of the town and was called the 'Golden Mile'. You can see how it once looked at the photo display in the council annexe building. The photos show smoke pumping out of chimneys and busy conveyor belts inside battery and bottle factories, men in overalls inspecting labels and working levers connected to cogs. One photo dated 1949 is entitled 'A Hive of Industry', and shows the mayor handing a large wooden key to the town planner, the Right Hon. Eric Rogerson. It was the town planner's idea to consolidate industry along the road and start the Blue Line bus service to and from the area. This period in the town's history is known as the Reconstruction Years. The mayor is wearing a large ceremonial chain in the photo and has his hand resting on the Right Hon. Rogerson's shoulder. His fingers are small and look like miniature party sausages.

Many of the factories had already closed by the time I was born. As a child I would sit at the window and watch the last of the workers as they headed to the bus stop each morning. They wore rough woollen clothes and walked with their heads down, carrying lunch boxes and thermos flasks. As I grew up, I saw fewer and fewer of them. Some bought popular cars like Honda Civics and did not use the bus service any more but most were eventually laid off as the factories closed down. People like my mother blamed the recession on the European Union, particularly on the French. Others said it was Margaret Thatcher's fault. These days, people blame bankers and many say the Chinese are the cause of Britain's problems. They argue that if Chinese labour was not so cheap, industry would not have relocated. I think we should not blame the Chinese. It cannot be pleasant to sew handbags for a few pence a day. Here in Britain you cannot even buy a sandwich for less than a pound.

Most of the former factories along Industry Drive have now been converted into warehouses for imported products, which is something I do not understand. Britain is rich by world standards but does not produce or export much of anything any more except weapons, of which it produces quite a lot. It is a surprising fact that the United Kingdom is one of the world's top arms exporters. How can Britain buy so many products from other countries when it does not have much to sell except armaments? This goes against the supply and demand principle of capitalism, a popular socioeconomic system based upon the ruthless control of the means of production.

Mr Tanderhill's house was wedged between two former factories. One had been converted into a carpet showroom while the other appeared to be a storage facility. Many of this warehouse's windows had been broken and wooden pallets were strewn over the pavement outside its large double doors. On the side of the building someone had used green chalk to write 'TRUST' in large capital letters. This was an unusual message to leave on a wall and I paused to consider its meaning. I was still considering when a loud noise sent a shiver up my legs to my sacrum, which is the triangular-shaped bone at the base of the spine. Somewhere inside the warehouse, a chainsaw had been started.

I quickly entered the gate of the bungalow. To get to the front door, I had to walk around a yellow Ford Escort without wheels. The car was sitting on blocks with its windows open. Someone had painted 'FOR SALE' on the windscreen from inside so it read back to front. The lawn had not been mown for a long time and was littered with things like old shoes and food wrappers. There were several wine bottles on the front steps.

The doorbell had a small chrome arm. I pulled it but did not hear a *ding*. I tried knocking but my knuckles produced only a dull sound on the door's wooden panel. I picked up an empty bottle of Australian Cabernet Sauvignon and used it to pound the door several times. The sound was loud and had an immediate effect. I heard running from inside. The door was yanked open.

A tall man appeared in the doorway. He looked at me, blinking. 'What?' he said. His manner was unfriendly.

'Good morning,' I said. 'Mr Tanderhill?'

He nodded and then seemed to think better of it and shook his head. His eyes were large and bulbous, which made me wonder about the condition of his thyroid gland. I might have become preoccupied with this gland if I had not noticed another unusual facial feature. The area between his top lip and nose was expansive and made me think of Robert Mugabe. I took a step back and realised the man was dressed in a blue towelling bathrobe open in a V at the chest. My mother would have described the hair on his chest as a 'thatch'. She believed that hair on a man was a sign of virility and was partial to Portuguese men for this very reason. It was her opinion that hairy men have classic good looks. I am not sure that I agree but body hair must be a comfort in winter.

'I don't live here,' he finally said.

'I've come for my treatment.'

'Treatment?' His expression changed. He glanced at a large gold watch on his wrist. 'But you're an hour early.'

'Correct.'

'I'm in the middle of a business meeting.' He hesitated, noticing me glance at his bathrobe. 'It's a conference call. I'm an internationally busy man. You'll have to wait in the vestibule until I've finished my affairs.'

I was led into the entrance hall and told to sit on a guest stool, which was a wooden box with several newspapers on top. Mr Tanderhill went out another door at the far end, leaving me alone in the dark. The hall was narrow and in the gloom I vaguely made out several other boxes and belongings stacked along the opposite wall. From the far end, I heard a door shut and then silence, and then the flush of a toilet. This was followed by footsteps, which moved in an arc to the room behind my back. I heard movement, a *click* and then a *bang*. It sounded as if furniture was being rearranged.

Five minutes later, a door opened to my right. Mr Tanderhill appeared with his hands in prayer and said, '*Namaste*', which is a word derived from Sanskrit and a popular salutation among practitioners of yoga. He was dressed in a wrinkled grey Indian caftan with matching trousers. The grey did nothing to flatter his complexion, which had the puckers and dull veneer of a smoker. I averted my gaze and found myself looking at his feet. These were clad in sandals and on each of his toes was a bristling tuft of hair. Noting my interest in his appearance, he patted his chest.

'I'm an Indian and a Hindu. This is my garb.'

I am no expert on the people and religions of the Indian sub-continent but Mr Tanderhill did not look like someone from that part of the world. His skin was pink and his eyes were murky blue. What was left of the hair on his head was sandy with grey around his ears. He did not speak with an Indian accent.

He tightened his lips in a determined, businesslike way. 'Kindly follow me to the therapy room.'

I was waved into what must have originally been the house's living room. It was furnished with a brown couch, a wooden chair and a battered vinyl massage table. There was nothing on the walls and no curtains. The room smelled of human beings and mentholated ciga-rettes. All the windows were closed. Outside I could see the Ford Escort and the warehouse wall with the graffiti. The car was not an attractive sight but it did block the view from the street, which was of some comfort to me. The couch rolled back and clicked as I sat down. Something blue was sticking out from under its base. It looked like towelling.

Mr Tanderhill remained standing with his hands behind his back.

He bent in my direction and opened his eyes wide, revealing his irises in their murky entirety. I took this to be the look of a professional hypnotherapist and reminded myself that I had come to him with a purpose. My bad habits were interfering with my work. Something had to be done about them.

'Tell me about yourself.' He moved his hands forwards and up the sides of his legs as if drawing pistols from holsters. He pointed his index fingers at me. 'Clear the air. Purge your chakras.'

'I did already on the phone.'

'It's natural to feel embarrassed.'

'I'm not embarrassed. I've come here because of Mr Chin.'

'I bet you have.' Mr Tanderhill smiled and closed his eyes, rubbing his hands together several times. He said, 'Hmm, hmm, hmm,' and then fell silent. He remained standing with his eyes closed, swaying on the balls of his feet for a full minute.

I coughed and his eyes flicked open.

'Climb on to the massage table. We'll get to the bottom of this Chin business.'

'I don't want a massage. I've come for hypnotherapy.'

'I know that! I'm a certified professional. Royal Academy.' He rolled his eyes impatiently and pointed to the table. 'If you would feel more comfortable in less clothing, go ahead and remove it. I'm not averse.'

'I'd prefer to keep my clothes on.'

'It'll make my work a lot harder.' Mr Tanderhill sighed and held out his long fingers for me to view. 'God has given me golden fingers. If you keep your clothes on I'll have to send my healing rays through the layers.'

I did not want to displease Mr Tanderhill, especially not before receiving hypnotherapeutic assistance. Reminding myself that he was there to help me, I removed my cardigan and climbed on to the massage table, which wobbled in a disconcerting way. I then lay back stiffly with my arms at my sides. To take my mind off the possibility of the table collapsing, I imagined myself as a soldier on duty outside Buckingham Palace. These soldiers are called Grenadier Guards and wear a controversial headdress called the busby, which is made from the fur of the Canadian black bear. I was trying to guess the weight of one of these large, impractical hats when Mr Tanderhill told me to shut my eyes; he was going to perform a 'Chakra Flush' in preparation for hypnotics. As I closed my eyes, I told myself that all my bad habits would be flushed out of my system forever.

I remained still with my eyes closed for several minutes listening to the swish of his movements until the desire to know what he was doing got the better of me. I opened an eye and was surprised to find him making circular motions in the air over my torso. He could have been polishing a Ford Escort or, the thought occurred to me, doing an air massage over my chest. I opened the other eye and crossed my arms over my chest.

'What are you doing?' I asked.

'I was working your higher chakras but you've ruined it now,' he replied with a sigh. His shoulders sagged. As he bit his top lip, I noticed that his teeth were stained and uneven. 'We'll have to skip the flush. I only hope you'll be more cooperative with the hypnotics.'

'You were standing very close.'

'I'm a professional!'

'That's reassuring.'

'When I look at you I don't see a nondescript young woman in an unattractive woollen top and tartan trousers. I see unhappy chakras. I see spiritual blockage, corporeal malfunction, psychological disarray. To my professional eye, you're a soul in a sac and your sac is leaking energy. It's called soul fatigue.'

'I do get tired in the evenings. I thought it might be iron deficiency. I'm a tea drinker and tea is known to rob the body of iron. Do you think you can help?'

'Friends are angels who lift us to our feet when our wings have trouble remembering how to fly.'

'Sorry?'

'Listen this time, for God's sake! Friends are angels who lift us to our feet when our wings have trouble remembering how to fly.'

'We're not friends.'

'I'm thoroughly aware of that. Strict professional distance is part of my creed.'

'Perhaps it would be better for me to sit on the couch.' It was unsettling to lie on a table without a cardigan.

'Stay right where you are. The soul is more receptive when the body is prone.'

He leaned over and stared with his bulging eyes into mine. A shiver travelled up my spine and tightened my jaw. My face became hot. Either I was alarmed or Mr Tanderhill's hypnotherapy was taking effect. Again, I reminded myself that he was a certified professional and tried to relax.

'I am now removing this valuable Hindu medal from around my neck. I want you to keep your eyes on it. Concentrate, and keep your eyes on the medal.' His voice was firm and his movements were slow as he removed a chain with a metallic disc from around his neck. He began swinging it over my face.

'Concentrate! You are going to feel sleepy, so sleepy that you will fall asleep. You will hear my voice and remember only what I tell you to remember. You will tell me all there is to know about this Chin and I will cleanse your mind of its psychic toxins. When I say, "Hello, anybody home?" you will wake up and feel that no time has passed. Now concentrate on the medal.'

I willed my body to relax and my pulse rate to slow. I concentrated on the disc swinging above my face. It was the size of a thumbnail and the colour of aluminium. My eyes moved up the chain to Mr Tanderhill's fingers, which were thin and hairy. His nails were grimy and short enough to be those of a nail biter. I thought of Mr Chin and blinked before bringing my eyes back to the medallion, willing myself to concentrate on its movements. On its surface was an embossed pattern that made me think of Mr Da Silva. The butcher had been a serious Catholic who closed his shop on Fridays and kept plaster figurines of the Virgin in the meat display of his window. At Christmas, he would create a full nativity scene with mounds of sausages and rows of lamb chops as a backdrop. My mother was a big fan of these displays and called Mr Da Silva an artist. She also said it was a shame he was Catholic and a tragedy that he had married. He was a swarthy man with very hairy forearms. I brought my attention back to the medallion and reminded myself to feel sleepy.

Mr Tanderhill noticed my restlessness. 'For God's sake, just concentrate on the medal! I haven't got all day.'

'Sorry.'

'The medal. Watch the medal. You're feeling sleepy, very sleepy.'

Strangely, I did feel sleepy. My body seemed to sink into the massage table. As my eyelids fell shut, an image of Mr Chin flashed before me. He was sitting in his Komfort King executive chair, shouting. When I tried to work out what this unsettling image could mean, my thoughts would not align. I struggled to stay alert but sleep, like one of those enormous Hawaiian surfing waves, knocked me down and pulled me under.

'Hello, anybody home?' The words were like an alarm clock going off in the centre of my brain. This area is known as the third eye and is the seat of the pineal gland, a small endocrine gland shaped like a pine cone.

The question had come from a strange man in the doorway. He was of medium height and wiry, and had the sharp features of an operator of a sideshow shooting gallery. He was dressed in flared blue jeans, cowboy boots and a John Wayne hat. His checked shirt had press-studs and pointed pocket flaps. He could have passed for a country and western singer if not for the haloes of grease around his pockets. There were dark smudges on his hands and face, which made me wonder whether he was a bicycle mechanic. He winked at me. I looked away.

Strange!

I was no longer lying on the massage table but seated on the couch next to my handbag. Its zipper was undone and the bag was open. I could not remember opening it or getting off the table. I pushed my knuckles into my eyes and rubbed hard until neon points of light appeared. When I opened them again Mr Tanderhill was striding over to the cowboy.

'How dare you!' He was trying to whisper but the absence of furnishings gave the room excellent acoustics.

'Didn't know you were entertaining,' said the cowboy. He called out to me. 'Howdy tooty, darling.'

'Get out, Shanks!' Mr Tanderhill made a wild pointing gesture. 'You're interrupting a professional session.'

'I can see that.' Shanks howled like an American coyote, which was appropriate given his Wild West clothing.

'Get out!'

'Well, pardon little ol' me.' He winked at me again and flattened a hand against his greasy chest in the manner of an apologetic duke. He smirked at Mr Tanderhill. 'I need your *professional* opinion on some merchandise. A van load of very nice Husqvarnas.'

Mr Tanderhill threw the balls of his palms on to Shanks's chest and shoved him into the hall. Shanks was still protesting as the hairy hand of the hypnotherapist snaked around the door and pulled it shut. I could hear them talking loudly as I hunted for my cardigan.

'You're ruining everything!' Mr Tanderhill's voice was shrill.

'They're very nice Huskies. He says he'll take them somewhere else.'

'You're not listening, you fool! I'm telling you, I've struck gold.'

I stopped moving, my stomach gripped by the urgent feeling that accompanies vomiting, an upward rushing sensation from my duodenum to the base of my tongue. I had to get out of the bungalow. I pushed myself to my feet and realised my hands were damp with perspiration.

Outside the door, there was scuffling.

'What the hell are you doing?' Shanks sounded surprised.

'Look at this. It's a valuable Hindu medal.'

'Looks like crap to me.'

'Take a closer look.'

'How can I look with you waving it about like that?'

'For God's sake, just keep your eyes on the medal.' Mr Tanderhill's words were followed by a slap.

'Ouch!'

'Concentrate. Keep your eyes on it. You're feeling sleepy, very sleepy.'

I heard a loud thud followed by confused movements. A door opened somewhere. There was shuffling and dragging. I found my cardigan rolled up next to the arm of the couch and stuffed it in my bag. I could feel my heart beating in the back of my throat as I opened the door and peered into the empty hall before slipping out of the therapy room. Taking care not to make any noise, I pulled open the front door and stepped outside. The day was still overcast but the sun had moved higher behind the clouds. A chunk of time had elapsed. I felt disoriented as I stepped over the wine bottles and around the Escort to walk swiftly down the path.

At the gate, I glanced at the side of the neighbouring building and saw something I had not noticed before. 'TRUST' was only the first part of the message. Below in smaller letters were the words, 'NOT THE FALSE PROPHET'.

A stocky man in overalls was leaning against a white van parked next to the warehouse. As I broke into a run, he called out: 'Ten quid on the chestnut nag. Ha, ha.' I did not look back and kept running until I reached the bus stop on Industry Drive. There I opened my bag and removed my cardigan.

Strange!

My purse was gone. I rummaged inside the bag, taking out my notebook and pens, two multigrain cereal bars, town map, lip balm, tissues, three hair clips and the large colourful handkerchief I carried for rainy days. My passport was still tucked in the side pocket but the purse had disappeared. There was only one place it could be but the thought of returning to the hypnotherapist's bungalow made me feel nauseous.

I held out my hand as the number five Blue Line bus approached the stop. The bus door opened but I did not move. The driver gave me an impatient look.

'I've lost my purse,' I said, shaking my head.

'You mean you've got no money,' he said, revving his engine.

I nodded.

'Take a bloody hike then.' The door closed with a hiss.

As the bus pulled away I noticed a large banner advertisement printed along its side. It showed the head and shoulders of a man in a tuxedo resembling Sir Winston Churchill. He was holding up a hand and flashing Sir Winston's famous V sign but instead of regular fingers he had two fried fish fingers. Coming out of his mouth was a speech bubble: 'Nack's Fish Fingers. The winner's gold medal dinner.'

As I walked home, I tried to make sense of what had just happened. Something had occurred between Mr Tanderhill's massage table and the couch. Time had passed, at least half an hour. But the harder I thought, the more elusive this period of time became and the more uncomfortable I felt. There was a blank where there should have been a memory of events. I had no recollection of what had occurred or what had been said.

Industry Drive is a long road and I was quite disheartened by the time I reached my flat.

3

I have seen the man in the fuchsia trench coat every morning this week. He must be quite public-spirited because he always brings a plastic bag to pick up his dog's droppings at the rose gardens. Many dog owners do not bother with such precautions, which is not very responsible. Excrement is unpleasant but in the worst-case scenario, it can kill. In France, thousands of people slip on it every year. Most victims are mildly injured but some actually lose their lives. The government of France publishes annual statistics on such tragedies. The figures do not speak positively about French dog owners.

For several decades, Laos was part of the French empire and probably had a problem with dog excrement until the Japanese arrived during the war and created other, more complex problems. Japan does not publish statistics on dog-related deaths and is by all accounts a very clean if not severe nation. I imagine the footpaths of Laos were reasonably clean until the French briefly reclaimed the country after the war. When the Americans started bombing Vietnam decades later, they also bombed Laos for good measure. From 1964 to 1973, the American air force dropped two million tons of bombs on Laos. This is twice the amount of bombs dropped on Germany during World War II, which is quite a lot when you consider the small size of Laos and the fact that the Americans were not actually at war with the country.

This morning, after cleaning up his dog's business, the man in the fuchsia trench coat stood looking at the floral clock for a long time. The minute hand moved from seven to ten while he shuffled his feet and the dog sniffed at the flowerbeds.

The clock is a very attractive timepiece and a legacy of the Beautification Drive pursued by the town council during the Benevolent Years of the fifties. According to the information panels at the council photo display, it was during this period that many trees and flowerbeds were planted around public facilities to 'enrich the lives of residents with verdant niches'. You can still find traces of garden structures near the old library building but very few of the original trees remain standing. Beautification was not a priority under Jerry Clench who was mayor throughout my childhood and adolescence and might have kept the post if he had not bankrupted the council. He was sacked last week for gross financial mismanagement. His black Range Rover was impounded and his personal financial assets were frozen.

This weekend an election will be held for a new mayor. The *Cockerel* has dubbed it the 'Ballot of the Bloody Knight' because of the ancient bylaw on which the town's unique electoral system is based. The bylaw is the only one like it in Great Britain and dates back to the thirteenth century, which is quite a long time ago when you think about it. It gives the townspeople the right to hold a weekend election to elect their own mayor and was enacted during the ill-advised Crusade of 1271 when the local lord and all the churchmen rode off to the Middle East on the town's finest horses. The bylaw was supposed to be a temporary measure but remained in place when the town leaders were ambushed and killed before they reached Jerusalem. Two of these unfortunate knights are featured on the town's coat of arms. One has an arrow through his chest and the other is missing his head. Both are bleeding profusely.

For the first time in my life, I am old enough to participate in an election. But voting is a civic responsibility and I do not feel ready to accept this mantle. It does not seem right for me to participate in choosing a leader when I am not a bona fide member of the local society. Observing is not the same as engaging, as well I know.

At five minutes to nine, the man turned to leave, pausing as he passed my bench. 'Time is a like a fowl,' he said. 'But does it fly towards us or do we fly towards it?' He did not wait for a reply but turned on his heel and headed for the gate with the dog trotting after him and a delicate floral fragrance lingering in his wake.

As I stood and prepared to leave the gardens, I was surprised to find new graffiti on the pavement below the CCTV camera. The message had been scrawled around the base of the pole in green chalk. By now, I recognised the bold hand and capital letters. Removing the notebook from my bag, I copied down the words under today's date.

This new chalk message and the man's poignant comment about time were on my mind as I waited for Mr Chin to unlock the office door at the foot of the stairs. It is my habit to talk to him as he does this and I found myself repeating the man's words. Since Mr Chin is not a native speaker of English and I did not want a misunderstanding, I substituted the 'fowl' with 'chicken' to avoid confusion with the word 'foul'. I had not wanted to upset Mr Chin but that is exactly what occurred.

'What you mean?' he asked.

'It's a comment about time,' I said.

'Not just comment! Very intelligent and wise. Even tricky twist at end.' His eyes narrowed and he stared at me without moving. 'Someone tell you Chin is chicken?'

'No.'

'You visit Mandarin?'

'No.'

'You visit Jade Dragon?'

'No.'

'Chin not chicken!'

'Correct.'

I could not explain about the man in the gardens without admitting that I had been too early for work. I tried smiling but Mr Chin did not smile back. He observed me as I sat down at my desk and went through the motions of opening the phonebook and turning on my computer.

It is difficult to avoid Mr Chin's gaze because our desks are directly opposite each other. Mine faces the window and on the wall behind it hangs a large mirror that provides Mr Chin with a view of my back. There are only two of us in the office but we have enough furniture, computer equipment and telephones for ten. These furnishings were purchased in a liquidation sale and are arranged at one end of the large room like a circle of covered wagons on a prairie. In the centre of the circle is a decorative wooden table with a floral arrangement of silk flowers. The only other ornamentation in the room is a large fish tank with a bubbling oxygenator. The tank sits on tall metal legs against the far wall and contains several aquatic plants but no fish. Next to this is a standard lamp with a pink conical lampshade. The fish tank came from a Chinese restaurant that closed down but the lamp was in the office when Mr Chin moved in.

He was still watching me as I dialled up my first customer of the morning, a dentist from Dundee with the faint, whispery voice of an elderly person. The dentist was not friendly at first but warmed up once I explained our business and made my proposal.

I find this is often the case with dental professionals. Dentistry is a respectable profession and dentists are often proud and standoffish as individuals. You have to approach them in the correct manner or you get nowhere. The technique I use is called the Honey Trap and was invented and taught to me by Mr Chin. It is a simple yet effective technique: if the dentist is a man, which is often the case, I use a very soft voice and take a big gaspy breath every ten or so words. By the eleventh word I usually have his attention. With female dentists, I simply introduce myself and immediately start talking about financial incentives. The Honey Trap involves a strict set of prompts and responses and I am not permitted to diverge from this formula. This technique works over the phone but it would not work in person because I do not have a convincing personality. Mr Tanderhill was correct when he described me as nondescript. People often do not recognise me, even after several meetings. An effective salesperson needs recognisable charm and a winning smile. I do not smile often and I have never won anything in my life. Small talk is another thing I have yet to master. It is on my 'To Do' list along with most other social skills.

The Honey Trap is an effective business tool but will not be helpful once I finish calling all the dentists in the UK and Republic of Ireland and must find a new job. That is when I will need a university degree to launch a new vocation.

Since I joined Mr Chin's office, I have called virtually every dentist in the lowlands of Scotland to the city of Dundee. According to *The Greatest Cities of Great Britain*, Dundee was founded on the three J's: jute, jam and journalism. Today it is a vibrant modern city and popular tourist destination. The guidebook says the people of Dundee are naturally generous and among the friendliest in the world: 'Gracious and polite, the charming folk of this bonny wee city greet you with dazzling smiles and open arms. Forget the old adage about the Scot being a stingy hoarder. The hearts of Dundonians are warm and their sporrans are deep and generous.'

My work is always easier when dentists respond positively to the Honey Trap. It can be upsetting when someone shouts in my ear or hangs up abruptly. I came across quite a few disgruntled dentists when I first tried calling clinics in London. The manners I encountered certainly put me off having any dental work done there.

The official title of my job is Gold Purchase Consultant. Mr Chin says we make a lot of dentists very happy and I believe he is right. We take unwanted gold off their hands and give them cash in return. I have noticed that people appreciate cash, especially dentists who nearly always have some gold in a drawer or cabinet. The dental industry's attachment to this precious metal is historical. For centuries, gold was the best tooth filling money could buy. People even used to insert chips in their front teeth for decorative purposes but these days it is mainly rap music enthusiasts who seek this kind of dental augmentation. The most popular fillings are now made from composite materials or high-quality ceramics. Unfortunately for Mr Chin, these have no resale value.

Nearly all the gold I purchase comes from crowns in teeth that have been extracted. Dentists often keep this gold because most people are too upset after having teeth pulled to ask about it. I doubt that I would remember to ask about mine. Tooth extraction can be painful and is often traumatic for the dental patient.

As a gold purchase consultant, my job is to make the first contact and break the ice using the Honey Trap. Once I have established the existence of surplus gold and the dentist's willingness to sell it, Mr Chin takes over and handles negotiations. We are a team but the relationship is strictly a boss-assistant one. Mr Chin has very fixed ideas about business and has no interest in my opinions. I am forbidden to take initiative or deviate from the Honey Trap. This arrangement is ideal for me because I work best within set parameters. Decision-making is something I find difficult, especially when I am dealing with an aggressive dentist.

Mr Chin had kept his eye on me while I talked to the Dundee dentist and was still watching when I pushed the hold button and signalled for him to pick up the phone. The elderly dentist had just agreed to sell a shoebox of gold crowns. He told me he had been collecting them since 1958, which is the year the first parking meter was installed in England. The dentist said he would be happy to get rid of the box. It was taking up cupboard space and was now too heavy for him to lift.

I thought the purchase would make Mr Chin happy and I was right. When he got off the phone he took his personal chopsticks from his drawer and drummed on the desktop for at least thirty seconds. He was smiling with his mouth open and I could see the glint of gold fillings in his molars. The smile was still there when he left to eat an early lunch at the Mandarin restaurant.

There are two Chinese restaurants within walking distance of our office, which is located near the centre of town above the old Babylon Cinema. The Babylon was closed down in 1981 because of an electrical problem but had been a popular venue in its heyday. Its entrance is very ornate with a large metal awning and pillars designed to resemble the façade of a Roman bathhouse. I know precisely when it closed because you can still see the faded stills for *Cat People* in the display case on the wall next to the cinema entrance. The showpiece of the

24

display is a length of dusty fake fur with the caption: 'Actual replica of tail worn by Nastassja Kinski.' I never saw *Cat People* but apparently it was a popular movie with nude scenes about people who turned into large cats. It was released before I was born.

The door to the office stairs is located behind one of the ornate pillars and is reinforced by steel rails to prevent access with a crowbar. Mr Chin had another steel door with a powerful spring hinge installed at the top of the stairs. He monitors the doorway from where he sits which happens to be directly above the trapdoor to the old projection room. This trapdoor is locked and covered with a colourful Chinese carpet square. Mr Chin's desk and chair are positioned on top of the carpet. He says the projection room is dangerous and has forbidden me to go anywhere near it. I obey his instructions but do not understand his decision to sit above an unsafe trapdoor.

By the time Mr Chin returned to the office, I had called two more dentists and set up purchases of several more crowns. Mr Chin looked very different after his early lunch. His cheeks were red and shiny and his eyes were bloodshot. In his hand was a plastic bag from the Mandarin restaurant. It clinked as he placed it on his desk. Licking his lips, he circled the furniture, saying, 'Yes, yes, yes.' The only time I had seen him so agitated was during the Chinese New Year celebrations when he won a bottle of plum liquor in a raffle. I had not been working at the office very long and was quite surprised by the sudden liveliness of his manner. He was now showing the same vivacity and looking very pleased with himself.

'Today now holiday. Chin require rest and relaxation,' he said, waving his small hand around. He sat down on his Komfort King and pushed his head against its vinyl cushion. 'Go home. Go shopping. Go find boyfriend. Do what normal girl do.'

'Normally I work,' I said. 'Today is Friday, a normal working day.'

'Normally, normally, normally. What normally? You not normal girl. Very abnormal in fact.'

'Abnormal?' I sat up straight and made a mental note to record the word in the COMMENTS subsection of my OBSERVATIONS ring binder. It is the Chinese custom to criticise and I have learned to take such criticism as encouragement. Mr Chin's assessment was like a red flag.

'Certainly abnormal. No friend. No boyfriend. No dog. Not even small dog that is high-quality Pekinese. You very peculiar girl.'

'Peculiar?' Another word to file away.

'Peculiar. Abnormal. No matter what.' Mr Chin closed his eyes and smiled to himself. Opening them again, he pointed a finger at me. 'You come to office too early, work too late. Never complain. Never thieve ballpoint pen. Never make private phone call and email. What English girl do such? Certainly not normal English girl.'

'But as you said, I have no friends to call or email. And you don't supply pens so I couldn't steal one even if I were that way inclined.'

'Crazy and nuts. I supply petty cash box of ten pounds sterling in rolling drawer. Normal person buy pen with petty cash then thieve. That is most regular English solution.' He looked at me and shook his head. 'You like house of too many window. Wind blow through house always. Take force and energy. House too empty. You too yin, too damp-cold. Need yang.'

'My feet do get cold in winter.' In fact my feet were cold as I spoke and it was not even winter. 'Is there a cure?'

'Eat meat of pork and so on. Take more yang force. Warm up feets.'

'I couldn't eat pork and so on. Modern animal husbandry is not humane and mass-produced meat is full of chemicals. You never know what you might find inside a sausage.' I did not bother to tell him that my mother believed sausages were stuffed with sweepings from the floor of the abattoir.

'Abnormal.' Mr Chin pursed his lips into a point and shook his head. 'Sausage is traditional English. Normal English love sausage and so on.'

'Correct.' Despite my mother's beliefs about their contents, she bought pork sausages every week from Mr Da Silva. 'I am partial to vegetarian sausages.'

'You need professional expert. American Jewish make highest-quality expert for head. Go find such person.' He hesitated a moment, as if thinking over something important. 'I give you present of one hundred pound liquid cash.'

'One hundred pounds! That's a very handsome gift!' I was stunned by the offer. Mr Chin never gave money away, ever. My condition had to be a lot more serious than I imagined.

'One-time only investment.' Mr Chin lifted his heavy money belt out from under his shirt. It was made of flesh-coloured leather and perfectly camouflaged against his skin. He removed a wad of banknotes, counting five twenties across the table in a fan. With a thumb and forefinger, he then pinched each note to make sure it was a single. Mr Chin was a great believer in the power of money and liked to say that 'cash is king'.

'Here, take as bonus. Now leave premise. Come back Monday for work at normal time. Come back more normal. Normal girl with friend and so on.' He leaned back in his Komfort King and patted his chest with authority. 'Order of kind and generous boss.'

I felt a jolt. The chalk message from the gardens flashed through my mind: 'HAIL TO THE KING OF KINGS. HE IS THE KINDEST BOSS.'

'One-time offer only.' Mr Chin zipped up his money belt and tucked it back inside his shirt where it protruded like the stomach of an Australian lager drinker. He looked at me again but with an expression flickering between kindness and irritation. From experience, I knew that irritation was the more dominant of Mr Chin's moods and sprang into action before it could settle over him.

I slipped on my cardigan and, leaning down, opened my file drawer, taking care to roll it slowly. The hypnotherapist had not cured me of my bad habits but I had discovered that with concentration, I could control my impulse to yank the drawer open. I had also been training myself to chew my cuticles instead of my nails. This habit gave me almost the same pleasure as nail biting but allowed my fingernails to grow. In the week since my visit to Industry Drive, my nails had developed a ridge and I was now able to pick up coins and even scratch my forearms where the wool of my cardigan rubbed. It was a new sensation and thoroughly enjoyable.

Mr Chin nodded as I removed the fan of twenty-pound notes from his desk and folded them into my new vinyl purse. Neither of us spoke but I had no illusions about the gravity of the moment. He had set me a formidable task and had given me the means to achieve it by Monday. It was a challenge and I knew from reading about Sir Edmund Percival Hillary that challenges were an integral part of character building. I wanted to be a better person and win Mr Chin's approval. Indeed, my future depended on it.

It was Sir Edmund who once said, 'It is not the mountain we conquer, but ourselves,' which is quite a profound statement when you think about it. He certainly knew what he was talking about. He was the first person to reach the summit of Mount Everest, the highest mountain in the world. Mountain climbing is a rigorous activity and carries considerable risk. I would not like to die on a mountainside or lose a nose or fingers to frostbite. Fortunately, Sir Edmund never lost any facial features or extremities. After his adventures, he returned to beekeeping, which is a job that requires considerable manual dexterity.

4

The idea of normality was flashing in my mind's eye like the rotating beacon of a lighthouse as I made my way down the office stairs. The stairwell was pitch dark but I knew the width and squeak of every stair by heart. I used to run up and down the stairs until Mr Chin forbade it: 'This run, run, run get on my nerve. Walk up stair at normal human speed or forget interesting and exciting job.'

The stairwell lights do not work because their electrical supply is connected to the faulty circuitry of the cinema. It would cost hundreds of thousands of pounds to rewire the Babylon and make the building fireproof, which had been the original plan when the council purchased it from its bankrupt owner in 1990. The Babylon was going to be refurbished and turned into a centre of local culture and history with photo panels and audiovisual displays. This plan was one of the first things to go when Jerry Clench became mayor. Mr Clench was not interested in the cinema's architecture or its historical value. It was an eyesore and a fleapit, he said. He not only refused to allocate funds for its renovation but also said there was no budget to have it pulled down.

Mr Chin is more than happy with the dark stairwell because it discourages people from visiting the office. He had the reinforced metal doors installed after a boy scout carrying a plastic donation bucket made it to the landing with the aid of his pocket torch. The boy's arrival had sent Mr Chin into a frenzy. He began screeching and waving a length of green bamboo around his head. After the boy had fled, I asked Mr Chin why he was so upset.

'Foolish and stupid!' he shouted, shoving the bamboo back into his personal storeroom. 'You understand nothing.'

'About boy scouts?'

'About criminal people.'

'Criminal? Boy scouts assist the elderly.' I had read only good things about scouts and their love of the outdoors. 'They know their roots and berries.'

'Root and berry! Ha!' Mr Chin wagged his finger at me. 'Never trust such person. Maybe such person is spy and thief.'

'He was wearing an official uniform.'

'Uniform mean nothing. Worst crook in Hong Kong that is so-call police and military wear uniform.' Mr Chin pounded the top of his desk with a fist. 'Here office for private and personal business. Trespasser and other strictly forbidden.'

'But—'

'Enough of but! This but, but, but get on my nerve!'

He chopped the air with his hand to end the conversation. His face had flushed angry red and stayed that way for several minutes. Later that evening, I made a note in the CHIN subsection of my OBSERVATIONS ring binder: 'Scouts upset Mr Chin. Suspicious of uniforms. To be followed up.'

The door clicked shut behind me and I paused for my eyes to adjust to the dim light under the awning. Out of habit, I turned to examine the old movie stills in the display case but as I did this, my foot touched something solid and organic. I looked down and saw a boy, curled up asleep on a square of cardboard. It is not unusual to find people sleeping in doorways in the centre of town. Unemployment is high and the list for council housing is long. But I had never seen anyone so young sleeping so unprotected.

'Hello,' I said.

The boy's eyes flicked open. He scrambled to a crouch.

'You're not a cop,' he said, looking me up and down.

'No.'

'Social services?'

I shook my head. 'I work in the office upstairs.'

The boy assumed his full height, which was at least a head shorter than me. He was thin and pre-pubescent with fierce blue eyes and a tight lipless mouth. I could not see the top of his head for a dirty red baseball cap but the stubble around his ears was blond. He looked about ten years old. On his cheek was a furry birthmark. It was brown and perfectly round like a two-pence piece.

'Got a spare fiver?' He wiped his nose with the back of his hand.

'Why do you want five pounds?'

'Why do you think?' The boy scowled at me from under the cap.

I had just read an article in the *Cockerel* about boys sniffing industrial chemicals. The newspaper referred to them as 'feral' and said they terrorised the town in gangs and vandalised public property. I had never encountered a gang of savage children but I was very familiar with vandalism. 'To buy paint thinner?'

'Do I look that stupid?'

'It's hard to tell.'

'Well, *you* definitely look stupid.' The boy pointed to my trousers. 'What the hell do you call those?'

'Tartan trousers.' I did not bother commenting on the boy's grimy, oversized white T-shirt and baggy jeans. Fashion is a matter of personal taste and people can be sensitive to criticism. 'Do you need money to buy clothes?'

'I'm hungry, you idiot.'

My purse contained Mr Chin's one hundred pounds in addition to the one pound eighty I keep on hand for purchasing spiral note-books. 'I don't have five pounds in change but if you come with me I'll buy you a sandwich and a beverage.'

'Why should I trust you?' The boy squinted at me. 'You could be one of those molesterers. I'm a minor.'

'I'll take you to a public place.' I hesitated. An idea was forming in my mind. 'And rather than give you five pounds, I'll employ you and pay you to do something for me.'

'I'm not nicking anything.'

'I'm not a lawbreaker and would never encourage a minor to become one either.' I offered the boy my hand. 'My name's Sherry.'

The boy eyed my hand suspiciously. He kept his arms at his sides. 'That's not a real name.'

'It wasn't my choice.' I let my arm drop. 'What's yours?'

'Nigel, but that's not my real name either. And I don't want a sandwich.'

'What would you like?'

'A cup of tea and a cake.' He thought a moment. 'And a Coke.'

As we set off down Harry Secombe Parade, the boy hung back, trailing me along the pavement.

'You don't want to walk beside me?'

'Not when you walk like that.'

I stopped swinging my arms to chest height and slowed down but the boy continued to follow several steps behind. I glanced back to check on him as I passed under the old rail bridge. His shoulders were hunched and his hands were in the pockets of his baggy jeans but he was light on his feet and made no sound as he walked. At the high street he paused, scanning it before continuing.

Several people were milling around in front of the council buildings but they took no notice of us as we passed. Ten years previously the town hall square had been furnished with iron benches and rubbish bins stamped with the town's coat of arms but these had been ripped up under Mr Clench's drive to give the council a new face. Cobblestones had been imported from Italy and laid in a circular pattern. A marble fountain of a semi-naked woman in a clamshell was installed as a decorative centrepiece. The nozzle of this landmark has not spouted for several years but its clamshell is always filled with rainwater.

As I neared the betting shop, a man stepped out of a doorway and blocked my way. He was my height and looked about thirty-five. His head was small and his dark hair was oily and uncombed. He was wearing a black T-shirt printed with a skull and bones design and blue nylon sports trousers with a mismatched green nylon jacket. His face had an unhealthy pallor and he did not look like someone who practised sport. Smouldering between his fingers was a hand-rolled cigarette.

'Spare change, love?' he asked, crumpling his face in a tragic way and holding out his free hand. 'Down on my luck.'

I turned to see what Nigel was doing only to discover that the boy had disappeared.

'Are you hungry?' I asked the man, removing one pound from my purse.

He eyed me as he snatched the coin. 'Nope.'

'Why do you need money?'

'The derby.' He turned to go.

'You're going to bet on horses?'

'As soon as I get five quid together.'

I watched him slouch off and wondered where he would get the rest of the money. It was not uncommon to observe people asking for cash or cigarettes from townspeople but I did not often see them rewarded.

Nigel was waiting for me on the corner in front of the betting shop. I had not seen him pass me and had no idea how he had got there. He pointed to an electronic signboard hanging in the window of the pawn shop next door. Running across the board in red diode lettering were the words: 'We buy used gold! Divorcees trade in those wedding bands then double your cash on the nags.'

'That does not seem very ethical,' I said.

Nigel laughed. 'The punterers will be cutting the ring fingers off their grannies.'

There was truth to what the boy said. Gambling is a compulsive activity and can prompt an addicted person to engage in desperate behaviour. Mr Chin had told me he would never employ a gambler. 'Policy of office strict,' he explained during my job interview. 'Gambler forbidden and not permitted. Chin never trust such fool. Gambler worst kind of weak and stupid person. Never care for family. Only care for money and more money.'

I motioned for Nigel to follow and led him down the side street towards Ted's Famously Fine Coffee and Teas. The café is a small place with colourful plastic tablecloths and solid wooden chairs. It serves an all-day breakfast of fried bacon, mushrooms, tomatoes and eggs on a pool of baked beans. The price of breakfast includes a large mug of tea or coffee. There is a sign above the counter that reads: 'Our teas and coffees are made the old-fashioned way – by Ted's very own fine hand'.

For a month now I have been going to Ted's every Monday and Thursday after work to observe people and collate my notes. I would like to go every day but I do not want to overstay my welcome. This has happened to me before in other places and I have learned to pace myself. Most people are able to pace themselves without thinking but pacing does not come naturally to me. If I like a place, I want to go there all the time. I would spend many more hours in the office if Mr Chin were not so strict.

Twice a week seems about right for Ted because he always raises his eyebrows and greets me with a familiar, 'You again'. It is not often that I am recognised and greeted as a regular customer. Ted lets me spend as much time as I like in his café but insists I use a small table and buy at least one drink per hour. 'House policy,' he says.

This time, however, Ted did not give me his usual greeting. He looked at the boy beside me.

'I've got my eye on you,' he said.

'Aren't I the lucky one,' replied Nigel. He winked.

'Don't try any funny business.'

The boy snorted. 'A funny thing happened on the way to a funeral.'

'That's not funny!' Ted pushed his large stomach against the counter and tapped its surface with a stubby finger. 'The recently bereaved come in here.'

'Did you hear the one about the bishop and the button mushroom?'

'Watch your mouth! I'll not have Roman Catholics offended. Buy something or get out.'

'Keep your hair on, Teddy boy.' Nigel pointed to me. 'She's buying me one of your fine teas.'

'What the hell are you doing with this delinquent?' Ted turned to me, shaking his head. 'I didn't think your sort had friends, especially not his sort.'

'He's not a friend,' I said. 'I've hired him to help me.'

'I doubt he helps anyone but himself.' Ted's eyes shifted to Nigel and then back to me. 'So, what will Her Ladyship be having?'

'I'll have one of your famous milk coffees and my employee will have a Coke and fairy cake with his tea.'

'Fairy cake?' Ted's thin lips parted in a smile. It was a tight smile that did not reveal any teeth. 'That's a turn-up for the books.'

I used one of Mr Chin's twenty-pound notes to pay the four pounds forty for the order before leading Nigel over to a table for two near the window. As I sat down, I noticed a message had been scratched into the glass with something hard like a diamond ring or glasscutter. Each letter of 'Chantelle Corby Luvs it' was made up of multiple scratches. Nigel sniggered at the graffiti.

'Bet that pisses off old Ted,' he said.

'He doesn't seem to like you,' I replied, sliding the tray over to the boy. I removed the notebook from my bag and began noting down the graffiti.

'He's a prick.'

'He's always very welcoming to me.'

'You call that a welcome?' The boy took a bite of the cake and screwed up his nose. 'This must be fifty years old. Probably crawling with salmonellera.'

'Ted makes all his cakes and beverages by hand.'

'I don't want to know that.' He frowned but kept eating.

'He says that his coffee is superior to machine-made espresso and cappuccino.' I took a sip of my instant coffee. It was tepid and weak, just how I liked it. 'Ted says the steam jets of modern machines destroy the flavour of the beans and can lead to cancer.'

Nigel stopped chewing and frowned at me. 'Are you really a wally or is this an act?'

'Wally?' I glanced over at Ted who was wiping a tabletop with a grey washcloth. 'I prefer the coffee here. It's light and remarkably thirst-quenching. Even more thirst-quenching than a glass of tap water. It doesn't prevent me from sleeping at night.'

'I bet it doesn't.'

Ted's café is one of the few places in town still furnished with a payphone. It is an old pink ring-dial model with a slot for coins. Around its base is a strip of brown tape with the words 'FOR PAYING CUSTOMERS ONLY' written in red marker. The phone is often in use and not always by customers. There are not many phone booths left in the town and it is often difficult to find one in working order.

I walked over and brought back the Yellow Pages. The phonebook was dog-eared and its cover had been defaced with doodles and swear words. I opened it at P and ran my eye over the page before sliding it across the table to Nigel, who was unscrewing the lid of the sugar dispenser.

'I'd like you to choose a psychological expert from this list.'

'Why can't you do it yourself?'

'Decision-making is difficult for me. I have a problem with choices.'

'That's not normal.'

'Correct.'

'You'll be wasting your money. All those psychologicalists are pricks.'

I nudged the phonebook closer to the boy. 'I need to see a therapist as soon as possible. I have no time to lose.'

Nigel finished pouring the contents of the salt container into the sugar dispenser and then screwed the lid back on. He looked up, pleased with himself. 'You'd better pay me.'

'Of course I'll pay you! I've been given money to get normal by Monday. This afternoon tea and your salary are my first investments.'

'Whatever.' The boy shrugged and ran a finger down the listings, stopping at the name Poulet. He sniggered. 'Here's one for you. Pooh-let.'

'Could you call and make an appointment?' I did not bother to explain the challenges of telephony without the prompts and responses of the Honey Trap.

'Give me your mobile.' He held out his hand.

'I don't have one. It's a personal policy.'

The boy frowned.

'I don't want to expose my body to unnecessary radiofrequency radiation. Testicular cancer poses no danger to me but I prefer not to take any risks with my brain.'

The boy shook his head but did as I asked. He was feeding coins into the phone when someone tapped me on the shoulder and said, 'Excuse me.' It was the large man from the table behind me. He was wearing overalls with 'Paradise Plumbing' embroidered on the pocket. In front of him was an all-day breakfast and a mug of tea. 'Love, pass me the sugar,' he said. I did as I was asked but my attention was on Nigel who was talking into the phone.

The boy came back to the table, smiling. 'Tomorrow at three o'clock.' He pointed to the name in the phonebook. 'Bijou Poulet Psy Dram.'

I was about to thank him when a dog started barking loudly behind me. I twisted in my seat again and found the plumber coughing violently over his mug of tea.

'Give me the five quid, quick!' Nigel was standing next to me with his hand out. 'I've got to go.'

I had barely removed the banknote from my purse when it was snatched out of my hand. Before I could say anything, the boy was gone. The next thing I knew Ted was thumping the plumber on the back. Once the coughing fit had subsided, he gave the man a fresh cup of tea and a curled-up ham sandwich on a plate. 'Compliments of the house,' he said as he put the plate down in front of him. The plumber looked over at me and shook his head. Ted approached my table.

'Did that little bastard just nick your money?' he asked.

'No,' I replied.

My response did not please Ted who exhaled noisily through his nose. The sharp whistling sound made me wonder about the presence of hair inside his nostrils. Abundant nostril hair is not uncommon in men of a certain age. Quality chemists stock nose-grooming tools but I did not think Ted would appreciate this information. I have found that people are not very receptive to grooming or healthcare advice. Ted's nostrils made an even shriller sound as he exhaled again.

His mouth was a tight line and he was looking at me in a disappointed way as if I had just dropped a bottle of sticky red cordial over his linoleum floor. I decided to change the subject.

'I notice someone has scratched your window.'

'Bloody vandalism!'

'The original Vandals were a Germanic tribe that sacked Rome in 455.'

'You think I don't know what a vandal is?' Ted pointed to a security camera peeking out from a small hole in the wall above the payphone. 'Cost me a fortune to get that installed.'

'Many people believe that CCTV surveillance is an invasion of privacy. It might interest you to know that there are at least one hundred and seventy-seven CCTV cameras in the centre of this town, which is a lot of surveillance when you think about it.'

'Roger Bottle is going to double that number and, if you ask me, he's got the right idea.' A crimson flush had gathered around the grimy collar of Ted's T-shirt, inflaming the shaving rash on his neck. 'They come in here and rip holes in the tablecloths and write filth over the phonebook.'

'Who?'

'Who do you think?'

I surveyed the patrons in the café. At the table next to the plumber were two grey-haired women. I could not imagine plumbers having the time or energy to rip up the tablecloths or scribble on the phonebook. That left the pensioners.

'Pensioners?'

'Are you taking the piss?'

'Sorry?'

'Two can play at that game, little lady.' Ted filled his chest and lowered his voice. 'What's with the tartan trousers?'

'I have an affinity for the tartans of Scotland. I've made a study of them.'

'You know it all, don't you.'

'Not all, but I do know quite a lot. I have several books on the clan system and own a complete set of the *Encyclopaedia Britannica*.

I used to be an active member of the public library.' I looked down at my trousers. 'This tartan comes from Angus, an agricultural and maritime district near Perthshire. I've never visited either district but apparently they are both very scenic. I've just been reading about the jute, jam and journalism situation in Dundee. It's fascinating.'

'If you're so bloody smart you can go drink your coffee in the bloody public library.' Ted raised a hand from his hip and pointed to the door. 'I don't want to see you or the likes of that little bastard in here. Do you understand?'

'No. Mayor Clench closed the library five months ago.'

'Piss off. You understand that?'

I understood well enough to know that I was being asked to leave. Ted's words would have been a blow if I did not have an appointment with a psychological expert. The idea of normality was like an orange lifesaver ring bobbing on the ocean. It gave me hope for my personality and my future with Mr Chin.

The lifesaver image made me smile, which seemed to surprise Ted. He glanced at my hands and moved out of my way as I pushed myself to my feet and left the café.

On another day, I might have crossed the square and visited the council photo display but earlier in the week I had encountered a particularly unfriendly council worker. I had arrived at the annexe during regular opening hours only to find the door closed. When I knocked, the woman had opened it a crack and shouted at me that the building was closed ahead of the election before slamming it in my face. This was not the first time I had experienced unpleasantness at the council. The workers are disgruntled and do not appreciate enquiries or suggestions from the public. This attitude is something I do not understand. Why have a suggestion box if no one is supposed to use it?

I stopped at the corner and glanced inside the betting shop, where several men were clustered in front of a large flat-screen television mounted on the wall. The town is not known for its tolerance but the group watching the horse race was a picture of racial harmony. One thin white man, two Chinese and someone from the Indian subcontinent were standing shoulder to shoulder, united by a common cause. This is called the Dunkirk Spirit and is very helpful in times of war when British soldiers are trapped on a coastline and require the assistance of fellow citizens in small vessels. Dunkirk was a tragic moment in the nation's history but it did highlight the British capacity for rallying around a common cause.

As I headed towards the rose gardens, I thought of the man in the fuchsia trench coat. His comment about the fowl of time had made me curious and I wondered whether I would meet him again. He had not been unfriendly, which had to be a good thing.

5

Someone had been busy while I was in the café. As I passed back under the rail bridge, I discovered four damp campaign posters pasted along the brick wall of the underpass. The posters showed a man in his late forties with a robust red moustache the size and shape of a hamster. His shoulders were squared in a military manner and his expression was severe: 'Roger Bottle – a Hard Man for Hard Times.' Below the mayoral candidate's photo in smaller print were the words: 'When the Going Gets Rough, Rog Gets Tough.'

I jotted down the campaign messages in my notebook and as I left the underpass, I discovered that it was drizzling. By the time I reached the Babylon, the drizzle had turned into rain and I decided to step under the awning to wait it out. What I found there took me completely by surprise.

Tied to the double doors of the cinema was a large official-looking notice printed in bold type. My pulse rate increased as I read its contents. I immediately thought of Mr Chin and wondered whether he knew about this new turn of events.

A second surprise was waiting for me when I tried the door to the stairs. It was unlocked. Mr Chin had forgotten to follow me down to lock it after I had left. This was very unusual behaviour for my employer, whose policy was to 'Lock ruffian and rascal out. Guarantee security and safety for kind boss and office.'

I entered the dark stairwell and quickly climbed the stairs to the landing where I paused to take the door handle in both hands. The heavy reinforced door had a habit of flying open on its German

41

spring hinge and I did not want to give Mr Chin a fright. He does not appreciate surprises as I learned one day when I vacuumed the office and inadvertently shifted the position of his desk by two inches. The reprimand I received must have exceeded the safety guidelines for decibel levels because my ears were still thrumming when I put them on my pillow that evening.

I poked my head in the doorway and found Mr Chin reclined in his Komfort King, sleeping with his mouth open and making a 'hukka-hukka-hukka' sound with each exhalation. On his desk were a glass and a half-empty bottle of plum liquor.

I slipped inside and eased the door closed with a faint *click* before tiptoeing over to my desk. Taking care not to make any noise, I lowered myself on to my chair. It was probably the familiar comfort of the neoprene padding against my buttocks that made me forget myself because the next thing I knew I was rolling the file drawer open at high speed. The heavy cash box inside slid along the bottom of the drawer, hitting its metal interior with a loud *clang*.

'Best quality!' Mr Chin sat bolt upright in his executive chair, shaking his head in confusion. His eyes fell on me, darted to the clock above the door and then flicked back to me. They were watery and bloodshot, red like his cheeks. He blinked. 'What?'

'Good afternoon,' I said.

'Why you here?' He rubbed his face in an irritated way and made a long 'Ahhh', which was both a yawn and a sigh. 'Chin enjoy calm and peace, sleeping and so on. Now pop go weasel, here you again. Irritating and most annoying girl.'

'I'm here within business hours.' I pointed to the clock and wondered how best to tell him about the notice on the cinema doors.

'I give you sudden holiday. I tell you vacate premise. Now what?'

'I've followed your advice about my abnormality and have an appointment with a psychological expert. She has Psy and Dram after her name.'

'Expert best idea. Chin never joke or say nonsense thing. Chin always right.' He nodded and let out another yawning sigh. 'What name?'

'Bijou Poulet.'

'Jewish?'

'I'm not sure. Poulet is a French word. It means chicken.'

'Chicken!' He snapped to attention and threw his forearms on to the desk. His expression was fierce. 'What this chicken business again and every time?'

'It's the name of the therapist. You told me to find a professional for my head.'

'Head.' He tapped his temple fiercely. 'Get into head now and permanently. In world, two kind of people: hero and chicken.'

'I thought it was normal and abnormal.'

'Interrupt, interrupt. Always interrupt! Quiet now!' Mr Chin waved his hand in front of his face as if shooing a hornet. 'Two kind of people: hero and chicken. Hero fight always. Brave and good, many sacrifice for family, so on and so on. Chicken sneaky and cunning. Gambler and so on.'

I nodded but wondered where this was leading. What was it about chickens that inflamed Mr Chin so?

'Sometime stranger come with stick and gun and knife, beat and stab, thieve precious ornament and so on.' He narrowed his eyes and shook a finger at me. 'What chicken do in such case?'

I did not know how to respond, aware that an incorrect answer might put me in the wrong category.

'Chin tell you. Chicken run always.' He leaned further across the desk and lowered his voice. 'Do Chin run always?'

'No.' This was true. Mr Chin never ran anywhere. His way of getting from A to B was either to drive his 1979 lime-green Ford Fiesta or walk. As a walker, he was alert yet relaxed. His head and torso appeared to remain motionless while his legs forged ahead.

'Correct and true. Chin completely *not* chicken.'

He exhaled in a satisfied way and reclined his executive chair. It seemed like a good moment.

'Have you seen the notice downstairs?'

'Chin tired now.' His eyelids closed. He waved a hand as if to dismiss me. 'Take one hundred per cent free holiday. See expert and so on. Come back Monday for work at normal hour.'

'But the cinema might be pulled down.' By announcing this information, I made it more real and by making it more real, I made myself more anxious.

'Who say pull down?' Mr Chin jerked upright again. He looked at me in an accusing way as if it were my idea to demolish the Babylon.

'Roger Bottle wants to tear it down and build a public surveillance centre in its place.'

'Wrong and rubbish!' His voice was shrill. He brought his fist down on to his desk. The empty glass jumped up and bounced sideways, hitting the bottle with a *clink*. 'Chin have lease from council that is foolproof. Why you tell wrong and false information?'

'Roger Bottle is running for mayor and will control the council if he wins.'

'Who say Bottle win such election? Why you talk so?' Mr Chin's expression changed from accusing to dangerous, like traffic lights flashing from amber to red. If I had been a motorist, I would have heeded the sign and braked hard to avoid hitting a pedestrian or colliding with another vehicle. But I was engaged in a discussion and the rules of social intercourse are not as straightforward as the UK Highway Code. My next comment was a logical extension of the subject but it was probably the worst thing I could have said.

'Roger Bottle already has a lot of support. The *Cockerel* says he's winning hearts and minds with his security and employment promises.' At this point I should have stopped but I was too focused on Roger Bottle to heed the warning signs on Mr Chin's face. 'He wants to create local jobs for local people and is calling for compulsory English tests for immigrants.'

Mr Chin squawked. 'Chin one hundred per cent British citizen. Passport foolproof British. English speaking excellent and perfect.' He slapped his chest in a proud way. 'You think Chin have wrong English?'

I thought for a moment. 'I wouldn't say it's wrong English but you often conjugate verbs incorrectly.'

My comment was like a shot fired from a starter pistol. Mr Chin bolted out of his chair and sprinted around to my side of the office. Before I could move, he had grabbed the back of my chair and yanked it away from the desk, spinning me around so that my nose was almost touching his.

'Incorrectly! What incorrectly?' He gave my chair an angry shove and pushed himself upright, assuming his full five feet three inches and crossing his arms over his chest. 'Why Chin employ such peculiar girl as you? Many people want excellent job. Chin too kind and generous.'

It was true what he said but it was discouraging to hear it stated so clearly. Local unemployment was high. I did not have people skills or qualifications and would be hard-pressed to find another position. I needed my job with Mr Chin. My future depended on it.

'But I can change. I'm determined to crack the normality nut by Monday.'

Mr Chin threw up his hands and groaned.

'I'm seeing the psychological expert tomorrow afternoon.'

'Go see expert for head. Go see fortune-teller or astrology person. Whatever necessary. Just vacate premise immediately. Leave Chin now. You forbidden here today and weekend.' He stopped and narrowed his eyes. 'Come back Monday at normal hour or—'

'—or what?'

'—or Chin find new worker for replacement!' He made a whisking motion with his hands. 'Go now!'

I jumped to my feet and hurried over to the doorway, my heart thumping against my ribs. I turned. 'What will you do if they demolish the cinema? What will happen to the office?'

'Vacate premise immediately!'

Mr Chin advanced on me and grabbed the door handle. The door sprang open and hit the wall with a *clang*. I stepped out on to the landing.

'But I've been following the election campaign. Roger Bottle might get elected.' I started descending the stairs. 'Do you have a contingency plan?'

'Question, question, question drive me crazy and nuts!'

My head was whirling when I reached the awning. I blinked as my eyes adjusted to the light. My nostrils flared. The air was heavy with the dry, sickly smell of a mentholated cigarette. I looked around for the smoker but the space under the awning was empty apart from some litter and Nigel's cardboard square. I glanced across the road to the bus stop. My scalp tingled.

A man dressed as a cowboy was leaning against the bus shelter. It was Shanks and he was looking at me in a friendly way. He doffed his hat and whistled.

Without waiting to see what he would do next, I stepped on to the pavement and hurried away. I wanted nothing to do with the cowboy or Mr Tanderhill. The bungalow experience had cost me my purse and left me with a deep fear of hypnotherapy.

When I finally dared to look back, Shanks was gone and a bus was pulling away. Printed across the back of the vehicle was a large advertisement featuring a woman dressed like the Queen of England. On her head was a jewelled crown but around her neck was a string of deep-fried hash browns. A speech bubble was coming out of her mouth: 'All that glitters is gold. Nack's Hash Browns, the majestic snack.'

I made a mental note of the advertisement and set off again, walking briskly and swinging my arms to chest height to maximise cardiovascular activity. This is called power-walking and is very popular in Australia, a country renowned for sports enthusiasm and Rolf Harris.

My head was down as I entered the rose gardens and I did not see the man in the fuchsia trench coat coming the other way. We collided with considerable momentum, which is the sum of mass times velocity. He let out a high-pitched 'Oh!' His tiny dog started barking. It was a sharp, ear-piercing sound.

'I beg your pardon!' I said.

'O-là-là.' He wheezed and grabbed the gatepost. The dog stopped barking and sniffed his master's ankle.

'I hope I didn't injure you. I was power-walking at high speed and hit you with considerable momentum.'

He took a deep breath. 'Don't worry, my dear, I'm quite accustomed to brutality.'

He released his grip on the gatepost and as I reached out to steady him, I noticed his face was dusted with beige powder. It is not unusual for male actors to wear stage makeup but there was no theatre in the rose gardens, not even a bandstand for outdoor musical performances. I had never seen a man so made up in a public setting. His lips were cherry red and his eyelashes were thick and dark.

'You spoke to me the other day.' I removed my hand from under his arm as he righted himself. 'You said time was like a fowl.'

'So I did.'

I nodded and waited for him to continue.

'Time is an elusive bird, my dear. I have less of it every day.' He coughed in a delicate way, using a floral handkerchief to cover his mouth.

'Do you suffer from lung cancer?'

'Not yet.' He rummaged in a trouser pocket and removed a bag of old-fashioned sweets. They were hard-boiled Everton Mints with black and white stripes. He held out the bag and shook one into my hand. 'I'm an alcoholic.'

'I've not observed you drinking.' I did not bother to add that I had seen plenty of other people doing so in the gardens. I put a mint in my mouth and tasted peppermint and pocket dust. My nasal passages cleared with a crackle.

'Good to know I'm not at it behind my back. I've been on the wagon for a week. That's seven days for a normal person but about three years for an alcoholic.' He put two sweets in his mouth, clicking them against his teeth with his tongue. He noticed me looking. 'The sugar, my dear. It's one of the few thrills left to me since the doctor gave me my orders. No alcohol. No stimulation. Fresh air, moderate exercise and plenty of sleep. I've been advised not to get myself worked up. Excitement, apparently, can drive the vulnerable back to the bottle.' He held out his hand. 'It's a pleasure to meet you.'

I shook his hand, which was soft and warm. 'My name's Sherry.'

'Makes my mouth water.'

'Sherry Cracker.'

'You must have suffered every Christmas.'

'I have never celebrated Christmas but it is on my To Do list.'

'Worth it for the tinsel if nothing else.' He smiled. 'I'm Jocelyn.'

This was an unusual name for a man but as I was rapidly realising, Jocelyn was an unusual person. He was polite and spoke in a gentle, reassuring way. Alcoholism is known to afflict sensitive people and often those with artistic tendencies. Francis Bacon was an alcoholic. So was Tennessee Williams. Jocelyn certainly looked like he had an artistic personality. His clothes were brightly coloured and styled for a much younger man or woman. The fuchsia trench coat was over-stitched in orange and had large mother-of-pearl buttons. His shoes were black suede and his trousers were made of a shiny blue-black material. Knotted around his neck was a turquoise silk scarf. These vibrant clothes combined with the soft grey hair he wore tucked behind his ears created the effect of a Roman Catholic cardinal on holiday. Perhaps it was his ecclesiastical appearance that loosened my tongue. As he strolled back into the gardens with me, I found myself confessing my fear of unemployment and explaining my lack of social skills.

'My problem is that I feel isolated, as though I were suspended over human society in a Perspex pod.'

'How novel!' Jocelyn laughed a small tinkly laugh. The powder on his cheeks was thick and made the skin crinkle like crepe paper. 'I have difficulty picturing you in a pod, my dear, but I do find those tartan trousers rather dashing.'

I felt heat rise in my cheeks as we sat down on a bench. No one had ever said anything complimentary to me before. 'You have a very agreeable temperament for someone your age.'

'Thank you, I'll take that as a compliment.' He removed a rolled-up copy of the *Cockerel* from his coat pocket and opened it to page three, which was not difficult because the newspaper only had four pages. 'Shall we check our stars?'

I nodded and thought of Mr Chin's suggestion of an astrologer as Jocelyn read his horoscope.

'Apparently I'm going to meet a stranger.' His powdered cheeks crinkled again. 'Someone tall and dark.'

'Is that a good thing?'

'At this point, it would be a godsend. What sign are you?'

'Sagittarius.'

'How wonderful. You're also going to meet a tall and dark stranger.' He laughed and held the page open for me to read.

The column was called 'Astral Acorns' and was written by Andromeda Mountjoy, world-renowned stargazer and lunar minstrel. The horoscope for Sagittarius had a frame around it and a title, 'Nut of the Day'. It was short, half the length of the other star forecasts: 'Think tall, dark and strange. You're in for the ride of your life!'

'I don't understand.'

'I don't either, dear, but it does sound exciting. I do find his tall, dark strangers rather thrilling.'

He adjusted the scarf around his neck and beckoned his dog. As he pushed himself to his feet, I found myself wanting to delay him and extend our discourse. I stood, trying to think of an engaging conversation topic but my mind was blank. I had no repertoire and did not know the first thing about small talk.

'Do you think we could meet again?'

I was not in the habit of asking such questions because I have learned that people generally do not want to meet me more than once. But Jocelyn had allowed me to finish my sentences and had even addressed me as 'my dear'. My mother never called me by my name, let alone by a term of affection.

'Mais bien sûr.' He slid the paper back into his pocket and picked up his dog, tucking it under his arm like a clutch purse. 'I'm often here. The fresh air keeps me out of the gin bottle.'

I watched him stroll out of the gardens and realised I was feeling lighter, as if I had been relieved of a heavy suitcase or bag of groceries. The lightness had something to do with optimism and I wondered how best to maintain this feeling as I sat down to consider the task before me. Mr Chin had set a goal and given me the means to achieve it. I had to remain positive and keep my eye on the ball. This strategy is called positive thinking and is very helpful for running corporations and battling terminal illnesses.

'Birdy, birdy, birdy. Ho, ho, ho.'

I sat up straight at the sound of the melodious baritone and saw a tall, dark man heading towards the gate. He was dressed in loose, colourful clothing and walked in a free, relaxed manner. On his head was a hat shaped like a Pope's mitre, which added another foot to his height. He glanced at me before leaving the gardens and made a fluttering gesture with his hands.

I was wondering what this could mean when I noticed new chalk graffiti on the wall behind the CCTV camera: 'TAKE COURAGE. THERE IS GOOD AS WELL AS EVIL.' I was making a mental note of this message for my OBSERVATIONS ring binder when I realised that the lens of the CCTV camera had been masked with duct tape.

Strange!

This was the sixth masked camera I had seen in a week.

6

Saturday afternoon began in a damp way with light drizzle that eased off as I power-walked towards the centre of town. I reached the high street and was moving swiftly past Quality Pies and Confectionaries when a campaign poster caught my eye. I stopped and took a new notebook out of my bag.

The windows of Quality Pies and Confectionaries were boarded up and pasted over with layers of advertising and posters but in its heyday, the bakery was renowned for its 'Pie of the Day' specials and 'fine English baked goods'. The shop had been a favourite of my mother's who liked to buy herself a celebratory Victoria sponge every benefit day. This she ate from her armchair with a tea towel spread over her knee and a glass of port at her elbow.

The campaign poster was printed on matt, off-white paper with a small horizontal note along the lower right edge: 'Made from 100% recycled paper.' The photo was of a man in his forties dressed in a safari shirt done up at the neck. In his breast pocket was a pen and pencil. He was wearing wire-framed glasses and his hair was parted on the side in a three-to-seven ratio, which is considered the ideal hair parting among Japanese businessmen. But Warren Crumpet was not Japanese or a businessman. He was an organic farmer and member of the British Soil Association who was promising to clean up council corruption and put the town's finances back in the black. One of his more progressive ideas was to turn unused council land into market gardens and grow organic vegetables for commercial sale. His 'Go Organic' initiative would employ and retrain local residents and generate income for municipal projects. The poster's message was simple: 'Warren Crumpet for Mayor – Because Honesty Is the Best Policy.' The first thing he had vowed to do if elected was to halve the mayor's salary.

Mr Crumpet's political platform made complete sense to me but clearly he had at least one detractor. Someone had defaced the poster with a thick black marker, drawing crude women's breasts over the pockets of his safari shirt. 'Tofu eater' had been scribbled around his head like a halo or crown of thorns. The destruction of campaign advertising was a crime but I had yet to find an undamaged poster of Warren Crumpet.

When I reached the address of Bijou Poulet Psy Dram, I had to remind myself to remain positive. Her office was located in a dilapidated building above a fish and chip shop called the Sea Breeze. This was not a very prestigious location for a psychological expert. The white paint was peeling on the front door and litter had collected in the doorway. The handwritten card next to the buzzer read: POULET Psy Dram Therapeutic Chambers. As I held my finger down on the plastic button I noticed that someone had scratched 'ITCH' into the paintwork. The intercom crackled and a woman's voice shouted, 'Enough already!'

The door clicked and I climbed the stairs to a scuffed carpeted landing. There I found a second door. This had a peephole and a large framed photograph of a popular American actress. The photo had a caption in gold lettering, 'Jodie Foster, Hollywood Screen Legend, Etcetera.'

The door opened and Bijou Poulet beckoned me inside. Her nails were long and made me think of the empress dowager Cixi who reigned over China for several decades and earned a reputation as a ruthless tyrant and dog lover. One of Cixi's diplomatic initiatives was to give away toy dogs as gifts and she once bestowed a Pekinese on the daughter of American President Theodore Roosevelt.

Bijou Poulet was a stout woman with wide shoulders, chest and pelvic girdle. Her hair was very blonde except near the scalp where it was dark and streaked with grey. She was dressed as if for a French cabaret in a ruffled blue synthetic gown and silver shoes with very high heels. Around her neck was a glittery necklace with several of its paste gems missing. She did not appear to be American and I could not tell if she was Jewish but she did have a lot of framed documents on her walls. I could not read their contents but they appeared to have the seals and swirling signatures of academic diplomas. The qualifications would have pleased Mr Chin, who believed in getting 'bang for buck'.

Bijou Poulet announced that a half-hour session would cost thirty pounds. I was asked to pay upfront before being led to a reclining sofa.

'Remove your shoes and stretch out,' she said, putting on reading glasses.

'Can I keep my clothes on?' I asked.

'Do you enjoy nudity with women?' She stepped back from me, frowning over the top of her glasses.

'I thought it might be expected.'

'Uh-huh.' She pointed again to the sofa with the end of her pen before sitting on a swivel chair and placing a stenographer's pad on her knee. 'Ho-kay, I'll need some background info-data for my files. Are you affiliated with the motion picture industry?'

'No.'

'Film, TV, docu-dramas, mini-series, pilots, commercials?'

'I go to the cinema sometimes.'

She frowned and noted something down. 'Are you married or homosexual?'

'I'm single.'

'So you're *not* homosexual?'

'One never knows, I suppose. I've read that people sometimes discover homosexual relief in mid-life.'

'Uh-huh.' She wrote something else down. 'Allergies, phobias, unresolved anger?'

'I'm not allergic to anything but I am afraid of spiders. Especially those large, hairy bird-eating spiders that live on tropical islands. I have a horror of a bird-eating spider falling from a coconut palm, down the back of my cardigan.'

'That's fear of the vagina.'

'I'm not frightened of the vagina. It's spiders.'

'Psy 101: Fear of snakes is fear of the penis. Fear of spiders is fear of the vagina. It's the ABC of my trade. You've probably had a traumatic birth or a brush with a forceful lesbian. Sometimes it's a distant aunt or over-friendly neighbour. Fear and shame drive the female child to internalise the incident and bury it deep in her subconscious. It takes multiple sessions with a highly trained expert to normalise a traumatised victim. It's a baptism by fire, catharsis, rebirth. I have a time plan to ease the financial burden of payments.'

'But I thought most people were scared of spiders. And snakes for that matter.'

'Leave the thinking up to those licensed to do it.'

This statement was not very encouraging but it was not my place to question a certified professional. It seemed like a good moment to clarify my goals. 'I've been told by a reliable source that I am abnormal. I'm looking for relief by Monday.'

'There are two types of abnormal, the chronically abnormal and the averagely abnormal. My professional guess is that you're the former.' She shook her head and exhaled noisily. 'I've heard it all in my game. Violence, torture, murder, rape, damage to private property. I carry it with me. It's all up here.'

Bijou Poulet tapped her temple and sighed in a significant way. She had not chosen an easy career path. I knew for a fact that suicide among psychotherapists was uncommonly high. So was suicide among veterinarians. I was glad I had not opted for a career in veterinary science. It cannot be easy giving animals injections.

'At least you don't see animals suffer.'

Bijou Poulet seemed startled by my comment. 'What does the word *beaver* mean to you?'

'Dam.'

'Ho-kay, I'll take that as a hostile response.' She folded her lips and wrote a lengthy paragraph on her notepad. She then reread her notes, frowned and scratched her scalp with her long fingernails.

When she finally looked up, her expression was serious. 'Your illness has a name.'

'That's helpful.'

'Joan of Arc complex.'

'But Joan of Arc was a soldier. She led armies into battle against the British. I don't agree with fighting. I think it does more harm than good.'

'That's only what you think you think. What goes on inside your mind is a different kettle of fish.' She pointed to her temple again before motioning in the general direction of my groin. 'You're a victim of unnatural impulses, dangerous impulses if left unchecked. They've got to be controlled, suppressed, suffocated, metaphorically held down and beaten with a stick. Electric shock therapy is no longer available but there are other psychological routes we can pursue.'

'This is not very good news.'

Bijou Poulet held up a hand. 'Describe a recent dream.'

I would have liked to pursue the Joan of Arc theme but it seemed prudent to do as instructed. 'I dreamed this morning that I lost my job. I woke up with pins and needles in my legs. Would you like me to describe it?'

'No.'

I was taken aback by this abrupt response but reminded myself of the 'Psy Dram' after Bijou Poulet's name. 'Earlier this week, I had another dream. It was quite strange.'

'I'm sure it was.'

'In the dream I was sitting in the therapy room of Mr Harrison Tanderhill, a registered hypnotherapist.' I looked at her. She nodded for me to continue. 'I was speaking indiscreetly.'

'Filth, shame, childhood guilt. The hypnotist takes away your sense of responsibility. You're under his control, free to pursue sexual fantasy.'

'Mr Tanderhill then said, "I just love the Neapolitan lifestyle". That's the part I don't understand.'

'Suppressed sexual feelings for the maidenhead. Textbook case.'

'He then started asking about money.'

'Pure greed. It starts at the breast.'

'I was bottle fed.'

She glared at me. 'Get on with it.'

'Then the dream seemed to jump ahead. The hypnotherapist was laughing and doing the Macarena.'

'Release, sexual freedom, cork popping. You're frustrated, craving sexual expression. If you dig deep into your subconscious, you'll find that the hypnotist in your dream was actually a woman dressed as a man.'

'I'm not sure it was a dream.'

'The dreaming mind can be compelling but reality is reality, full stop.' She clicked her fingers to emphasise the full stop. 'An averagely abnormal person knows the difference. A chronically abnormal person should be put on high-quality psycho-pharmaceuticals to suppress the imagination, to kill it dead in the parlance of psychotherapeutic dramatology. I'm not licensed to prescribe but I can point you in the right direction. For a fee, naturally.'

'The thing is, I did go to see Mr Tanderhill last week. He's a certi-fied hypnotics expert.'

'Poppycock.'

'I was mesmerised with a small medallion.'

'In your dreams, sister.' She raised her eyebrows and made a whistling gesture with her lips without actually whistling.

'He said the medallion was of Hindu origin but I recognised its image. My mother's butcher had worn the same talisman. Mr Da Silva was Roman Catholic and Portuguese. He had considerable body hair.'

Bijou Poulet frowned and shook her head at the mention of body hair. 'We're wasting time. Have you ever dreamed you've forgotten to put your underpants on?'

'No.'

'You dream you're back at school and suddenly realise you're not wearing underpants.'

'No.'

'You're sitting an exam and panic when you realise you've forgotten your underpants.'

'I have never dreamed about underwear, with or without.'

'For God's sake!' Bijou Poulet exhaled loudly through her nose and slapped her notebook on her knee.

I did not need to be a psychological expert to recognise frustration when I saw it.

She let out a long, irritated sigh. 'Tell me about your anxieties, worries, qualms. Give them to me in a nutshell.'

I tried to think of something to say. What I was most worried about at that moment was displeasing her but I doubted this was what she wanted to hear.

'Hurry up!' She tapped her wrist. 'You're over halfway through your session.'

I was thinking how best to describe Mr Chin and explain that my education and career plans were in jeopardy when Bijou Poulet's words cut through my thoughts.

'Hello, anybody home?'

I felt a jolt as if an alarm clock had gone off next to my ear and a small flash bulb had popped inside my brain. I started talking rapidly. 'Dirty washing worries me. If I think about the way it piles up, I get an empty feeling in my chest. No matter how often I wash my clothes, there's always more. The clothes I wear while doing the washing will be the dirty clothes I wash tomorrow. It's endless, like infinity, the universe. It makes me feel small and meaningless.'

'Ridiculous.' She tilted her chin and tapped her lips with a palm to demonstrate a false yawn.

'Could we discuss abnormality?'

'No.'

'I'd like to talk about how I feel disconnected from the human context, encased in Perspex.'

'Think of a family member, a key family member with breasts.'

'Sorry?'

'Starts with M. Sounds like "other".'

'Mother?'

'It's like pulling teeth with you.'

It felt good to get something right. I smiled at Bijou Poulet and received a frown in return.

'Describe a traumatic incident with this woman.'

'You mean my mother?'

'Whatever. Just pick up the pace. I haven't got all day.' She click-clicked the fingers of one hand and made an upward swirling motion with the index finger of the other.

My mind whirred, went blank, whirred, went blank. There had been many traumatic incidents but at that moment I could not think of a single one. I watched Bijou Poulet tap her pen on the notepad with impatience. I closed my eyes and heard her snort, a long 'Hnihhh.'

Suddenly I could see my mother's face. It was poked between the curtains of the fitting booth in the ladies department of Trout and Son and she was breathing heavily through her nose. I was naked from the waist up, struggling with the clasp of a Miss Teen Starter. Perspiration was running between the two things that had brought me there. They were as round and hard as walnuts and burned on my chest under my mother's gaze.

'Stop sweating. You'll soil the thing and I'm not paying for soiled goods.' She spoke in a hoarse whisper, twisting her neck out of the booth to make sure the shop assistant was out of hearing range.

The plastic clasp, slippery with perspiration, miraculously clicked shut. I pulled up the straps and raised the twin apricot cups over my breasts where they puckered for want of fill. My mother moved in close, breathing relentlessly through her nose. Her eyes were fixed on the cups.

'Just lean forwards and fall into them.'

I bent at the waist and urged whatever flesh there was on my chest and underarms to fall into the cups. Nothing fell. I had no moveable flesh on my fourteen-year-old body. My mother looked at the empty cups and sucked air between her teeth before expelling it through her nose in a dissatisfied 'Hnihhh.' It was clear by the way she frowned that my chest was not good enough and never would be.

'That's it?' Bijou Poulet raised her eyebrows and gave me an incredulous look.

'Correct.'

'That story has no entertainment value whatsoever. You need to learn the value of a good punch line. It makes all the difference.'

'But I wasn't trying to entertain. I didn't think it was expected.'

'What do you think it's like listening to someone ramble on about personal problems? Psychotherapeutic dramatology is a two-way street. What did you expect from me?'

'Mental therapeutics. I was hoping you could help me iron out the kinks of abnormality.'

'I'm not a magician. It's session number one and we haven't even scratched the surface. Someone with your psychological profile needs extensive analytical attention. There's layer upon layer of chronic disorder in your psyche. I'm seeing obsessive-compulsive behaviour and classic female hysteria. Then, of course, there's the Joan of Arc business, the nub of your psycho-sexual problems.' She leaned back in her chair and smiled professionally. 'The good news is, you're not alone with your psychoses. I treat sick people like you every day. The bad news is that your psychology needs reprogramming from the brain stem up. That sort of overhaul doesn't come cheap. We're looking at four, maybe five figures.'

'I don't have that kind of money. My funds are limited.'

'I have an instalment plan with attractive rates for bulk purchase. You'll need to buy bulk. I can assure you.' Bijou Poulet smiled in an unnatural way and made a T with her hands. 'Let's take some time out. I'll give you a minute or two to think over my generous offer.'

I should not have been disappointed by Bijou Poulet's evaluation. Criticism is not new to me. I have heard it all my life and am vaccinated against it to some degree. But what surprised me was the finality of her assessment. I had naively expected some sort of miracle cure. The gift from Mr Chin and the timely assistance of Nigel had convinced me that something groundbreaking was about to happen. I should have known better. The brain is a complex and powerful organ. It consists of one hundred billion neurons and can generate enough energy to illuminate a twenty-watt light bulb. Psychology is not a simple science.

'I'm afraid I can't afford more psychotherapeutic dramatology but it would be helpful to know where my central problem lies.'

'That would be revealed in session seventeen. Not before. Professional reasons, you understand.'

'I don't, no.'

'I'm writing a screenplay, tentatively titled *Cat Fight*.'

'About me?'

'What kind of a psychological professional would I be if I couldn't keep secrets?'

'For a moment I did wonder.'

'The content of my screenplay is private and personal, subject to copyright, patent pending.' She looked at her wrist. 'Your session is terminated.'

Without warning, she slipped a hand under my armpit and pulled me to my feet. I was fumbling with the laces of my shoes as I was bundled out of the door and escorted to the bottom of the stairs. The door was opened and I was ejected on to the street, blinking at the sudden whiteness of the overcast afternoon. I turned to protest but the door was slammed in my face. My eyes fell on the buzzer and I saw something I had not noticed before. The word scratched into the paint was not 'ITCH' as I had first thought. In front of this was the letter 'B'.

Something hard poked into the small of my back but before I could react, a familiar voice spoke: 'Hand over your crocodile bag and make it snappy!'

7

'Nigel!' I said, turning. 'I didn't expect to see you again.'

'How's Ted?' he asked, smirking. The boy was wearing the same clothes as the previous day. The T-shirt was dirtier and the cap was pulled even lower over his brow.

'I was told to vacate the premises.'

'Shame.' Nigel's smirk became a smile, causing the birthmark on his cheek to crease into an oval.

'Yes.'

'And Pooh-let?' He jerked his thumb at the door.

'She was not helpful.'

'Told you it was a waste of money. Those psychologicalists are either nutters or pricks, or nutty pricks.'

'You've had experience with them?'

The boy's face hardened. He did not say anything.

'I'm not sure what to do now. I'm trying to stay positive but my hopes were riding on a personality change before Monday. I've got a deadline.'

'You hungry?' Nigel's eyes slid in the direction of the fish and chip shop. Condensation had collected on the large windows, making it impossible to see inside.

'No, I began my day with a substantial bowl of Swiss muesli, fruit and soya milk with a tub of yoghurt. This breakfast is highly recommended by nutritionists and very popular in the German-speaking world.' I did not bother describing the tofu, root vegetables and unpolished rice I had eaten for lunch. My digestive system was still processing the fibre. 'Have you had lunch?'

'What does it look like?'

It looked like Nigel had not eaten well since infancy but I did not think this was something he needed to hear. His body was thin and angular and the large T-shirt hung from his narrow shoulders like a rag on a coat hanger. The skin on his arms and face was the colour of aged newsprint. It had a dusty quality that suggested eczema.

The boy glanced at the fish and chip shop again.

'Would you like to go inside?'

He shrugged and headed for the door.

I had never been inside the Sea Breeze but I was very familiar with its smell. On a windy day, the odour of boiled animal fat would waft out of the shop and travel as far as the Babylon, which was a good five minutes' power-walk away.

Above the door was a sign: 'Proud to be battering your quality favourites since 1982.' A bell tinkled as Nigel pushed against the door. It jammed partway across the faded blue linoleum floor and took another shove to open fully. Inside, the shop was hot and stuffy. The membrane inside my nostrils contracted at the intense fatty smell and I opened my mouth to aid breathing. A man was standing in front of two large deep-frying vats and turned as we entered. He was pink and very fat. What was left of his hair was combed over his head like a barcode. He swallowed and removed his hand from a basket of chips.

'What'll it be?' he asked.

He moved to the counter and as he wiped his mouth with his hand I noticed that each of his fingers was tattooed with a letter. The letters on the four visible fingers spelled H I P S, which was an unusual message to ink permanently on a hand. His hips were hidden behind the counter but judging by the width of his belt line, they were broad and well-padded with adipose tissue.

'This young man would like something to eat,' I said.

The chipman frowned at Nigel before addressing his reply to me. 'Deep-fried pizza in batter,' he said. 'We highly recommend it.'

I looked around for the other person or persons of the 'we' but the chipman was alone. The shop was large and sparsely furnished with two white plastic tables and three green plastic chairs. The walls must have been painted pastel lemon at some stage but were now yellow-grey. Paint was peeling from the brown ceiling, which was fissured with a network of darker brown cracks. A thick layer of grime had collected on the long menu board hanging over the vats, obscuring the list of food and prices. At the back of the shop was a recess with two doors bearing handwritten signs: 'PRIVATE & PERSONAL' and 'EXCLUSIVE CUSTOMER TOILET.'

'If you're after something fancy, we recommend battered pickled eggs and chip spice.' He held up a plastic container of brown dust that I took to be chip spice. 'The party saveloy in batter is always nice. Served with a toothpick. Novelty value.'

'What would you like?' I turned to Nigel who was studying the food items in a non-refrigerated glass cabinet next to the counter. They had all been battered and pre-fried into lumpy nondescript forms.

'Are those Scotch eggs?' Nigel asked, pointing to five ovular objects the size of tennis balls. They were stacked in a neat pyramid and decorated with a piece of plastic parsley.

'What do they look like?' The chipman's tone was unpleasant.

'You really want to know?' Nigel cocked his head and gave him the same provocative look he had given Ted.

The chipman glared at the boy and threw his hands on the counter, spreading his thick and very pink fingers. I now saw that his left thumb bore a large C and that his tattoos made sense. They were the tattoos of a person proud of his vocation like an anchor on a sailor's arm. The left hand spelled C H I P S, while the right spelled F I S H &.

The chipman was still glaring at Nigel. I did not want a repeat of the previous day's conflict and decided to intervene on his behalf.

'I think they look like meteorites.'

Nigel burst out laughing. The chipman hunched lower, narrowing his eyes at the boy. The fingers of his F I S H & hand bunched into a fist.

I decided to try again. 'I see you're proud to be battering quality favourites since 1982.'

The chipman unhunched himself. He looked at me in a wary but proud way. 'Everything is double deep-fried to crispy, sanitised perfection. Our secret is hair-trigger timing.' He glanced at my tartan trousers. 'You won't find a better Scotch egg this side of Glasgow.'

Battering was clearly a subject close to the chipman's heart. I decided to expand upon it. 'Do you batter chips?'

'Don't be stupid!' He looked shocked as if I had just suggested battering a table leg. 'You can't batter chips.'

I did not understand the rules of deep-frying but it was not a subject I needed to pursue since I had no intention of eating anything made on the premises. Neither did I think double deep-fried food was suitable fare for anyone, much less a malnourished boy, but it was clear that Nigel was not going to listen to nutrition advice from me. I paid four pounds fifty for his Scotch egg, chips and orange drink and watched as the chipman filled a metal basket with the food and plunged it into the vat. He then gave the boiling fat a satisfied nod before reaching over to flick a switch on a small red panel next to the deep-fryer. The powerful ventilator fan inside the metal hood roared to life, filling the room with noise and lifting the chipman's barcode of hair into a vertical position. The noise of the fan made conversation impossible. I could not hear Nigel but I could see him laughing at the chipman's hair as he opened his can of orange drink.

He finished the beverage before the order was ready and grabbed the tray from my hands as we made our way over to a table. Once there, he wasted no time with his meal, tearing open the paper wrapper and shovelling chips into his mouth. I watched in amazement as he swallowed without chewing. I wondered when the boy had last eaten.

'Who looks after you?'

Nigel stopped chewing and gave me a fierce look. 'What's it to you?'

'I'm interested in your welfare.'

'I know how to look after myself.' The boy jutted out his chin and pulled a face. 'You're the one who needs looking after.'

'My mother used to be my legal guardian but it would be incorrect to say that she ever looked after me. She emigrated to New Zealand last year to pursue agricultural life with a sheep farmer. His name is Barry Bunker and he has a large farm with three thousand Perindale sheep. It might interest you to know that sheep outnumber humans by at least ten to one in New Zealand, which is quite a high ratio when you think about it.'

'I like my sheep on a kebab.' The boy laughed and wiped the grease from around his mouth with the back of his hand.

'Do you have a mother?'

'No.' He stopped wiping.

'A father?'

His face tightened but before he could respond, the doorbell tinkled. I turned.

The door opened a crack and a black boot ventured into the shop followed by a thick leg in synthetic black trousers. The owner of the leg gave the door another shove and threw it open wide.

The tall, powerful-looking woman in the doorway let out a jet of air from between a gap in her front teeth. She had broad shoulders and muscular arms and would have looked at home on the Bulgarian national shot put team had she not been wearing the uniform of the British Police Force. Her trousers were tight across her solid upper legs and rode up at the ankles to expose thick black woollen socks. She was strapped into a stab vest, which compressed her wide torso and gave her the look of a jack-in-a-box about to burst. Her skin was rosy pink and freckled. The hair showing under her cap was almost orange. She strode up to the chipman and slapped a thick freckled hand on the counter.

'You want to get that door fixed,' she announced in a booming voice.

The chipman swallowed whatever he had been chewing and moved from the vats to the counter.

I turned back to the table only to discover that Nigel had gone.

As I looked around, my eye caught movement near the back of the shop. It was the small dial on the toilet door. It flipped from 'Vacant' to 'Engaged'.

'What can we do you for?' asked the chipman, wiping his fingers on the grey apron tied around his large waist.

'I'm making a round robin of local eateries,' said the policewoman. 'We've got a missing juvenile.'

'A kid?'

'Juvenile.' The policewoman's broad shoulders straightened. She expelled air from between her teeth.

I glanced over at the toilet door. It remained closed with its dial turned to 'Engaged'.

'We get a lot of little so-and-so's around here. Gangs of them. Armed to the teeth. They smash streetlights and puncture car tyres.' The chipman pointed to the camera mounted above the door. 'Had that installed.'

'The missing juvenile in question is on his own.'

'I don't care about kids on their own. It's the gangs you want to stop. They work in relays; a couple on the lookout while their mates rob you blind. They'd steal the gold out of your teeth.'

'I repeat, he's on his own. Blond, blue eyes. Ten years old. He's in trouble.'

I resisted the urge to glance at the toilet door again.

'The gangs have started writing nonsense on the pavement.' The chipman coughed in an oily way. 'Found a message in chalk outside the door this morning: "FIGHT THE GREED DISEASE." That sort of thing will put good paying customers off their chips. Little so-and-so's. I know what I'd do if I got hold of them.'

'Uh-huh.' The policewoman moved her hands to her waist. It was thick and powerful looking, like the trunk of a healthy *Pinus radiata* tree. She raised her voice. 'What would you do?'

The chipman's eyes followed the policewoman's hands to her utility belt, which was packed with several serious-looking objects sheathed in nylon and leather. He raised an eyebrow and coughed again. 'Naturally, I'd call the police.'

'Call the station if you see a boy on his own. Ask for Big Trish.' She let out another jet of air before tapping the glass cabinet on the counter. 'Is that a pork sausage on a stick?'

'A mouth-watering combo of battered British pork and mature cheddar. We double deep-fry them. Highly recommended.'

At a nod from the policewoman, the chipman picked up a sausage by its stick and dropped it into the vat. He flicked the switch to the ventilator fan and its loud growl filled the room, sending vibrations up the legs of the plastic table to my elbows.

Big Trish looked around the shop, her professional eyes taking in the vats, price list and misted windows before noticing me at the table. She blinked and did a double take. I felt my neck flush as her sharp policewoman's eyes scanned the table, noting Nigel's unfinished food and empty chair before moving back to me. She looked at my tartan trousers and frowned. Before she could make eye contact again, I removed the notebook from my bag and began jotting down the chalk message the chipman had described.

I felt prickly and uncomfortable under her penetrating gaze. It was the same discomfort I had once experienced in a supermarket when I was accused of stealing a bottle of VO5 shampoo. The checkout girl had refused to listen to my explanation and paged the manager over the public address system, announcing, 'Theft at till three.' This had caused a delay at the checkout and customers had become disgruntled and said unpleasant things in loud voices. No one had apologised when the mistake was straightened out, not even the checkout girl who told me to 'get on with it' as I packed my groceries. I left the supermarket under a cloud, feeling as if I had committed a crime despite having proved my innocence.

I was still jotting with my head down as the fan died and the cash register *ding*ed. The door was yanked open and then slammed shut with a *bang*.

The next thing I knew, Nigel was tapping me on the shoulder. His eyes darted from the counter where the chipman was tonging something out of a vat to the door and then back to me. He stuffed the Scotch egg in the pocket of his jeans and scooped up the parcel of chips. With a tilt of his head, he indicated that he was leaving and that I should leave, too. Without knowing why, I stood and followed him out of the shop. I continued following him as he swiftly made his way through a gap in a fence and down a side street that connected the backyards of several shops. This thoroughfare fed into yet another narrow street I had never seen before.

I was breathing heavily by the time we got to the base of the old rail bridge. We were in a dark cul-de-sac whose sole purpose was to provide access to the service steps leading up to the top of the bridge. The rail bridge had not been in use since the 1960s when services to the town were axed under a national drive called 'rationalisation'. You can see the role the bridge once played in local transportation in a photo at the council display. It shows people standing below its brick arch, waving small British flags at a highly polished steam train passing overhead. Out of one of the train's windows, a small gloved hand can be seen. The photo has a caption: 'Royal treatment for our cherished new rail bridge.' It has been a long time since people cherished the rail bridge but the council has not pulled it down because dismantling such a well-constructed piece of architecture would be a costly endeavour.

The steps up the side of the bridge were fenced off with a spiked iron railing and a gate with a chain around it. A sign was bolted to the side of the bridge: 'ACCESS PROHIBITED. PREMISES UNDER 24-HOUR SURVEILLANCE.' I looked around for the CCTV camera and found it mounted midway up the side of the bridge, its lens masked with duct tape.

Nigel dropped to his knees and tugged the bottom of the gate. It screeched and swung out on one hinge to create a small opening. He slipped through the gap and held the gate out for me.

I hesitated. Not sharing information with a police officer was one thing but entering a prohibited area was definitely against the law. I had never done anything illegal in my life. I did not even cross the street on an orange light.

'Hurry up!' Nigel made an impatient face.

Again, I found myself acting impulsively and scrambled through the gap to follow him up the steps. At the top, I used the metal pegs bolted into the wall to ease myself over the brick edge and down on to the tracks.

The bridge was not much wider than a freight train and had a narrow ledge running beside its rails. I followed Nigel along this to the middle of the arch where he stopped in front of a large metal box, which was open and contained a tangled mass of electrical wires. He threw his packet of chips on top of the box and scrambled up to resume eating.

We were not the first people to have trespassed on the bridge. Across the tracks someone had spray-painted 'Chantelle Corby is a big fat lyer' on the brick wall. I looked up and saw something familiar in the distance. It was the decorative 'B' on top of the cinema's façade. I crossed the tracks and, picking up a large piece of wood that had come loose, I wedged it against the wall. I stood on it and craned my neck. The wall was high but by pulling myself up on to my toes I could see the top of the office windows.

Strange! The office was ablaze with light.

Mr Chin never turned on all the office lights and certainly not on a Saturday. Lighting was restricted to the four fluorescent tubes directly over our circle of desks. The office was closed on weekends. I knew this because when I had asked about working Saturdays, he had replied that his business was a nine-to-five operation, five days a week: 'No overtime available or permitted. This office obey rule of EU and other.'

'You could do some damage with this,' said Nigel. 'Knock someone out cold.'

I lowered myself on to the balls of my feet and looked across at the boy who was tossing the Scotch egg from hand to hand like an American baseball pitcher.

'That wouldn't be a good idea,' I said.

'Keep your hair on. Just joking.' He laughed and stuffed another handful of chips in his mouth.

I pushed myself back up on to my toes again, stretching my neck until I could see into the office. It looked different from the bridge, like a normal office with furniture for ten employees. I was straining the arches of my feet and craning my neck when a figure appeared in the window. But before I could make sense of this, Nigel called out 'Cow!' at the top of his lungs.

I twisted around in time to see him hurl the Scotch egg over the bridge. There was a dull thud followed a woman's scream. The boy jumped off the box and took off, sprinting along the narrow ledge at high speed.

I hesitated. After living within the parameters of British law for nearly nineteen years, I had now become a party to two crimes within five minutes.

Nigel made it to the metal foot pegs and glanced back at me before disappearing over the side of the bridge. I had already crossed the tracks and was running along the ledge towards him. I reached the pegs and scurried over, quickly making my way to the service steps and down off the bridge.

The boy was waiting at the bottom, holding the gate open. I slipped underneath and took off at a run, following Nigel as he bolted out of the cul-de-sac, across a backyard and through a car park. We emerged on a familiar street, panting for breath. I recognised the empty shop fronts of Harry Secombe Parade and felt my spirits lift.

I was still struggling to get my breath as I trailed Nigel to the pedestrian crossing in front of the rose gardens. The back of my tongue tasted of metal and my legs were trembling. The run had been frightening and exhilarating but it was not just our escape that had stimulated the adrenal glands on top of my kidneys. It was what I had seen from the bridge.

The figure in the office window had not been Mr Chin.

8

The scene I had witnessed replayed over in my mind as I crossed the pedestrian crossing: a tall man had appeared in the office doorway and walked over to Mr Chin's executive chair, inclining his head as if to converse with its occupant.

I had been too far away to make out the features of the man's face or the details of his clothing but his presence in the office had left me with a sense of foreboding. Mr Chin never entertained. He had no business partners. Neither did he have any friends or family as far as I knew. His policy was clear: 'Office for office staff only. No other permitted or allowed.' Unless he had changed this policy in the last twenty hours or was receiving a delivery of some kind, the newcomer had to be a candidate for employment or a new recruit.

Nigel did not wait for me and had disappeared into the gardens by the time I reached the other side of the road. My mind was on Mr Chin and I was not paying attention to my surroundings, which is an unsafe way to conduct yourself on a public thoroughfare. You never know when the brakes of a vehicle might fail or a motorcyclist might lose control of his handlebars. Vehicles knock down pedestrians every day in Britain where driving under the influence of alcohol, illegal drugs and prescription pharmaceuticals is not uncommon. You take your life in your hands when you leave the door of your home. It pays to be vigilant, which is not what I was being when I arrived at the gate.

For the second time in two days, I collided with another person leaving the gardens. The shock of impact forced the air out of my lungs and left me stunned and gasping for breath. It took me a moment to realise that my face was pressing against the sternum of another very tall human being. It was a man and he was producing a humming sound from deep within his chest. He smelled of patchouli, a pungent herb native to Asia but cultivated extensively in the Caribbean. As I pulled away, I found that I had to tilt my head back at an uncomfortable angle to see his face. I stepped back in surprise, stumbling then righting myself. It was the tall, dark stranger from the previous day.

'Look right, look left and then look right again,' he said, waving a bony finger in my face like a windscreen wiper. The wiper stopped and he held my gaze for a moment before continuing out of the gardens. His limbs were long and his movements easy and graceful. He hummed in a melodious way as he moved but there was stealth and purpose in his manner.

As I watched him walk away, I realised that it was not a Pope's hat on his head but an elaborate hairstyle. Sticking out of this was a piece of wire with a bead on top like the aerial of an old-fashioned transistor radio. His hair must have been extremely long because it had been matted into dreadlocks and then twisted into a spongy tower that added at least twelve inches to his height.

Dreadlocks are popular among certain religious groups and environmentalists but they have a long history and were probably the first hairstyle known to humankind. John the Baptist is said to have worn his hair in dreadlocks. He was a prophet who was born around the time of Jesus Christ. He lived in the desert on a diet of locusts and honey and wore a garment made of camel's hair. I imagine that camel's hair is itchy against the skin but the life of an ascetic is often not a comfortable or dignified one. Neither is his death. John was executed in a most undignified way. His head was cut off and served on a plate to a dancing girl, which is quite unfortunate when you think of it.

The tall, dark man did not look like a religious zealot or an environmentalist but it was difficult to know with certainty without further observation or even contact. As he disappeared around the corner, I noticed a roll of duct tape on his wrist.

'Oy!'

Nigel was standing near the park bench beckoning me. On the bench was a man lying on his side. I recognised the fuchsia trench coat and hurried over.

'He looks pissed but I think he's sick,' said Nigel. 'He's gurglering.'

Jocelyn was curled in a foetal position with his face hidden in his hands. His coat was covered with grit as if he had been rolled in breadcrumbs. Nestled in the V formed by his thighs and calves was his small yellow dog. It opened one eye at my approach but did not move or make a noise.

'Jocelyn,' I said, reaching out to touch his shoulder. 'Are you alright?'

He shivered and murmured something that sounded like '*Maman*'.

I shook his shoulder again, prompting the dog to growl protectively. Nigel edged closer, extending his arm and offering the Chihuahua the back of his hand. The dog sniffed and then began licking the boy's fingers.

'Jocelyn.' I shook him again, harder this time.

He groaned, turning his head to look at me with his hand raised as if to ward off a blow.

'Oh!' I dropped to my knees beside him.

His face was covered in grit and streaked with tears. He twisted around on the bench with effort, upsetting the dog, which leaped down only to be scooped up by the boy. Jocelyn's eyes were bloodshot and his coat was undone. The top two buttons of his lavender shirt were missing. The silk scarf was gone and his neck was red and streaked with scratches. His hair looked like he had been standing in front of a wind machine or riding on the open deck of a lorry. It was wispy and wild and made me think of Farrah Fawcett, an American actress who helped popularise the blow dryer in the 1980s.

'Have you had a fall from a lorry?' I asked.

'I'm fragilised,' he said in a weak voice. 'No lorry, dear, but I feel like I've been dragged behind a motorcycle.'

I waited as he roused himself, swinging his feet to the ground with a delicate sigh. His attention shifted to Nigel, who was holding the dog against his chest and rubbing it under the chin.

'Have you been assaulted?' I scrutinised the scratch marks on his neck. It looked as if someone had tried to strangle him.

'Abused.' Jocelyn's red-rimmed eyes flicked back to me. 'Terribly abused.'

'When did this happen?'

'*Il y a quelques minutes.*' He nodded towards the dog in Nigel's arms. 'That dog saved my life.'

'Your Chihuahua?' It was no bigger than a teapot and did not look violent or capable of saving anyone's life.

'He's called Herb Alpert and he's terribly brave. He made mincemeat of my attacker's ankles.'

'What did your attacker look like?' I thought of the tall, dark stranger but immediately rejected this idea. The man had not reacted in a desperate or violent manner despite being head-butted in the sternum.

'He came at me from behind. I did the only thing I could.'

'You crushed the arch of his foot with your heel and then drove your elbow into his abdomen?'

'I closed my eyes.' He fluttered his eyelids as if to demonstrate what he had done. 'I didn't see his face and he probably didn't even see mine.'

I looked around the gardens for signs of criminal activity but apart from the taped-over CCTV camera, nothing seemed out of place or suspicious. The only other people in the gardens were two grey-haired women. They were taking a cutting from a rose bush with a pair of secateurs and seemed more like petty thieves than assailants.

'Those pensioners might have seen something.'

'I doubt it, dear. It happened inside the gents.'

The rose gardens did not have regular public toilets, but they did have an authentic open-air French urinal. This was constructed from decorative wrought iron and painted green to blend in with the garden scenery. Its iron panels were cemented into the ground and came up to shoulder height to provide a view of users' heads.

The urinal is the last of several that were erected under the Modernisation Drive, which characterised local government policy from 1969 until 1973. An entire wall of the council's photo display is devoted to this period, which was dubbed the 'Maverick Years' after Jim Snick. Mr Snick earned a reputation as a flamboyant and reckless mayor despite initiating several progressive policies that improved the quality of life for the community. In the council photos he is wearing flared trousers and his trademark tasselled leather waistcoat. His hair is high and wide and he has large sideburns.

'Was the prick after money?' asked Nigel. The boy had pushed his cap back to allow the Chihuahua to lick him below the ears.

'Yes,' said Jocelyn, looking from the boy to me. 'Who is this young man?'

'Nigel,' I said. 'He's been helping me.'

The boy shrugged. 'Did he nick anything?'

'He stripped my pockets: purse, handkerchief, even my peppermints. I don't care about the money but the purse was my mother's. Vintage Dior. A keepsake.'

I waited for Jocelyn to wipe his eyes before asking the obvious question. 'Shouldn't you call the police?'

'No!' Jocelyn and Nigel both answered at once.

'You're forgetting where I was attacked, my dear. They'd draw the wrong conclusions.' Jocelyn's eyes were wide. 'Doesn't the name George Michael mean anything to you?'

The name did mean something to me. I had read about George Michael in the 'Pop Culture' section of the public library before it closed. Mr Michael favoured leather trousers and had been part of a male singing duo called Wham! that had several popular musical hits. Early in his career he had changed his name to George Michael from the polysyllabic Georgios Kyriacos Panayiotou, a decision that probably helped avoid spelling errors on record labels. I was about to share this information with Jocelyn when Nigel abruptly announced he was leaving.

He kissed the dog's tennis-ball head and handed the creature to Jocelyn. 'Nice dog.'

'Where are you going?' I asked.

But the boy was already walking away at great speed. At the gate, he gave a backwards glance. It was aimed at the dog and he did not respond when I waved.

'Interesting,' said Jocelyn, shaking his head. 'Herb Alpert doesn't pop his cork for just anyone.'

'Nigel is interesting.'

'Could you help me up, dear?' Jocelyn was struggling to push himself off the bench with the dog tucked under an arm.

I put my hand under his other arm to steady him, and as he leaned against my shoulder I realised he was trembling. He was in no condition to walk home alone. I offered to accompany him and we set off at a slow pace, pausing in front of the floral clock where he released my arm to put down the dog, which had begun to squirm. It trotted over to the base of the CCTV camera pole to cock its leg.

Jocelyn glanced at the masked camera and shook his head. 'Why must we live in fear? What's happened to the world?'

'Karl Marx would say that wealth has accumulated in the hands of the owners of the means of production,' I replied. 'People are disgruntled.'

'It's all so difficult without liquid comfort.' His eyes filled. 'When I don't drink, every day seems the same as the one before, but each passing day leads cumulatively to days and weeks with remorseless inevitability.' Jocelyn turned away from the clock and looped his arm through mine as we walked towards the gate. 'It's those disappeared days that silently measure out the ageing process. I've reached fifty-nine and am scratching my head.'

'You don't seem old.'

'I'll take that as a compliment.' He ran his fingers through his unruly silver hair, tucking it behind his ears. 'My liver is in its nineties, my dear. Occupational hazard, I'm afraid.'

'What is your occupation?'

'Gentleman alcoholic.'

This was an unusual occupation but Jocelyn was an unusual and sensitive man. I decided not to press him for details.

'I have my sights set on a career in criminology. It's a vocation with a future. Crime is on the up and up. Your assault is a case in point.'

'Heaven help us.'

When we reached the gate, we found our way blocked by a short, wide woman dressed in pale blue stretch-cotton sports clothes. She looked about thirty and had dull sandy hair that was pulled back tight in a severe ponytail. Her face was pink and putty-like. In the middle of her forehead was a large lump. It was coloured the electric blue of a fresh bruise.

'You seen a kid here?' she asked. Her voice had the moist roughness of a cigarette smoker. 'A boy.'

Jocelyn and I looked at each other. Neither of us spoke.

'A little bastard in a baseball cap.' The woman had raised her hand to her brow and was scanning the gardens. 'He took off Friday. Hasn't been home since.'

'Is he your child?' I asked.

'Of course he's mine.'

'But you called him a little bastard.'

'I can call him whatever I like.' Her small eyes flashed.

'You didn't marry his father?'

She dropped her hand and took a step closer. 'I wouldn't marry a jailbird.'

'Sorry?'

'You heard me.' She scowled at my trousers and leaned in close, breathing hard through her nose. 'You Scotch git.'

'I'm not Scottish. I just have an affinity for tartan.'

Her breath smelled like stomach problems and bad teeth and as I backed up to avoid it, Jocelyn wedged himself between us.

'Dear lady,' he said, holding up a shaky hand like a Native American chief. 'I can assure you, we've not seen a little bastard.'

The woman's attention shifted to Jocelyn. She stopped scowling. Her mouth softened into a coy smile. I'd seen my mother do the same thing when Mr Da Silva offered her a meat sample.

'A gentleman.' She thrust out her chest. Her breasts were substantial, the size and shape of two Welsh turnips.

'And you, my dear, are a lady. I wish you every success in your endeavour.' Without waiting for a response, Jocelyn took my arm and manoeuvred me around the woman and out of the gate. We were some distance from the gardens before he turned to me.

'Surely that wasn't Nigel's mother.'

I shook my head. 'He said he doesn't have a mother. I'm inclined to believe him.'

I was about to describe what the boy and I had got up to together when Jocelyn stopped at a bus shelter to read a campaign poster for Roger Bottle. The sides of the mayoral candidate's moustache had been twirled into points to resemble Lord Kitchener's and his finger was pointing directly at the camera like the politician's World War I recruitment poster. But instead of Mr Kitchener's 'Wants You!' tagline, the poster urged: 'Your Children Need You! Vote for Rog. Vote for Family Values.'

'Here we go again.' Jocelyn sighed and bent down to pick up his dog, which was pawing his ankle.

'Again?' Roger Bottle was a newcomer to the local political scene. The *Cockerel* had described him as a retired international businessman returning to save his hometown from economic ruin: 'Former High-flyer Returns to the Nest'.

'The unpleasantness, my dear. The name-calling and public jostling.' He sighed. 'There was a time when I couldn't buy groceries in peace.'

'People jostled you in supermarkets?' I had witnessed a lot of repressed anger in supermarket queues but never physical violence.

'I've been jostled everywhere, all my life.'

'I'm very sorry to hear that.'

'One grows accustomed.'

Jocelyn lived on Des O'Connor Crescent in a house my mother would have described as palatial before criticising it as showy. It was a three-storey Edwardian terrace with large windows and tiled steps leading up to a lacquered blue door with a polished brass knocker in the shape of a woman's hand. The small front garden was trimmed with a neat hedge and contained colourful flowerbeds and bushy herbs in terracotta pots.

I recognised the smell of Bulgarian rose as Jocelyn opened the door and led me through the hall to the parlour. It was a pretty but crowded room furnished with French furniture, shiny brocade curtains and hundreds of cushions. The walls were covered with embossed wallpaper and featured several paintings of an attractive woman with the dark lips and blonde crimped hair of a film star from the 1940s. The mantelpiece and surfaces of tables and dressers were crowded with framed photographs of the same starlet.

'You have a very decorative house,' I said.

'Money may not buy happiness, my dear, but it does buy nice things,' he said with a sigh. 'If you'll excuse me for a moment.'

Jocelyn said he needed to freshen up. He pointed to a door off the parlour and kindly asked me to make a pot of tea.

The kitchen was large and did not look like it had been used in a very long time. Its tiled bench tops were spotless and its chrome was highly polished. The refrigerator was empty apart from a Tetra Pak of long-life milk and several bottles of Indian tonic water while the cupboards appeared to contain nothing but cakes and biscuits. I thought about Jocelyn's pancreas as I filled the kettle and put two teabags of Lady Grey into a large floral teapot. The pancreas is located behind the stomach and secretes enzymes and hormones that play an essential role in digestion. Jocelyn's high-sugar diet must have been punishing this organ but he was not the only person I knew with a dangerous sugar addiction. Mr Chin's consumption of Chinese sweetmeats was phenomenal. His sugar intake had to be at least five times the recommended daily allowance.

I became aware of Mr Chin's sweet tooth during my first week at work when he had led me over to the cinema's former film room. This was his personal storage area, he had explained. I was not permitted to enter or take anything from the tall cupboard, which contained a stockpile of cakes and sweets in brown cartons stamped with the name and address of a Chinese wholesale outlet in Liverpool.

'Delicious moon cake and speciality sweet sesame cracker and so on forbidden for low-grade and ordinary staff,' he said. 'Privilege for rank of boss.'

'I would never touch your cakes,' I replied.

'What wrong with delicious Chinese cake?' Mr Chin narrowed his eyes. He reached inside a carton and laid a proprietary hand on a red and gold presentation box. 'Chinese moon cake famous and glorious.'

'It's the sugar content. I don't want to compromise my organs.'

'Crazy and nuts.' He shook his head in disbelief, as if a life without moon cakes was one not worth living. 'What crazy girl such as you eat?'

'Root vegetables.'

'Nuts!'

'Those, too.'

Jocelyn's pipes stopped rattling overhead as I arranged a selection of biscuits on a tray with the teapot and matching floral cups. I was carrying it into the parlour when he appeared through the other door. He had changed into rose-coloured satin pyjamas and a burgundy robe. On his feet were burgundy slippers with a white faux-fur trim. He looked fresher and happier. His eyes were shining and his face had been washed and redusted with powder and blusher. A light floral fragrance wafted up from him as he sat on the sofa. I bent forwards to pour the tea and caught another smell, something tangy that made me think of juniper berries.

'The woman in the portraits is very attractive,' I said.

'My dear mother,' he replied. 'Life is not the same since she left me.'

'Did she emigrate to New Zealand?'

'She passed away.' He dabbed his eyes with the sleeve of his robe. 'The call of the bog.'

I thought of the mummified Vikings found in northern European marshes and waited for him to explain.

'Irish whiskey, my dear.' He placed a hand on the right side of his chest. 'The warmer the heart, the harder the liver.'

'A hard liver is never a good thing.'

I would have liked to mention the risks of an overburdened pancreas but this did not seem the right moment to bring up another internal organ. Organ failure is a sensitive issue and I have learned to pace myself on this subject during conversation.

I watched Jocelyn take his sixth biscuit and break a corner off for the Chihuahua on his knee. His hands had stopped shaking and despite the red scratches on his neck, he looked remarkably relaxed. The satin pyjamas gave him a regal air, like that of a kindly monarch about to bestow a favour on a knight. It seemed like a good moment to seek his advice.

'I have a problem.'

He looked at me, another biscuit poised over his teacup.

'I need to find an expert and right the wrongs of my personality by Monday.'

'What's wrong with your personality?' He dunked the biscuit in his tea. 'I find you positively delightful.'

The compliment made my throat constrict. I had to swallow several times before I could continue. 'I'm abnormal.'

'That's probably why I like you.'

A muscle or valve near my duodenum fluttered. I paused to consider this physical disturbance and realised that I was experiencing something quite alien and possibly pleasant. I had to force myself to set aside these feelings for later examination in order to continue the conversation.

'But I need to change camps. There's a lot riding on my getting normal by Monday.'

'Normality is overrated, my dear. Like sanity.' He raised an eyebrow. 'I prefer desperate eccentricity myself.'

'You don't seem desperate.'

'You haven't seen me trying to decide what to wear. It's very limiting to live in a town like this. A gent cannot wear anything with flair in public and expect to remain in one piece.' Jocelyn glanced at my trousers and smiled. 'Unless of course he's wearing the colours of the Macnee.'

'You know the tartan!' A thrill went through me. 'A clan is a place to hang your hat.'

'And a tartan kilt is one of the few safe options for a gentleman of my calling.'

The tartans of Scotland were a fascinating subject and I would have liked to talk at length about their history but I had noticed Jocelyn stifling a yawn. He was the nicest and most logical person I had ever met but he had just been assaulted and needed to recuperate.

'Could we meet again?'

'With pleasure.'

It was getting dark when I left his house. The streetlights were on but many of the bulbs were smashed or missing. I was feeling positive and energised after my conversation with Jocelyn and power-walked to the end of the street where I paused under a streetlamp to catch my breath.

The curtains of the house on the corner were open and a woman with fluffy dark hair was sitting in front of a large television. The screen showed a reporter holding a microphone in his hand. He cringed as something exploded behind him. The image disappeared and then reappeared. Smoke was billowing out from behind him as he stumbled and disappeared from the frame.

I was absorbed in the scene on the television and did not notice the woman leave the room or open her front door.

She called out to me. 'I've been waiting.'

I shaded my eyes from the glare of the streetlight and noticed a metal nameplate attached to the wall of her porch: LADY LUCK.

9

'Your future lies in my hands,' called the woman from the porch.

'Sorry?' I replied.

'Lady Sybil Luck.'

With a bow, she moved out from under the porch and I saw that she was dressed in a shiny black one-piece that would have been described as a 'cat suit' if worn by Dame Enid Diana Rigg. A vinyl cat suit was an unusual choice for anyone in the town, especially for a woman of mature age. It had a large silver zipper running from the groin to the neckline and its tight trouser legs and sleeves were trimmed with metal studs. She tapped the place on her wrist where a watch should have been and raised an eyebrow.

'I don't wear a timepiece.' I lifted my cardigan sleeve to show the absence of a watch. 'I don't like any sort of strap or belt. It's the pressure. I couldn't bear sock garters, for example.'

'Are you coming in or not?' She rolled her eyes and motioned for me to enter her house with a twitch of the fingers.

On another evening, I might have hesitated but I was feeling upbeat and could find no reason not to accept the invitation. I followed her into the room I had just viewed from the pavement. It was dim and smelled vaguely of dog and stale cigarette smoke. The only light source was the television. Its volume was turned up very high and I found myself shouting to be heard.

'How did you know I was outside?'

'Why do you think I'm called Lady Luck?'

'Because it's your name?'

Instead of answering, she emitted a clicking sound, which made me wonder whether she had loose dentures or was rolling a ball bearing around inside her mouth.

Her hand swooped on the remote control on the arm of a chair. I looked at the screen as she waved it and saw the reporter's dusty head emerge like a ghost amid the smoke. The image died with an electrical zip and apart from the faint glow from the streetlamp, the room was dark. I could make out the silhouette of the cat suit as it moved away from me but I could not see what the woman was doing. It was disconcerting to find myself in a darkened room with a stranger and not know whether she had recently been discharged from a mental asylum.

'Who are you?'

'A *voyante*.'

Strange! Mr Chin had suggested I see a fortune-teller and here was one inviting me into her home. A thrill went through me.

'Take the settee.' Mrs Luck's voice came from the other side of the room. 'His Highness Gaikwad requires personal space.'

'There's someone else here?' I squinted into the gloom but saw nothing with a vascular system amid the many shadowy objects and furnishings.

'Gaikwad's here in spirit. He's an Indian spirit guide.'

'From the Indian subcontinent or the Americas?'

'Indian Indian.'

'Native American Indian Indian?'

'Indian Indian, tandoori Indian Indian!' The source of the voice had moved to near my elbow. She sounded irritated. 'Just sit down!'

I felt the grip of a hand on my elbow and was propelled towards the couch. As my buttocks touched down on a cushion, I found myself sinking low. Either the springs had gone or part of the stuffing was missing. From my new low position, the room looked even more cluttered and shadowy.

The armchair beside the couch creaked as Mrs Luck settled herself and switched on a lamp on the coffee table between us. The bulb must have been less than twenty watts because its weak circle of light only reached as far as our feet and cast a faint glow over the rest of the room. I could now make out the outlines of the television, dining table and bulky desktop computer. On each surface were piled other objects: boxes, papers, ornaments, clothes, plastic bags and half-dead plants. The room was full of belongings, more like a storeroom than a living room. The only clear space on the floor was an equilateral triangle of carpet between the open door, lounge suite and television.

Mrs Luck clicked again. I turned towards her and in the meagre light of the lamp I realised that she was not of pensioner age at all. She was probably about fifty but had the premature puckers and wrinkles of a cigarette smoker or Australian surf lifesaver. She did not appear to be either of these, which made me wonder whether she had a nervous or angry disposition that entailed a lot of facial expression. The vertical lines on her forehead were like the pleats of a concertina.

Her knees cracked as she bent forwards and rifled through a pile of papers near her feet.

'There you are!' she said, picking up a round, hollow object and banging it free of dust. As she thrust her head into it, I saw that it was an oversized turban, pre-wound with the solid appearance of a massive cloth coconut. Its centrepiece was a large green jewel that twinkled weakly in the light of the lamp. The enormous turban gave the fortune-teller a magisterial and impenetrable look, something between Barbra Streisand and an official of the Ottoman Empire.

'That's a very impressive turban,' I said.

'Genuine,' she replied with obvious pride, tilting it away from her ears which had become engulfed by the cloth. 'It came with a certificate.'

'From India India?'

'eBay. It had a peacock feather but the dog got it.'

'You have a dog?'

'Had.' She clicked again. 'German shepherd. Had to get rid of it.'

'My mother never allowed dogs inside the house.'

'Did she get bitten, too?'

I shook my head. 'She had a strident personality and an aversion to animals.'

'Poor woman.'

Mrs Luck's reply did not correspond to my statement but this was not new to me. My mother virtually never responded to anything I said because she did not listen when I spoke. 'You remind me of my mother.'

'She must have been very attractive.'

I frowned and did not respond. Mrs Luck gave me a fierce look. 'The sooner we start, the sooner we can get this over and done with.' She adjusted the turban and pointed to my shoes. 'Now do as I say.'

'What do you have in mind?'

'Just do as I say.'

Mrs Luck's manner was domineering, another personality trait she shared with my mother.

'Place your feet flat on the floor and fold your hands in your lap. I will now work myself up into a trance. My body will shake and I'll make channelling noises. Take no notice. Do not interfere.'

I reminded myself that Mr Chin had suggested I see a fortune-teller as I placed the soles of my Hush Puppies on the carpet and folded my hands in my lap.

Mrs Luck closed her eyes and mumbled, 'Gaiiik-wad, Gaiiik-wad, Gaiiik-wad', and then commenced to blow air through her lips and make them vibrate. The sound she made was like a refrigerator and I was enjoying the mechanical-like hum when it suddenly stopped. Her shoulders jumped and her body bucked in the armchair. She opened her eyes and mouth and made a noise between a growl and a cough. Her eyes reddened and bulged from their sockets. She growl-coughed again.

Stifling a desire to assist, I watched her grip the armrests and open her mouth wide enough to hold a tangerine between her teeth. Her tongue emerged and flopped over her bottom lip. Her face dissolved into wrinkles and her upper body shook violently.

Raising a hand from the armrest, she punched herself in the

middle of the chest. She coughed and then punched again. A projectile, small and oval like a broad bean, shot out of her mouth at high speed and skimmed across the carpet. I glanced down and recognised the black and white stripes of an Everton Mint.

Gulping air, she flopped back against the armchair. There she remained, moaning and breathing raggedly for at least a minute. When she finally spoke it was to accuse me.

'You didn't lift a finger!' Her voice was hoarse.

'Correct.' I did not add that it had been extremely difficult to remain immobile while she was bucking and coughing.

'I was choking to death!'

'You said you'd make noises and shake. You told me not to move.'

'That was the death rattle.' She shook her head. The turban tilted to one side.

'But the death rattle occurs at the moment of death.'

'Just shut up!' She shook her head and shot me a hard look. 'I'm not risking another near-death experience. We'll use the cards.'

Mrs Luck lifted a buttock and felt around under the cushion of the armchair. Again I was reminded of my mother, who used to keep a block of Dairy Milk under the cushion of her chair. She purchased all her chocolate in family blocks but always consumed them on her own. The first time I tasted chocolate was after she had left for New Zealand. I was looking for lost coins to buy bread when I came across a half-eaten block under her cushion. Its surface had whitened and gone dry and its taste had been disappointing, like dusty cucumbers sprinkled with sugar.

'There you are!' Mrs Luck slipped on a pair of reading spectacles. The frames were bent and sat askew over her nose. She picked up a stack of playing cards from the table.

Until that moment, her movements had been erratic, even clumsy. But with the cards in her hand, her manner changed entirely. The deck was shuffled from hand to hand, stretched up one arm and down the other, fanned out and finally, thrown from left to right in a graceful arc. She then reassembled them into a tight pack and handed this to me.

'Have you worked in a casino?'

'Just pipe down and shuffle.' She nudged the turban off her forehead. 'Then lay six cards face down on the table.'

I had never handled playing cards before and struggled to divide the pack in an orderly manner. It was even more challenging to reassemble them. I was wedging one half into the other when she squawked.

'Stop shoving! That's a Belle Karma Arcana deck. Cost me an arm and a leg on Amazon.'

As I loosened my grip, a card slipped out and fluttered to the floor. It bore a decorative medieval image, a skeleton wearing a tall hat.

'You've let death slip between your fingers!' She picked it up in a significant way and placed it on the table.

'Is that a bad sign?'

'The cards never lie.'

'About what?'

'Just zip it and pick another five cards. Place them face down.' She rapped the tabletop with her knuckles. 'As you choose the cards, clear your mind and visualise the thing you seek.'

I sat up straight. How did she know I was seeking something?

'Hurry up.'

I closed my eyes and tried to visualise normality but what came to mind was a man sitting in a Ford Mondeo eating a meat pie. I tried again and got the pie man once more only now he had thrown the pie wrapper out of the window and was rummaging in the glove compartment for his cigarettes. How could I visualise normality when I had no idea what it entailed?

'Hello, anybody home?'

I felt a jolt like an electric shock and opened my eyes to find Mrs Luck waving a hand in front of my face. She pulled it away as I peeled off the top five cards and laid them face down on the table.

She began turning them over, muttering with each turn. The images on the cards were colourful, stars and figures of royalty.

Muttering louder, she pushed the turban to the back of her head and scratched her damp hairline with her fingernails. She stopped scratching and examined her nails.

'Is there a problem?'

She shook her head again and tapped the tabletop. 'These could be the cards of Mahatma Gandhi.'

'Oh!' My chest tightened. 'But Mr Gandhi was a visionary and a hero. It takes determination and courage to lead a subcontinent to independence. I doubt I have the necessary vigour.'

'I doubt you have much of anything. Something has gone wrong with my channels.' She shook her head and the turban swivelled, tilting to one side. Grabbing it with two hands, she ripped it off her head and tossed it on to the floor. 'I should've paid attention.'

'To what?'

'Signs and messages.' She raised her eyes to the ceiling. 'You wouldn't understand.'

'But I do understand! I've been finding a lot of messages lately. Something's going on in this town. People are disgruntled and restless. You'd be surprised what someone is writing about Chantal Corby.'

'What?' Mrs Luck rocked forwards on her chair and gave me her full attention.

'Chantal Corby. Apparently, she loves it.'

She squawked.

'I've also seen an accusation of dishonesty.'

She squawked again, louder this time. 'That's my daughter you're maligning!'

'I thought your name was Luck.'

Mrs Corby slammed her fist on the table and hit the remote control. The television burst into life and the room brightened. The screen showed the same scene but now the reporter had lost his helmet and was staggering around in a disoriented way as if he had been hit by a piece of flying concrete. There was something else on the screen, too, the silhouette of a person with a handbag. I twisted around and realised that it was the reflection of a woman heading for the front door.

The doorbell chimed as Mrs Corby switched off the television.

I was rising to my feet when the newcomer appeared in the doorway. She was dressed in jeans with gold piping and had a tank top decorated with 'ONE VOTE CAN CHANGE THE FUTURE' in glittery embroidery.

'The door was open,' she said.

'Who are you?' Mrs Corby rose to her feet and pushed me aside.

'I had an appointment at eight o'clock.' The woman smiled in an apologetic way. 'Sorry I'm late but it was impossible to get away with all the election palaver. I'm at my wits' end with that lot down at the council. I'm hoping you might shed some light.'

My ears pricked up at the mention of the council but before I could ask the woman what she meant, Mrs Corby had turned to me. Her expression was fierce. Her wrinkles had compressed and her small eyes flashed anger.

'Then who the hell are you?'

'Sherry.'

'You're not getting anything to drink.'

'I don't imbibe.'

'I've had enough of this.' She held out her hand. 'Give me thirty quid and get out.'

'But I didn't engage your services.'

Mrs Luck's hand twitched. Her jaw moved as if she were chewing a piece of beef gristle.

'I've not received any guidance from you.'

'You haven't?' It was the client in the glittery top. She was looking at me with her eyebrows raised.

'No.'

'The cheek of it!' Mrs Luck's voice was high and threatening. She moved to block my exit. 'You've taken up my time. Time is money.'

'Correct.' I had heard Mr Chin use the same expression. I glanced at her small wrinkled hand and thought of something else Mr Chin liked to say. It was a line he used when negotiating gold prices with dentists.

'The most I can afford is ten pounds.' I hesitated before delivering another of his lines. 'I'm doing you a favour.'

The fortune-teller blinked in surprise and nodded as if without thinking.

I was handing over the ten-pound note when someone very wide and forceful barged into the room, knocking the client in the glittery top out of the circle of light and creating an exit route for me. I recognised the belligerent woman from the rose gardens and began edging towards the door.

'Who's this, Mum?' asked the newcomer, giving me an unfriendly look.

'Nobody,' said the fortune-teller. 'She's just leaving.'

I smiled to show peaceful intentions as I stepped around the wide woman.

She spoke again as I was heading out the door.

'I just got propositioned by a workman coming out of that old cinema. The cheeky bastard offered me twenty quid and promised me a good time.'

10

I stopped under the streetlamp at the corner and looked back at the living-room window. The woman whom I had now identified as Chantal Corby was waving her arms about and speaking in an animated way. The lump on her forehead looked grotesque in profile, like a second nose or enormous boil. The client in the glittery top must have retreated into the shadows because she had completely disappeared from view.

As I thought over what Chantal Corby had said about the presence of a workman at the cinema, I felt myself reacting with alarm as if I had just read a newspaper headline about rising unemployment. I knew from experience that I had to take action or I would become anxious and then fearful. As B.S. Pappenheimer aptly describes in *The Disempowered Drudgery of the Human Condition*, anxiety if left unchecked will transform into fear and then hopelessness, a downward progression of emotional states that ultimately leads to anti-depressants or, in the worst-case scenario, death by suicide. I needed to establish that my fears were unfounded. This I could achieve by walking briskly past the Babylon while keeping my eyes open like a policeman on the beat. Mr Chin would be none the wiser.

Night had fallen and it was now very dark and quiet on the street. According to the *Council Handbook on Women's Self-Defence*, muggers prey on a certain type of person and that type is more often than not a woman, alone at night with a bag under her arm. The handbook was printed during the Maverick Years but its contents are more relevant than ever since the council reduced street lighting in favour of CCTV camera surveillance. In its prologue, the handbook states that criminals are less likely to attack someone who walks with determination and it encourages women to walk fast and in a confident manner. I did not doubt the truth of this information but walking with confidence can be difficult when you know the victim profiles for such crimes.

By the time I reached the rose gardens, my pulse was elevated and I paused at the gate to catch my breath. The council handbook states in no uncertain terms that parks, playgrounds and docks should be avoided at night. I had been careful to stop next to a streetlamp and now noticed under its glow that a new campaign poster for Roger Bottle had been recently pasted to the wall. It showed the mayoral candidate dressed in a green military-style jacket, saluting the camera: 'Safety First! Vote Roger Bottle. More Surveillance. More Security.'

As I removed my notebook to jot down the line, I noticed something else. Written on the pavement below the poster was new graffiti in white chalk: 'BEWARE THE PEDDLER AND APOSTLE OF BALDERDASH.'

I copied everything down and set off again, swinging my arms to stimulate my heart and lungs. Power-walking is the king of exercises but it must be done in a natural manner. Stiff arm movements do more harm than good, as any soldier outside Buckingham Palace must know. Restricted arm swinging not only creates tension in the trapezius muscles across the shoulders but the weight of a busby must also cause chronic neck strain. Soldiering is never a comfortable career choice, especially in times of war.

I saw the lights even before I reached the cinema. The entire first floor was glowing fluorescent white like a medical laboratory. Every light must have been turned on, something I had never seen Mr Chin do in the entire time I had worked for him. Energy efficiency was a key office policy, something he had drilled into me from day one.

I keep a note of Mr Chin's cost-saving measures in the THRIFT subsection of my OBSERVATIONS ring binder. It is one of my thickest subsections. In one entry, I note his insistence on getting two cups of tea out of every tea bag and his natural preference for the first cup. When I once suggested making a pot of tea and sharing it, he protested: 'Second cup best for girl! Flavour gentle and softy.' He also insists that milk is a waste of money and uses sugar in sachets stamped with the dragon logo of the Jade Dragon restaurant. The deal he got on the office furniture is a particular source of pride. This came from an estate agency that went bankrupt when housing prices fell. Eager to clear his office before the bailiff arrived, the estate agent had sold everything to Mr Chin for two hundred pounds, cash. I still have documents in my computer under such listings as 'Foreclosure', 'Divorce' and 'Death'. The categories do not say very positive things about the dealings of the estate agency business. I often wonder what happened to the agent after his own bankruptcy.

I stood in the relative safety of the bus shelter across the street and observed the office. A bus came and went but nothing stirred in the window and no one emerged from the office door. With my handbag pressed under my arm, I crossed the street and as I entered the gloomy space under the awning I picked up the scent of a menthol smoker or pomade user. Something crunched underfoot. I stopped and squinted into the darkness.

Strange! The display case had been smashed.

Before I could consider the significance of this vandalism, I heard a cough behind me. It was the humid passage-clearing rumble of a smoker. I froze as the silhouette of a thin man appeared from behind a pillar. He was backlit by the streetlight and I could not see the features of his face. He moved towards me swiftly, cutting off my exit and cornering me next to the damaged display case. I did not want to be overpowered by a man in a dark space. This is called the Worst-Case Scenario and is described in detail in the red section of the council handbook.

'Got the time, darling?' he asked.

Page one of the red section flashed through my mind: 'Remain calm and keep a clear head!'

'I'm sorry, I don't wear a watch,' I said, trying to keep my voice calm and maintain a clear head.

'Ha, ha. A comedian, I like that.'

The man's voice made goose pimples rise on my forearms. His accent and manner of speaking were strangely familiar. It was a voice I had heard somewhere, on a bus or in the street. As he moved closer, I could make out the outline of a woollen hat on his head.

'I'm not in the entertainment industry.'

'I know what industry you're in, darling. Ha, ha.'

I wasn't sure what made the man laugh but I decided to humour him. Humouring is like bantering and can be helpful for reducing tension in a difficult situation. I had no comedic experience but I did recall the jokes Nigel had tried on Ted.

'A funny thing happened on the way to a funeral.'

'Ha, ha.' The man laughed again and leaned in close. 'So what happened on the way to a funeral, darling?'

'I don't know.'

'That's brutal. Ha, ha.'

His hand slapped the wall next to my head and stayed there. I willed myself to remain calm and keep my wits about me. The handbook does not provide tips on how to escape from under a darkened cinema awning but it does feature several illustrations on ways to subdue an attacker. These are found at the back under Helpful Hints. I considered my options. I could give the man's arm an upper chop with my forearm and cause him to fall against the wall or I could bring my knee up fast and compress his testicles. Alternatively, I could jab my fingers into his eyes or swing an elbow against his nose and crush his lateral nasal cartilage. The book offered one last possibility, 'The Old Fool's Gold Routine.' This involved asking the attacker a question: 'Is that your ten-pound note on the ground?' When the assailant followed the natural impulse to look down, the victim was then free to head-butt him across the bridge of his nose.

I had too many options.

'Tell us another one, darling.' The man moved his face close to mine. I felt his breath on my neck and could smell pickled onions and lager. There was another odour, too, a mechanical smell like the cogs of a racing bike. I decided to try humouring again.

'Did you hear the one about the button mushroom and the bishop?'

'No.'

'Neither did I.'

'Tease.'

The man's hand fell on my shoulder and squeezed. I tried to slide out of his grip but he held me tight. His thumb was pressed into my clavicle, which is the long, curved bone that connects the arm to the torso. This bone is located close to the throat. The hand's proximity to my windpipe was worrying but I was now out of jokes.

'How much do you charge, darling?' He increased the pressure of his thumb. 'I'm coming into money.'

'It depends on what you want to purchase.'

'No holds barred.'

'You must be a wrestling enthusiast. The ancient Greeks were proponents.'

'We could try it Greek style.'

I was mentally calibrating the force needed to sufficiently compress his testicles with my knee when a deep, melodious voice filled the air: 'Ho, ho, ho.'

My assailant gasped and released my shoulder. As he turned, I saw his face in profile. A tremor travelled up my spine. Shanks!

He took a step back and cried out. 'Jesus! It's the bloody Pope!'

The outline of someone very tall appeared before the streetlight. He held up his arm and moved his index finger like a windscreen wiper, singing in a deep voice:

I spy a spider,
Catching a fly,
Bide Mr Spider,
Fly Mrs Fly

Glass crunched beneath my Hush Puppies as I dodged around Shanks and made for open ground. I reached the pavement and broke into a run, and did not slow down until I was on the high street. When I got to the town hall, I stopped to catch my breath.

I was leaning against the clamshell of the fountain, marvelling at the arrival of the tall, dark man, when I became aware of rapid footsteps approaching from the other side of the square. I looked up and recognised Big Trish, the policewoman. She was running hard and her breathing was laboured. She noticed me and veered my way, slowing down and narrowing her eyes as she drew near. I steeled myself for a confrontation but as she reached me, a car alarm sounded in the distance. She stopped and shot me a warning look before turning on her heel and running back the way she had come. I waited for her to disappear from view before briskly power-walking out of the square and heading for home.

Cliff Richard Boulevard is one of the town's widest streets and runs perpendicular to the high street. The boulevard used to be known as 'the road out of town' until the Maverick Years when it was planted in plane trees and renamed after a popular British entertainer. In 1995, Cliff Richard became a knight commander of the British Empire but the 'Sir' was never added to the boulevard name. Jerry Clench had very different ideas to Jim Snick and did not believe in honouring British talent on street signs. Neither did he believe in tree planting.

Only two of the Maverick's original plane trees now remain standing on the boulevard. They are both visible from my first-floor flat and provide a comforting green vista during the summer months. My flat is located on a corner above a twenty-four-hour laundrette called Friendly Frank's Dirt Cheap Wash & Dry. This location is convenient for my washing requirements but I have learned to avoid the dryers, which tend to melt plastic buttons off garments.

I had just reached the open door of the laundrette when the sound of heavy boots once again became audible. I slipped inside and positioned myself behind a panel near the door, focusing my attention on a cork notice board. The sound drew nearer. The boot steps slowed. I could hear the heavy breathing of the policewoman but kept my eyes fixed on the cork board as she stopped outside the door and cleared her throat. Her feet shuffled and she sighed. As she moved off, I relaxed and realised I was looking at a name card headed with: 'Andromeda Mountjoy, world-renowned astrologer and lunar minstrel.' It was the author of 'Astral Acorns' from the *Cockerel*. The card had yellowed and collected laundrette grime but its message was still legible: 'Starry-eyed seeker, let Andy guide you to the brighter pastures of personal growth and inner transformation.'

My spirits lifted as I set about committing the mobile phone number to memory. This I did by mentally grouping the numerals into sets of twos before visualising them in the shape of a bell curve. The 'Pair Bell' is an invention of B.S. Pappenheimer and a very effective method for memorising anything from a recipe for cheese and onion scones to the names of British prime ministers.

I had just fixed the Pair Bell in my mind when someone coughed behind me.

'Evening,' said a male voice.

I turned and recognised the horse-racing enthusiast from the previous day. He was leaning against a washing machine and dressed only in a pair of grey synthetic underpants and sports shoes. I might not have noticed the state of his socks if he had been wearing trousers but in the absence of leg coverings I found myself examining their tatty condition. They were full of holes and rather than grip the ankles, they drooped over his shoes like grimy grey lace.

Despite the gambler's semi-naked condition, I did not feel vulnerable or threatened. The shop was brightly lit, I was near an open door and there were several washing machines between the man and me.

'Hello again,' I said but I could tell by the way he was looking at me that he did not recognise me.

'You seen a kid with a baseball cap?' He exhaled in a frustrated way and put his hands on his hips. He was slim but his flesh had the rubbery quality of someone unaccustomed to physical exercise. He did not have a lot of body hair.

'When?'

'Just now.'

'Why are you looking for him?'

'The little bastard's nicked my clothes.'

I did not understand. 'He overpowered you?'

'I said he was a kid.' The friendliness disappeared from the man's manner. 'You deaf?'

'No.'

He gave me an unpleasant look. I did not want to pursue conversation with the semi-naked man but it seemed impolite to leave him in such a predicament without showing some concern for his case.

'How did he steal your clothes?'

'I went outside for a smoke.'

It did not make sense to leave clothes unattended in a laundrette where large signs were posted warning, 'Underwear thieves operating on these premises', but nicotine is a powerful narcotic.

I pointed to a sign pinned to the wall above the powdered detergent dispenser. It had been written by hand on a sheet of cardboard with a blue ballpoint pen: 'If you're stupid enough to leave clothes unattended, you deserve to have them nicked. The proprietor takes no responsibility.'

The man shook his head in an irritated way. 'What are you trying to say?'

'That you are not the first victim of crime on these premises.'

'I don't give a toss about anyone else.'

The man looked more unpleasant than ever. I have found that this is often the case in conversation because I seem incapable of providing reassuring responses. One of my key problems is that in searching for conversation topics I invariably go 'off on a tangent', which is something that people do not appreciate. I decided to try a subject closer to home.

'I see you've had your appendix removed.'

The man seemed surprised by this. He put a hand over the scar, which was purple and quite recent. 'What the hell are you talking about?'

'The small finger-like organ connected to the large intestine.'

'Are you a pervert?'

'No.'

He was about to say something else when a digital version of the 'William Tell Overture' started playing. He reached behind him and picked up a mobile phone from a dryer, barking into it, 'Don't start!'

He then held the phone away from his ear as a female voice shouted something back. When the woman stopped yelling, he retaliated with, 'Don't blame me. I didn't force her to eat them!'

The woman had started shouting again as I edged my way backwards to the open doorway. She was still bellowing as I reached the door to my flat, which was adjacent to the laundrette. I was inserting the key into its lock when I heard the man shout, 'I *am* working, you stupid cow! Ask Rog!'

I dived inside and slammed the door behind me.

My one-bedroom flat is not large but it is clean and well-organised. Unlike my mother, I do not have a couch, television or display cabinet. Neither do I have ornaments. The central room, where I spend most of my time, is furnished with a desk, bookshelves and an ergonomic chair on wheels. On the shelf above the desk are the complete works of B.S. Pappenheimer, Sir Edmund Hillary biographies and my OBSERVATIONS ring binder and its appendices. The council handbook is on the reference bookshelves next to the desk along with the *Encyclopaedia Britannica*, dictionaries and the one thousand, six hundred and fifty-two books I rescued from a skip when the public library closed down. My desk is long and made of pinewood. On one side are my notepads and in-out trays with a receptacle for pens and on the other are a telephone and the desktop computer I found in the library dumpster.

It had been a long day and I went into the kitchen to refuel with grilled vegetables before sitting down at the non-computer side of my desk. I removed the latest notebook from my bag and got to work. I had just experienced the most stimulating period of my entire life. Never before had I spoken to so many people or engaged in so much activity, especially not activity that ran counter to the laws of Great Britain. I took down my OBSERVATIONS ring binder and opened it at R, adding a new entry under 'RASTAFARIAN', subtitling the page with 'GOOD SAMARITAN' in red marker. I then created several other personality files, 'LITTLE BASTARD', 'POLICEWOMAN', 'COWBOY', 'GAMBLER', and set up a 'RED HERRINGS' subsection with 'PSYCHOLOGICAL EXPERT' and 'FORTUNE-TELLER' subtitles.

Two hours later, I had finished filling in the details and created another new subsection. A tremor passed through me as I underlined 'FRIENDS' with a pink highlighter and smoothed the empty page with the palm of my hand.

I then wrote the astrologer's number on a piece of paper and placed it beside the phone before emptying my purse on the table. I had forty-six pounds seventy left, which did not seem like a lot of money to achieve normality by Monday.

I glanced at Andromeda Mountjoy's number again and told myself to stay positive. As B.S. Pappenheimer says, anxiety and fear are never helpful. In *Get Real and Get Ahead*, he proposes that most people lead 'pruned lives' out of fear of disasters that never occur. 'It's not the killer bees or exploding toaster that ultimately destroy a life, but the fear of them,' he says. 'Separate fact from phantom. Make the most of your seventy-nine years and stop enriching insurance companies.'

What were the facts?

I had not made any progress in the normality department and had spent over fifty pounds trying. But I did have a phone number and a day left in which to sort myself out. This had to be a good thing.

What were the phantoms?

Something was going on at the office but until I had hard proof, I could not be sure that Mr Chin had replaced me. The man I had seen through the window might have been a new recruit or, the thought occurred to me, someone delivering a meal of chicken chow mein.

Stick to the facts, I reminded myself as I replaced my ring binder and appendices. I repeated this again as I wheeled my chair back under the desk and turned off the light: stick to the facts and stay positive.

11

I awoke with a start, my heart racing. My eyes opened and fixed on the calendar pinned above my bed. The day was circled in red. Above the circle, I had written 'ELECTION'.

I swung my legs over the side of the bed and turned off the alarm clock before it began to sound. An anxiety dream had woken me but as I tried to recall its events, the dream lost shape and became formless. What remained were flashes of movement and colours and a sense that I had a task to complete against all odds. I glanced again at the calendar and thought of the day Mr Chin had presented it to me in a rare moment of generosity.

'Magnificent and attractive calendar. Improve *feng shui* every time,' he said. 'Present for Chinese New Year.'

'What a handsome gift!' I replied, unrolling the calendar scroll. Red and gold were not my favourite colours but I certainly appreciated the gesture. 'This is very generous of you.'

'Kind and generous boss every time.'

'Are you sure? It's from one of your favourite restaurants.' I knew this from the way he had praised Mr Ding's wontons at the Mandarin restaurant.

'Calendar from Jade Dragon restaurant better and more superior this year.' He narrowed his eyes. 'Ding gossip and chitchat get on my nerve.'

Mr Chin stayed on my mind as I did my morning star jumps and running on the spot. He was still there hovering over me like a helium-filled balloon as I showered and prepared a substantial breakfast of yoghurt and fruit followed by high-fibre grains and grated carrot. I could not remember if Mr Chin had been the focus of my dream but in my mind the two had fused together and I felt a sense of urgency as I hastily tidied the kitchen and moved my operations to the pinewood desk. There I noted down the fragments of the dream in the DREAM subsection of my OBSERVATIONS ring binder.

I make a point of monitoring what goes on in my subconscious by plotting the themes of my dreams against the events of daily life. After my mother moved to New Zealand, I began experiencing dreams of driving a fast car along a German autobahn. With each dream, the cars got faster and I became more confident behind the wheel. After several weeks, I found myself driving a convertible. As I pushed my foot down on the accelerator, I rose from the seat and started floating. I chopped my arms through the air and realised I could fly.

I did not start keeping records until after my mother had left but I have very clear memories of the dreams I experienced while she was still my legal guardian. When I finally got a broadband connection for my computer, I was not surprised to learn that cobwebs are a classic symbol of imprisonment for the dreaming mind.

The Internet has been very helpful for filling in the details but I was first drawn to the subject of dream analysis by a book I found in the skip. It was called *Freud and Jung – the Shattered Dream of Friendship* and contained several useful charts and illustrations.

Sigmund Freud and Carl Jung were world-renowned psychological experts who constructed penetrating theories on the activities of the subconscious mind. The two men were leaders in their field and enjoyed an amicable professional relationship until their famous dispute. At the height of the conflict, Jung dreamed of Freud dressed in the uniform of an imperial Austrian customs inspector. I am no psychological expert but I do know that Austrian officials have a reputation for being strict if not officious. Jung's dream did not say very positive things about Freud, who in turn said very unkind things about Jung.

I waited for the clock above my desk to strike seven before calling Andromeda Mountjoy. The morning is a very productive time for me but I have found that most people do not appreciate being woken before dawn, especially on a Sunday. The phone rang ten times and then clicked to the digital answer service: 'Andromeda Mountjoy is busy making the world a better place. For public speaking engagements or astral readings, kindly call back or leave your number.' I replaced the handset without leaving a message because I would not be home to field a return call. The clock was ticking and I was keen to get some power-walking done before residents started driving cars and filling the air with carbon monoxide and heavy metals. Vigorous exercise would also help clear my head and put me in a positive frame of mind to receive astrological assistance. As I laced up my air-cushion sports shoes, I planned a walking route that would take in one of the town's four remaining public phone booths. I would call Mr Mountjoy from there.

I was not surprised to find it drizzling when I got outside. Drizzle is an English phenomenon and often frustrates foreign visitors with its frequency and persistence. I took out the large, colourful hand-kerchief I keep in my bag for rainy days and draped it over my head, knotting it under my chin in a practical manner like the Queen of England. As I passed the laundrette, I glanced inside and was relieved to find it empty. The semi-naked man had been unpleasant but a laundrette is no place to spend a night without clothes.

When I reached the high street I began to see cardboard signs bearing arrows and the words, 'Polling Station'. The arrows pointed towards the town hall, which had undergone a transformation over-night. In the square there was now a makeshift stage platform with a wheelchair ramp on the side. I stopped in front of the betting shop to get a better view of this construction but found myself distracted by the flashing red diodes of the pawn shop's electronic signboard: 'Trade in that engagement ring before he stands you up at the altar! We buy used gold.'

A man emerged from the doorway of the betting shop with an aluminium ladder under his arm. He stopped and looked at me.

It was the man from the laundrette and I was relieved to see that he was now dressed in a black nylon sports suit. Over the top of his jacket was the iridescent plastic vest of a council road worker. I steeled myself for a confrontation but instead of saying something unpleasant, he raised his eyebrows in a friendly manner.

'Morning,' he said in a chirpy voice. His face showed no sign of recognition.

'Good morning,' I replied. 'It's unusual to find you working on a Sunday.'

This was an understatement. Under Jerry Clench, the town's urban beautification budget had been slashed and a sizeable chunk of the council workforce had been given early retirement. Funds were reallocated to 'key activities' such as transport and security. A considerable amount of the security budget had then been spent on the installation and maintenance of CCTV cameras in public places. I have recorded the locations of the town's one hundred and seventy-seven cameras in the SECURITY subsection of my OBSERVATIONS ring binder. They tend to be mounted at 'hot spots' such as bus stops and outside public houses but the cameras have done nothing to reduce the level of crime in the town, which continues to increase with the rate of unemployment. I was aware of the two cameras outside the betting shop recording my image as I watched the man prop the ladder against the shop window next to a broom.

'I'm flying the flag for Bottle.' He pointed to a coil of rope strung with colourful pennant flags. Each flag was stamped with 'Globcom' and a youthful caricature of Roger Bottle's face.

He moved the bunting aside with his foot and took a packet of tobacco from his pocket. I did not know what to make of his friend-liness but he was obviously keen to engage me in conversation. It seemed like a good idea to be courteous.

'I thought you were a council worker.'

'I'm Bottle's right-hand man.' He cocked an eyebrow in a proud way and proceeded to roll a cigarette. 'I only back winners.'

'Roger Bottle has not won anything yet. Voting hasn't even started.' According to the electoral bylaw, voting would commence 'three hours after the cock's crow of winter' or at ten o'clock by today's reckoning.

'He'll win. I'd bet my back teeth on it.'

This was a strange thing for the man to say because the back of his mouth appeared to be empty. The previous evening, I had noticed a lot of gum when he was shouting into his mobile phone.

'Rog has got big plans for Industry Drive. Factories and the like.' He lit his cigarette and expertly flicked the match into the gutter, which was already littered with racing stubs and several scratch-and-win cards from the betting shop. 'There's talk of a casino down the line.'

'I don't agree with casinos. I think they do more harm than good.'

'I gather you don't gamble.' The man glanced at the handkerchief on my head and smirked. 'It's probably not kosher with you lot.'

I ran a hand over my scarf, which was now damp from the rain. 'It might interest you to know that lottery winners often end up depressed. Depression is not a risk I want to take. It can lead to dependence on pharmaceuticals and, in the worst-case scenario, death by suicide. Apparently, money can buy nice things but it can't buy happiness.'

'Bloody religious nut.' The man scoffed and filled his lungs with smoke. 'Know what I'd do if I won the lottery?'

I shook my head.

'I'd buy a red Ferrari and park it on the high street. Then I'd wait for the dolly birds in their skirts and high heels to come up and ask for a ride. Then you know what I'd say?' He paused but it was clear he did not require a response. 'I'd say, NAH.'

He then laughed *ha-ha-ha* like a Bren gun, which was surprising considering he had not said anything funny. His mouth was open wide and as I suspected nearly every one of his molars was missing. He still had teeth in the front of his mouth but these were mottled beige and brown like desert camouflage. They stood out in vivid contrast to the inflamed pink of his gums. I wanted to leave but he was looking at me as if he expected a response to his anecdote. I decided to be polite and respond to his interest in cars.

'What kind of car do you own?'

His eyes narrowed. The bones moved in his cheeks. 'What's it to you?'

I was surprised by this hostile response since my question had been a logical continuation of the car theme. It seemed wise to try another mode of transport.

'Are you a cyclist?'

Instead of answering, the man grabbed the broom and started sweeping racing stubs towards me in a menacing way. I did not know where the conversation had gone wrong but it had now clearly been terminated.

I stepped over the bunting and quickly moved out of broom range. The man's hostility was unpleasant but at least I could walk away from him. This was not possible when Mr Chin became upset. He had a peculiar method of interrogating me when I made a mistake, which involved standing over my desk and shouting down at me: 'How now brown cow?' The expression itself was harmless but the way he barked it at me was mortifying.

The prospect of facing such an interrogation and having nothing to show for his one hundred pounds spurred me on towards the nearest public phone. When I reached the distinctive red booth, I was disappointed to discover that its handset was missing. The next public phone had been attacked with something heavy like a cast-iron lawnmower body. The phone unit was covered in dents and the slot for coins had been bashed shut. In the third, a more modern metal and glass booth, someone had started a fire.

At one point in the town's history, the streets were furnished with over fifty public phones. This was during the sixties when cramming people into phone booths was still a popular pastime. A decade later, Jim Snick revived this activity when he recruited eighteen local residents to join him in the booth outside the town hall. You can see their attempt to break the national record in a photo at the council display. It is entitled 'Slick Snick in Tight Squeeze', and shows Mr Snick wearing a bathing suit and smeared with cooking oil, crammed into the top half of a booth filled with other well-oiled residents. Mayor Snick has a cigarette between his teeth and appears to be either smiling or grimacing.

I examined the blackened booth and considered my options. I could push on to the fourth and final public phone or power-walk all the way back to my flat. I imagined encountering the man at the betting shop again and decided to try the last booth.

As I rounded a street corner ten minutes later, I was relieved to find the phone in use. Its occupant was wide and dressed in pink stretch sports clothes. She turned as I approached and I recognised Chantal Corby. The bump on her forehead had gone down slightly but the bruise had spread, yellowing around the edges. She frowned at me and shielded the mouthpiece with her hand but her voice was loud and I could hear her clearly.

'I'm being watched,' she said, shaking her head. She raised her hand and held it up to my face like a traffic policeman trying to stop a speeding motorcycle. 'She's one of the headscarf brigade. A Pakistani by the looks.'

I pointed to the handkerchief and shook my head, smiling to indicate peaceful intentions.

'You've got to do something about them.' With the back of her hand, she made whisking motions at me. 'They're taking over the country.'

I smiled again.

'The bitch won't leave.' Grimacing, she turned her back to me but did not lower her voice.

'I'm telling you, I haven't seen the little bastard for two days.' She raised a fist and thumped the small platform next to the phone. 'We've got to find him before that jailbird gets his hands on him.'

The person on the other end of the line must have answered in the affirmative because she nodded and said, 'You'd better scratch my back,' and then, 'I'll be there,' before hanging up.

She threw open the door and glared at me.

'What the hell do you think you're doing?' she asked. Her face was the colour of salted beef boiled over a medium flame.

'Waiting to use the phone,' I replied.

'Ear-wagging! That's what you were doing.'

'You were speaking very loudly.'

'I'm a British citizen. I can speak as loud as I want.'

'Acceptable sound levels have nothing to do with nationality. It's all about the decibels.'

'The cheek!' She raised her eyebrows, which had been plucked or shaved into non-existence and then redrawn with the same thick black pencil she had used to underline her eyes. Her cheeks purpled.

'I think you misunderstand. Decibels are a measure of noise. A barking dog, for example, produces sixty to one hundred and thirty decibels. At one hundred and forty, sound is painful to the average human ear. You were probably shouting at seventy decibels, at the volume of a motorised scooter.'

Chantal Corby wheezed and showed her teeth. They were small and uneven with gaps on either side where premolars had been removed. Her eyes fixed on my handkerchief and narrowed.

'Who the hell do you think you are, coming over here and telling us what to do?'

'You are now shouting at about ninety decibels. Imagine a pneumatic drill at ten yards.'

She stopped shouting and clutched the zipper of her pink sports jacket. Her face was now magenta except for the bruise, which was midnight blue with a bright yellow frill. I wanted to leave but she was occupying the only working public phone in the centre of town. My only hope was to pacify her.

'Do you suffer from dermatitis?'

She blinked but did not say anything.

'You mentioned back scratching.'

Her face seemed to bulge as she threw herself out of the phone booth, narrowly missing my chest with her fleshy shoulder. Bellowing, she spun around and swung the back of her hand at me. It swished past my face as I dodged to the side. Her arm reached the end of its backwards arc with a jerk and a crack. She shrieked at about ninety decibels.

'I've popped a joint!' She looked at me as if I had struck her with a boxing glove. She then swayed on her feet for a second or two before staggering away, clutching her shoulder.

I waited until she had disappeared from view before stepping into the booth, which was warm and smelled of underarm. Holding the door open with my foot to allow the air to circulate, I put the handset to my ear, inserted a coin and dialled.

'Romantic rigours revealed,' said a nasal male voice in a strange accent. 'Lonely hearts healed.'

'Mr Mountjoy?' I asked.

'Lunar minstrel and public speaker.'

'I'd like an appointment for an astrological reading.'

'The stars are sending a golden beam of fortune your way.'

My spirits lifted.

'I can just squeeze you in. Half an hour's time at the astral ambulance on Industry Drive, number fifty-two. *A*.'

'*A* what?'

The phone went dead.

I replaced the handset and took a deep breath. Why of all places was it Industry Drive? The thought of going anywhere near the hypnotherapist's bungalow made my chest tighten.

As I stepped out of the muggy stench of the booth, I counselled myself to take courage and conjured up an image of Sir Edmund Hillary sitting beside a small gas cooker. He was wearing snow goggles and an old-fashioned anorak with woollen mittens. He and Tenzing Norgay had just come down from Everest and were enjoying a cup of tea out of enamel mugs. In my imagination, the Sherpa turns to Sir Edmund and asks the adventurer what he plans to do with the rest of his life. 'I'd like to become the first person to go overland to the South Pole,' comes the reply. Mr Norgay laughs at this but Sir Edmund is already calculating how long it will take to drive a Ferguson farm tractor over the ice of Antarctica to reach the Pole.

A number five bus was approaching as I reached the bus stop. Along its side was a large advertisement featuring a lookalike of former French President Charles de Gaulle holding up a fork with several chips on its prongs. Coming out of his mouth was a speech bubble: 'French fries? *Mais non*. Nack's chips. As good as gold.' Monsieur de Gaulle was a French military commander and statesman who wore the same abbreviated moustache as Adolf Hitler during WWII. He was known as Le Général or Le Grand Charles in his day but his full name was Charles André Joseph Marie de Gaulle, which is an unusual combination of male and female names when you think about it.

As the bus door opened, I recognised the driver of the previous week. He glanced at my trousers and raised his eyebrows.

'Och aye, lassie,' he said. 'It's the tart in slacks again.'

'This is the MacDonald tartan. Yesterday I was wearing the lesser-known checks of the Macnee,' I said, encouraged by his friendliness. I stepped on to the bus. 'The Macnees are a sept of the MacGregor clan. Their motto is "My race is royal".'

'Woop-dee-do.' The driver made as if to whistle but no sound came out of his puckered lips. He revved the bus engine.

'One adult please.' I put two pounds on the tray.

He smirked. 'You've forgotten your bloody bagpipes.'

'I don't own any bagpipes.'

He laughed and I took my ticket. As I made my way down the aisle, a recorded message came over the loudspeaker: 'Closed-circuit television is in service on this bus.' I turned back to find the driver watching me in his mirror.

I looked away and chose a seat at the back of the bus, removing the headscarf and folding it into my handbag. I then took out my notebook and, after jotting down the de Gaulle advertisement, I tried to assemble my thoughts. My day had not begun in the most encouraging manner and I needed to put myself in a positive frame of mind. I had goals to achieve and very little time left in which to achieve them.

My gaze drifted to the window as I considered the questions I would ask the world-renowned astrologer and public speaker.

Something caught my eye and I blinked several times. It took a moment to register what I was looking at. It was the unusual colour that had drawn my attention, lime green.

I sat up with a jolt.

12

'Old golfers never die. They just lose their drive,' read the bumper sticker. Except someone had crossed out 'drive' and written 'BALLS' with a red marker. There was only one lime-green Ford Fiesta in the town with that message on its bumper. Mr Chin had bought the car from a family of a ninety-year-old golfing enthusiast who had died on the greens with a number eight iron in his hands. 'Family very happy and pleased with cash,' Mr Chin had explained. 'Give Chin extra bonus gift. Lucky eight golf club. Lucky for Chin. Not so lucky for grandfather.'

I jumped to my feet to get a better look but Mr Chin's car had already overtaken the bus and disappeared from view. Industry Drive was an odd place for Mr Chin to choose for a Sunday excursion. There were no parks or interesting architecture. It was a road you visited when you wanted new tyres fitted or to buy kitchen units or bunk beds. Mr Chin had not mentioned any large purchases and I knew for a fact that his car had already been fitted with retreads because he had complained about their cost. The man who ran the tyre outlet was from the Seventh-Day Adventist church and had told Mr Chin he was not interested in cash. He had insisted on full price and then issued him with a tax receipt.

'Closed-circuit television is in service on this bus.'

I glanced up at the sound of the recording and saw the driver observing me in his mirror. I sat down and noticed a copy of the *Cockerel* among the litter under the seat in front of me. Only part of the main headline was visible: 'Election a Tight'. Below this was a partial strapline: 'Bottle Pops Into'. I resisted the urge to pick up the newspaper. I did not want to read bad news and anything positive about Roger Bottle had to be bad news for the Babylon and my future at Mr Chin's office.

I pushed the red stop button and as I walked towards the door, I could feel the driver's eyes on me. His surveillance was disconcerting. It added to the sense of unease I was already feeling as the bus pulled into the same stop I had used the previous week. I called out 'Thank you,' and disembarked feeling exposed and vulnerable, aware that Mr Tanderhill's bungalow was a mere three minutes' power-walk away.

As the bus moved off, I examined the façade of the nearest building but could not find a street number. Mounted over its door was a life-sized fibreglass effigy of an obese topless man with his arms folded over his chest. Below the genie was a sign: 'Midge's Magic Carpets. Fly-away Prices.' The next building was a tile outlet 'For all your sanitary needs' and next to this was a plumbing warehouse called Reg Barker's Bath & Basins Bazaar. Adorning the wall of the building was an oversized number fifty-two. It had been fashioned out of plastic pipes and plumbing fittings and suggested that Mr Barker was a plumbing specialist with flair.

I crossed the empty car park and peered into the warehouse but the lights were off and there was no sign of life inside. I was looking around for the astrologer's office when I noticed an old white caravan wedged between the warehouse and the carpet outlet. It was sitting on a narrow strip of land that must have once served as a municipal access road. The caravan had been parked there long enough for weeds to sprout around its wheelbase. Moss was growing along its roofline and its metal panels were streaked with rust. At some point a graffiti artist had discovered it and tagged its side with the words 'Your dream holiday destination' and an illegible signature. I reminded myself to record this message as I circled the caravan, noting the words 'Council Property Do Not Remove' in faded lettering over the bumper and a badge with the town's distinctive coat of arms under the rear window.

The caravan looked abandoned. Its door was shut and all its

curtains were drawn. These were orange with horizontal yellow stripes, the same colour combination that Jim Snick had chosen for the mayoral Vauxhall Firenza at the height of his popularity.

There was no doorbell or buzzer but an 'A' had been scrawled on the door with a pencil. I lifted my hand to knock but before my knuckles touched the metal, the door swung open and the smell of my childhood rolled over me. It was boiled mincemeat and cabbage and immediately made my jaw stiffen and my stomach tighten. I had to swallow several times before I could take in the man frowning down at me from the doorway.

He was of average height with a narrow, bulbous forehead and a remarkably long, oblong skull. His scalp was bald and shiny and looked like the surface of a freshly peeled potato. I looked down and noticed that his yellow T-shirt was faded and had several holes, which seemed unusual for a professional with an international profile. Printed across the front of the T-shirt was the slogan 'Make a Meal of It with Pring's English Mustard' and a cartoon face of a man with smoke coming out of his ears. His jeans had a glossy quality as if they had been finished with latex or never been washed. On his feet was a pair of buff-coloured moccasins with decorative beadwork. Many of the beads were missing but the words 'Pocahontas the Movie' were still legible on the right moccasin.

'Mr Mountjoy?' I asked, swallowing again. I shook my head to dispel the image of my mother that had risen in my mind. She was standing at the sink, wiping her eyes with the heel of her hand as she cut onions for a pot of minced beef. Mr Da Silva had sold his butcher's shop to a Polish man called Slawek and was moving back to Portugal with his wife.

'Stargazer and lunar minstrel,' the man said. His voice was deep and his accent unusual, a geographically improbable blend of Sir Sean Connery and the Duke of Edinburgh.

'You have an unusual accent.'

'Elocution.' He smiled, exposing the gappy yellow teeth of a Border Leicester ewe. 'I can make my vocal chords sound like a pipe organ. Ear candy.'

'Pipe organs require a lot of wind.'

His smile disappeared. 'What do you want?'

'Astrological advice. A friend of mine reads your column in the *Cockerel*. He's very fond of your tall, dark strangers.'

'They're one of my specialities. The Mountjoy signature.' The astrologer raised an eyebrow and smiled with one side of his mouth.

'Your card said you provide guidance with personal growth and transformation. I'm at a juncture.'

'Give and thou shall receive.' He smiled crookedly again. 'One of my motivational lines.'

'Sorry?'

He glanced at the handbag under my arm. 'My standard fee is one hundred pounds.'

'Oh!'

His expression soured. 'I can do a basic for thirty-four quid.'

I opened my bag and felt around for my purse. 'It will have to be a basic.'

'Money is the physical manifestation of power and success. I tell all my clients that a generous spirit is always rewarded.'

'I'm afraid I don't have a lot of money.'

'That probably says it all. I accept cheques.'

'I don't have a chequebook or a credit card. Unbridled consumerism and personal debt are growing problems in Great Britain. I prefer to stick to cash and monitor my spending. I do not want to join the ranks of the debtors.'

He shook his head in an impatient way as I counted out thirty-four pounds, shaking my purse to examine its few remaining coins. Mr Mountjoy's fee was the last professional investment I could afford to make. It was a significant moment, one I would have prolonged if the money had not been grabbed from my hand. He gestured for me to enter.

I filled my lungs and, wishing I had the hermetically sealing nostrils of a hippopotamus, followed him into the caravan. The lights were off but the curtains cast an orange glow over everything, creating the effect of a tropical sunset. My eyes flicked around the interior, noting an unmade bed, a wardrobe with a broken door and clothes spilling out of a chest of drawers. Among the clutter on the bench top were several empty bottles of Quality White Table Wine with 'Not For Individual Sale' stickers around their necks. I glanced at the unwashed dishes piled in the sink and decided not to look any further.

Mr Mountjoy pushed several boxes stamped with 'Festive Christmas cake. Individually wrapped.' to one side of a padded bench seat and gestured for me to sit down before pulling out a flimsy folding table attached to the wall with a hinge. Its wood-grain Formica surface was covered with ring marks and sugary residue, which stuck to my cardigan as I leaned forwards on my elbows. I did not bother to unstick them because my mind was focused on blocking off my nasal passages and limiting airflow to my mouth.

I continued to focus on my breath as Mr Mountjoy filled a mug from a teapot and added eight spoonfuls of sugar. The folding table wobbled as he brought over the steaming mug and a square of fruitcake in a plastic wrapper and eased himself into the bench seat opposite mine.

Tea is a refreshing beverage and is often used as a 'social lubricant' in convivial settings. Mr Chin insists that we share a tea bag but never fails to offer me a cup whenever he makes one for himself. He calls these daily tea-drinking sessions 'Mixing business with pleasure' because all tea consumption during office hours must be done at the work desk. 'Kind and generous boss permit hot tea with sugar sachet but office policy clear and crystal,' said Mr Chin. 'Take drink, call client. Finish client, take drink. Refresh tongue and throat every time. Keep mouth healthy with no waste of office hour. Best policy.'

The astrologer sipped the tea before removing the wrapper from the fruitcake, which was printed with 'Merry Christmas Courtesy of Jerry Clench.' He took a large bite, chewing with enthusiasm.

'Fruity,' he said, swallowing noisily. He wiped his fingers on his jeans and then raised his hands with his palms facing me. 'Don't say anything. The stargazer will now reveal all.'

I nodded as he traced a heart in the air. His fingers were short and spatulate and his fingernails were crowned with dark ridges. If I had not been sitting in a caravan in an industrial car park I might have mistaken him for a municipal bus mechanic or someone with rose beds.

'You're looking for romance with a tall, dark stranger.'

'No.'

'What did I just say?' He dropped his hands and gave me a sharp look. It was the same look I had seen on the faces of council workers whenever I approached them about the photo display.

'Romance with a tall, dark stranger.'

'Before that.'

'That I shouldn't say anything.'

He gave a curt nod and filled his lungs as if he were about to cut a ribbon and make an inaugural speech.

'The heart is a wild boar, sniffing for truffles in a meadow.' He smiled to himself. 'That's another of my lines.'

I did not understand Mr Mountjoy but reminded myself that he was a public speaker and world-renowned astral expert. I sat up straight and tried to concentrate as he opened a large notepad stamped with 'Do Not Remove From Premises.' and began writing with a pencil. I could not see his astrological notes because the page was hidden behind the cover of the notepad but I could read the gold printing on his pencil: 'The *Cockerel* – News with a cock-a-doodle-doo.' Its end was dented with teeth marks, which made me wonder whether Mr Mountjoy was a recovering nail biter.

When he finally looked up it was to ask for the details of my birth. I could provide a date and place but I could not give him a time because this information is not included on a British birth certificate. My mother had refused to discuss my birth, referring to it as the worst day of her life. What I did know was that her tubes were tied within hours of my arrival. 'Never again,' she told me. 'All that wear and tear of my personal arena for absolutely nothing.'

The astrologer continued to write notes for several minutes. He smiled as he did this and said 'A-ha' twice, which gave me hope. I must have relaxed and let my guard down because I became aware of the caravan's smell. I coughed to clear my sinuses of the fatty, sulphurous odour.

Mr Mountjoy looked up with a sigh as if I had interrupted him at a key point in his astrological calculations. 'You're a Sagittarius.'

'Correct.'

'It's the sign of the— '

'—archer?'

He frowned. 'Kook.'

'Are you suggesting I'm a kook?'

I wanted to make sure I understood him correctly. After the confrontation over the suggestion box, certain council workers had taken to calling me 'The Kook' and openly sniggering in my presence. Being branded a kook is not necessarily a bad thing as B.S. Pappenheimer points out in his seminal work, *Kooks Make the World Go Round and Invent Some Very Nice Things Along the Way*. I would not have minded the moniker or the laughter but the label seemed to obstruct my efforts to have the photo display refurbished.

Mr Mountjoy let the cover of the notebook fall shut. He took a mouthful of tea and, swishing it around his gums, leaned back to look at me as if he were examining an armadillo for the first time. When he spoke, it was with finality.

'I'm not suggesting.' He put the rest of the fruitcake in his mouth and chewed in a vigorous way, clearly pleased with this statement. He swallowed loudly, his throat making a sucking sound like a rubber plunger clearing a drain. 'You're a kook of the Sagittarian variety.'

'Are there other varieties? More normal varieties?'

He shook his head. 'You're astrologically challenged. It's an affliction, like being born with one leg only a lot more unpleasant for those around you. No one likes a Sag.'

Mr Mountjoy's assessment was not very positive but it did explain my lack of social appeal and the resistance I had encountered over the photo display.

'I've been encountering resistance at the council.'

He blinked at the mention of the council. 'What kind of resistance? I have friends at the council.'

'Door slamming and name calling. My words fall on deaf ears.'

'You can't expect decent people to listen if you don't have anything to say.'

'I've got plenty to say. That's the problem.'

He cleared his throat. 'Try this one for size: when the chips are down, start peeling more potatoes.'

The potato reference prompted me to glance at the slick surface of his scalp. He noticed me looking and frowned. I looked away.

'I've made numerous suggestions for improvements but the council is resistant to change.' I did not bother to add that it was also corrupt, according to Warren Crumpet, who had promised to launch an 'Operation Squeaky Clean' to eliminate corruption and cronyism. Council spending would be examined and rationalised if he were elected. So would its administration and employment practices. 'Mr Crumpet says the council is an old boys' club of self-satisfied chumps, sycophants and parasites. That's a quote from one of his pamphlets. Its language is quite vivid. He doesn't pull any punches when it comes to the misuse of council funds.'

'He doesn't know what he's talking about. The man's a fool.'

'He's a leading light of the British Soil Association.'

'He'll never get elected. The voters love their council. Its good people keep this town running.' He smiled. 'Where would we be without the *Cockerel?*'

I could not answer that question. The *Cockerel* had been around since I was a child and I could not imagine life without it. The newspaper was funded with public money and published under the auspices of the mayor's office. It had been set up during the Maverick Years as the 'Cock's crow of the people' to give the community a voice but under Clench it had become the voice of the mayor and his supporters.

'The *Cockerel* is a pillar.' The astrologer smiled. '"Astral Acorns" is a column. Get it?'

His good humour was encouraging. It seemed like an ideal moment to clarify my goals.

'Is there anything in my astral arrangement that indicates a personality shift by Monday?' It was warm in the caravan and I was finding it hard to breathe through partially closed nostrils. I tried to lift a hand to fan my face but my cardigan clung to the sticky tabletop. I decided to leave it where it was and focus on convincing the astrologer of the urgency of my case. 'I've been told by a reliable source that I'm abnormal. If I don't crack the normality nut by tomorrow, I'm in dire straits.'

Mr Mountjoy closed one eye and tilted his head back. When he did not say anything, I decided to illustrate my case with examples.

'Cherie Blair is unusual, but Idi Amin was abnormal. Mrs Blair has unusual fashion tastes but Mr Amin did very cruel things to other human beings. He also gave himself the titles of King of Scotland, Lord of All the Beasts of the Earth and Fishes of the Sea and Conqueror of the British Empire in Africa in General and Uganda in Particular. I do not think I am in the same league as Mr Amin but my employer called me abnormal and I am obliged to change camps by tomorrow or I risk losing my job.'

The astrologer's head rocked back to its normal position. His mouth opened wide and his jaw clicked as his yawn reached its climax. His Border Leicester teeth snapped shut with a castanet-like *clack*.

I had to impress upon him the gravity of my situation.

'I need to get normal by tomorrow. My future depends on it.'

He seemed to consider this statement for a moment as he ran a hand over his long, smooth head. According to the study of phrenology, the condition of the skull is an indicator of intelligence, personality traits, pathological problems and possibly issues with scalp hygiene. Phrenology had its heyday in the nineteenth century and involved a lot of cranial fingering and measurements with instruments. Mr Mountjoy's skull was smooth and shaped like a bicycle helmet. I did not know what a phrenologist would have said about his personality but the shape must have made hat purchasing difficult.

'Mr Mountjoy? I've come to you for advice.'

The astrologer shook his head and roused himself. 'When life throws you a haymaker, you've got to pick yourself up and keep fighting.'

I looked at him for an explanation.

'The haymaker is another of my motivators. Catchy.'

'I'm already motivated. What I need is direction, a place to hang my hat.'

He raised an eyebrow and seemed to consider my predicament for a moment. His face softened and his expression changed. He smiled. 'Try a hat rack at the funny farm.'

It was humid in the caravan and as I waited for Mr Mountjoy to stop laughing I realised that perspiration was gathering along my hairline. Without thinking, I lifted my hand to my brow. My cardigan at first clung to the tabletop and then released, jolting the table and knocking Mr Mountjoy's notebook to the floor. I looked down as it fluttered open.

My armpits prickled.

There were no astrological notes on the page. It was covered with variations of a signature: 'Andy Mountjoy'. Its 'j' was dotted with a star.

A dark hopelessness descended on me like the gloom I experienced whenever I had been shut inside my mother's broom cupboard. I flared my nostrils and filled my lungs but immediately regretted this impulse as the smell of cabbage and mincemeat flooded my airways and accumulated on the gag trigger at the back of my tongue. My chest heaved and my knees jerked upwards, hitting the underside of the folding table. The tabletop leaped upwards and catapulted the mug of tea high in the air. It hovered there a moment before dropping with thud on to the chest of Mr Mountjoy, discharging its contents over his face like an erupting volcano. He cried out and screwed up his eyes as the table collapsed on his kneecaps with a loud *clunk*, missing mine by half an inch.

My handbag was already tucked under my arm and I was pushing myself to my feet when his eyes opened. His face was red and glistening with tea. Mr Mountjoy had been unhelpful and I doubted his credentials as an astrologer but it seemed impolite to leave him in such a predicament without a word of encouragement.

'When the chips are down,' I said.

He stiffened. His hands gripped the tabletop.

'Start peeling—'

'Get out!'

He need not have shouted because I already knew from the violence in his eyes that I was no longer welcome.

I left the caravan and walked briskly to the relative safety of the public pavement where I paused to clear my lungs and sinuses. I glanced back to make sure Mr Mountjoy had not followed and noticed a large signboard on the other side of the car park: 'Boil your blues away in one of Reg's sizzling Californian spa pools.'

The rain had stopped and the sky was now the colour of cigarette ash. As I surveyed the grey pavement and grey road, I felt no optimism or spark of possibility. I had virtually no money left and nothing to show Mr Chin for his investment. I looked in the direction his car had gone and felt something stir. He had forbidden me to return to the office but he had said nothing about me following or observing his vehicle. My spirits lifted at the thought of the Ford Fiesta. It was within its vinyl interior that I had been hired.

The day I found the classified advertisement in the *Cockerel* had been a difficult one. All the tinned food in my mother's cupboards had been consumed and the council had served an eviction notice. 'Purchase Consultant Wanted for Excellent Business' sounded ambitious but I was pleasantly surprised when the foreign man on the phone said he would visit the house that afternoon. At the appointed time, a lime-green Fiesta arrived. In the driver's seat was a short man from the Far East who tooted his horn several times until I came out. This was an unusual way to start a job interview but as I was to learn, Mr Chin was an unusual man. He told me to get in the car and shut the door. I might have been reluctant to follow these orders from another person but Mr Chin was a small man who looked more like an accountant or acupuncturist than a sexual pervert. His eyes were alert and his hands were small and sensitive. When he opened his mouth, I glimpsed teeth so white and well-formed that

I initially mistook them for dentures. He introduced himself as 'Chin' and immediately got down to business.

'You have experience in gold purchase?' he asked.

'No,' I replied, adding a phrase I had memorised from the Job Centre's *Guidelines for New Job Seekers*, 'but I'm a keen starter.'

'Keen starter not interesting. Chin want gold purchase consultant.'

'I'm willing to learn new skills.'

This was another phrase from the guidelines but it also failed to impress Mr Chin, who shook his head. His right hand reached for the keys in the ignition.

'I need to find a job and a flat. I'm being evicted.' I did not know what made me say this, or add the next item of information. 'My mother has left me for a sheep farmer.'

'No family?' Mr Chin raised his eyebrows.

I shook my head.

'Friend?'

'No.'

'You tell lie or cheat and steal?' His eyes narrowed.

'No.'

'Gamble?'

'Never.'

'You gossip or spread rumour?' His lips tightened.

'No. I don't know anyone with whom to gossip and most people I meet do not listen to what I say. I'm often not recognised even after meeting people several times.'

He nodded and then gave me the office address, adding that I was to turn up for work at nine o'clock the next morning. Before I could ask him any questions about the job, he had started the engine and was waving me out of the car.

Buoyed by this recollection, I set off after the Fiesta along Industry Drive. I had been walking for less than a minute when I came across a sign stapled to a wooden stake. On it was a large red arrow and the words: 'Roger Bottle meets and greets his voters at the proposed Globcom factory site. Free drinks.' I kept walking and passed several more of the signs before arriving at a former factory building. The car park and both sides of the road in front of the building were crammed with cars. I scanned the vehicles for a lime-green Fiesta but found nothing manufactured before 1980.

The building itself must have been a battery factory at one stage because near the roofline it was still possible to make out 'Best Batteries for All Your Motoring Needs' in faded lettering. A new sign had been erected over the double doors, 'God's Church of the Holy Burning Bush'. Above this was a flickering blue neon cross. I was wondering what kind of church would use a former battery factory as premises when someone tugged my elbow.

'You're like a bad smell.'

Nigel's words were harsh but his expression was not unfriendly. He was still wearing the cap and baggy jeans but the grubby white T-shirt had gone and in its place was a large black one with a skull and bones motif in the centre of the chest. The T-shirt's size and colour made him look young and vulnerable in the impersonal context of Industry Drive.

'What are you doing here?' I asked.

'Looking for someone.' He wiped his nose with the back of his hand and gave me a look that did not invite further inquiry.

'In the church?'

Nigel walked up the steps and tapped a small sign next to the doorbell. I stepped up beside him to read it: 'For men's hostel and halfway house, take first left after main doors'.

'Can I wait for you?' I doubted women were permitted inside a men's hostel and I had no desire to enter a church. My last church experience had been troubling.

'Whatever.'

Loud gospel music flowed out as Nigel opened one of the large industrial doors. I peered inside and saw a spacious open area with another set of doors that must have led to the church. The boy turned left and disappeared down a hall wide enough for a forklift.

I returned to the car park and was scanning the vehicles again when I noticed graffiti written in pink chalk at the base of the boundary fence: 'RISE UP AND SMITE THE BRISTLED DEVIL.' I added this message to several other mental notes as I approached the wooden fence and looked over.

The large rectangular industrial site was empty and had been recently bulldozed. Amid the tracks of the earthmover were piles of rubble, pieces of old brick and wire, evidence of the factory that must have once stood there. My eye caught something bright in the far corner. It was an inflatable beach ball and looked gay and out of place in the grim post-industrial setting.

I was considering how the ball might have travelled there from the seaside when I became aware of rustling on the other side of the fence. I peered through a gap in the timber slats and saw someone sitting at a trestle table reading a booklet. Taped to the front of the table was a cardboard notice: 'Proposed site of new factory. Globcom – providing safe, efficient cleanup solutions.'

I immediately recognised Roger Bottle, only he was twenty years older than his campaign photos. His eyebrows were bushier but his hair was thinner and coloured an unnatural chestnut tone with a dye that had leeched into his scalp. The most striking feature of his appearance was his moustache. It was the size of a bottlebrush and completely hid his top lip. The bristles were fiery red and did not appear to have been dyed.

I looked back at the church doors before following the line of the fence to the pavement. I was curious about Roger Bottle. Until the previous week, I had never heard of him. Now I was finding his face and the Globcom logo everywhere. His campaign platform was winning hearts and minds. This did not bode well for the town or my future with Mr Chin.

13

Roger Bottle did not notice me walk up to his table. He was too engrossed in the booklet in his hands. It was entitled *Fifty Pages of Forbidden Adventures for a Boiling Hot Summer of Love* and, according to the small print, it was a supplement of a women's magazine well-known for its frank content.

The table had been laid out with pamphlets and papers sorted into piles. At one end was a plastic tub filled with pink liquid and a stack of clear plastic cups. A small card next to the tub announced that it was 'Rog's exclusive adult punch.'

I was surprised to find the mayoral candidate alone on the morning of the election, especially alone at a trestle table on an empty building site. But then I had never participated in an election let alone witnessed the events leading up to one. My mother did not vote and the only times she had shown any interest in local politics was when Jerry Clench had promised something free. She would have appreciated the adult punch.

'Hello,' I said.

'Hell's teeth!' he exclaimed, almost falling off his chair. Righting himself, he hastily stuffed the booklet into the pocket of his tweed jacket. He then cleared his throat and, running a finger over his moustache, looked me up and down. 'You're out early.'

'I didn't attend the service.'

'A-ha! You must be the reporter from the *Cockerel*.' His hand moved to the collar of his ironed white shirt and adjusted a blue and red striped tie. As his fingers wrestled with the knot, his Adam's apple caught my eye. It was the largest Adam's apple I had ever seen, the size of a prize walnut or ping-pong ball. It made me wonder whether he had a throat cyst or rampant testosterone production.

'No.'

'Don't tell me.' He held up a hand. 'You're here because you're going to vote for me?'

'No.'

'Then goodbye to you!' His face changed and he flicked his hand as if cooling a beverage.

'Voting is a rite of passage. It's a symbolic act carried out at a certain age by members of a community. I have reached that age but do not yet feel connected to human society let alone to this community.'

Roger Bottle frowned. 'So basically you're old enough to vote but you're undecided?'

'In a nutshell, yes.'

He smiled in a large way, baring the bottom row of his teeth under the moustache. They were yellow but straight and in remarkably good condition for a man over sixty. He swept a hand across the papers on the table. 'Take a look at what Hurricane Bottle can do for the aspiring youth of this town.'

My eyes followed his hand from the tub of punch to the opposite end of the table. There they stopped and locked onto a stack of flyers. They were simple black and white photocopies designed like a bounty poster with 'WANTED' in Wild West typeface: 'Roger Bottle urgently seeks information on this vulnerable young boy. Keep children safe. Vote for family values.' The boy in the photo was Nigel. He was not wearing his baseball cap but his sneer was unmistakable. So was his birthmark, which looked like a chocolate button stuck to his cheek. I glanced over the fence to the Holy Burning Bush and then back to Roger Bottle.

'Why do you want this boy?' I asked.

'He's gone missing,' he replied, biting his moustache in a show of concern. 'A runaway.'

'What is he running from?'

'His mother, the poor woman.'

'What will you do if you find him?'

'Get him off the streets where he's prey to men in trench coats.'

'Which men in trench coats?' Jocelyn wore a trench coat.

'You know the sort I'm talking about.' He raised an eyebrow.

'No.'

'You will after I'm mayor and start beating my tom-tom.' He said this in a strange voice, as if speaking through a keyhole or reciting lines for a BBC radio mystery. 'I'm going to flush the perverts out of their bushes and cubicles. Roger Bottle will scrape the filth off the underbelly of this town, make the streets safe for women and children.'

The candidate nodded with satisfaction and fell silent. I glanced again at the church. The doors were closed and there was no movement in the car park. I had to keep Roger Bottle occupied.

'What's Globcom?'

'A big fish.' He tapped the side of his nose.

'But I Googled it and found nothing.'

'Let's just say that it's a British company dedicated to protecting British interests.'

'A security company?'

'This factory and my proposed public surveillance centre will bring prosperity and safety to local residents.'

'But why demolish the Babylon cinema?'

'Location, location, location.' He smiled, pleased with the expression. 'A central anti-crime surveillance unit. Citizen protection is high on my agenda.'

'CCTV cameras do not protect citizens from crime. They are after the fact.'

'Kindly keep your opinions to yourself.'

'It's not my opinion. It's a fact. Crime is on the up and up despite increased camera surveillance. People are disgruntled and restless.'

Roger Bottle shook his head in an unfriendly way. Our conversation had hit a snag and I was at a loss to get it going again.

I turned once more towards the Holy Burning Bush and thought of my last experience inside a church. It had been St Trevor's Catholic church, one of the few places my mother had taken me as a child. We were not Catholics but this did not prevent her from 'putting on the dog' and a string of freshwater pearls every Sunday and making for the pews behind the town's Portuguese families. The services had been the high point of my week. The Catholic priest had worn festive clothing trimmed with gold brocade and I was free to observe people and read the Bible without interruption. Like many aspects of our lives, our attendance at St Trevor's ceased when Mr Da Silva sold his butcher's shop and moved back to Portugal.

The next time I visited St Trevor's I was on my own and services had ended. The church building had been bought by a development company and converted into executive apartments. I had visited it on open day out of curiosity and was taken through by an impatient man wearing a striped suit and pointed leather shoes. Only one of the original stained-glass windows now remained, a round porthole in the upper apartment. The agent said the stained-glass depiction of Jesus bleeding on the cross gave the apartments an authentic touch. The other windows had been sold for a fortune, he said. So had the apartments, even without stained-glass windows.

For a week after the visit, a strange empty feeling had troubled me. I kept thinking about all the people who had passed through the church since it had been built in 1890. I pictured them praying for the health of their children, an end to war, a new pair of leather shoes. I pictured all these prayers rising up like steam and collecting in the gables of the church. The developers had lowered and insulated the ceilings and I imagined over a century of prayers trapped in the gables forever.

When I returned my gaze to Roger Bottle, he was stirring the pink liquid in the plastic punch bowl with a grim expression. He had not taken kindly to being challenged about his political platform. I decided to try a non-political subject.

'You have a very impressive moustache.'

'Biggest handlebar in this town.' He flashed his bottom teeth again and raked his fingernails through the red bristles. 'Warren Crumpet has no facial hair. It's a flaw.'

'My mother was a big advocate of male hair.'

'A sensible woman.'

'She abandoned me for a sheep farmer.'

Roger Bottle's eyes flicked over me, alighting on my tartan trousers. 'She probably did the right thing.'

I turned at the sound of choir music to see a woman emerge from the church holding a tissue to her nose. She was wearing a tight beige dress with a plunging neckline that revealed at least fifty per cent of her bust. She sneezed into the tissue and exclaimed, 'Jesus!'

'Bless you, dear lady!' Roger Bottle's voice called out from behind me.

The woman glanced up and gave me a puzzled look before sneezing two more times, cursing with each sneeze. After hearing another 'Bless you' from Roger Bottle, she made her way around the fence to where he was sitting.

'Don't mind if I do,' she said, ladling herself a plastic cup of adult punch. 'That new pastor is thirsty work.'

'I hear he's very popular,' said the mayoral candidate.

'He's a dead ringer for Timothy Dalton if that's what you mean.'

'Modern times call for modern leaders. Modern clerics *and* modern politicians.'

The woman refilled her cup without responding.

'A modern minister knows that Christians don't want an old sodomite in a frock. They want colour and movement. Ditto for politicians.' Roger Bottle sat up straighter in his chair. 'I'll be making a lot of changes around here once I'm sitting in the mayor's seat.'

'That hit the spot.' The woman dropped the cup on the table and made her way back to the church. She blew her nose loudly before disappearing inside.

When I turned back to Roger Bottle, he was talking into a mobile phone. 'Hurry up, for God's sake,' he hissed.

I waited for him to put the phone in his pocket before reviving our conversation. 'What do you think of Warren Crumpet?'

132

'A vegetarian and wimp of the highest order. He'd cultivate carrots in front of the town hall if you gave him half a chance. Ha, ha.' He laughed in short bronchial bursts. It was loud and unconvincing.

'Organic vegetables are very popular. There's enormous commercial potential in chemical-free agriculture.'

'Where do you think all his vegetable eating is leading?'

'To lower cholesterol?'

'To the brassiere rack of the ladies' department.' He laughed again. 'It's the tofu. His chest is sprouting whatnots. Ha, ha, ha.'

I did not want to contradict Roger Bottle again but I had seen no evidence of breasts under Warren Crumpet's safari shirt. The only obvious affliction in his campaign photo was myopia. The lenses of his glasses were thick and reminded me of the puppet called Brains from *Thunderbirds*, a popular children's television programme in the 1960s. The series aired before I was born but I had read about it in the 'Pop Culture' section of the public library before it closed. The character of Brains had appealed to me. He operated the control console of an emergency team and would often save the day with his logic and knowledge.

'What do you think these are?' Roger Bottle lifted his moustache to expose two very pointed eye teeth.

'Eye teeth?'

'Canines. Man is a meat eater. We were not put on this earth to eat vegetation.'

I would have liked to discuss bowel cancer with the mayoral candidate but I did not want to risk another flare-up. I have found that meat eaters are often passionate about the consumption of animals and do not take kindly to dietary advice. Roger Bottle had brought up the subject of public gardens. It seemed like a good topic to pursue.

'During the Benevolent Years, the town underwent a green revolution. This period is immortalised in the photo display at the council. You can't see any green because the photos are black and white but people do look happy. Apparently, the colour green has a positive effect on the human brain.'

'People have their own gardens.' He waved his hand. 'What this town needs is industry.'

There was truth to what Roger Bottle said but like many politicians' statements, it was not the entire truth. The town did not have much industry but neither did everyone have a garden.

'What will Globcom's factory produce?'

'Highly technological devices for the protection of British nationals.'

'It's an arms factory?'

He arched an eyebrow.

'I do not agree with weapons. I think they do more harm than good. Laos is a case in point.'

'You don't have to crawl over desert sands with a sniper behind every date palm.'

'But the world already has too many weapons. Thousands of children are killed around the world every year.'

'British children are my priority.'

'But you're campaigning under the banner of family values?'

'Just shut up.'

The doors of the Holy Burning Bush opened and church-goers began pouring out. The sneezing woman appeared and shouted for the others to follow her around the fence to the trestle table. They were all female and all dressed in tight clothes. The doors closed but Nigel did not appear.

I turned to observe the women jostling for the punch bowl.

Roger Bottle had risen to his feet. 'The beauty queens have arrived,' he said, stretching out his arms in welcome. 'Christian womanhood in full bloom!'

The sneezing woman took control of the ladle and began filling cups and passing them out.

'Ladies, let me tell you a sad story.' The mayoral candidate tapped a spoon against the plastic punch bowl to get attention. He furrowed his brow and held up one of the 'WANTED' flyers. 'This defenceless young boy has been missing since Friday.'

The women stopped bustling and eyed the flyer.

134

'The little nipper's mother is beside herself.' He made a sad face and pointed behind them. 'Here's the poor lady now.'

I turned to see Chantal Corby approaching at a high-speed waddle. One of her arms was in a sling and the bruise on her forehead was now a fierce blue-green. She walked past me without a flicker of recognition to take a place next to Roger Bottle behind the table.

'I was just telling these lovely ladies about your tragedy,' he said, slipping an arm around her shoulders. 'They need to know why a vote for Bottle is the right and good thing to do.'

'My boy ran off,' said Chantal Corby, stopping to wipe an eye with the hand of her undamaged arm.

'Young fool.' Roger Bottle's fingers squeezed her shoulder.

'Kids can be so ungrateful.' She bit her lip and looked at Nigel's photo. 'A mother gives and gives till it hurts.'

'But you're not his mother!'

The statement had burst out of my mouth without warning, surprising myself as much as everyone else gathered around the table. The church women turned, eyebrows raised. Chantal Corby sputtered and drove an elbow into Roger Bottle.

'Who the hell's that?' she asked.

'Ladies, ladies,' replied the mayoral candidate, letting out one of his forced laughs. 'Just a heckler. Nothing to worry about.'

'I'm not a heckler.'

'One of Crumpet's communists.' Roger Bottle shot me a dangerous look. 'Go back to your commune and bake some soda bread.'

'I don't live on a commune.'

'Then go back to the nuthouse before I call someone with a straightjacket to take you away.'

I did not wait to see if he would make good on this threat and, turning away, I followed the fence line to the pavement. I was moving quickly across the church car park when someone whistled loudly behind me. It was a wolf whistle, a sound commonly made by drivers of white vans and workers on construction sites.

I stopped to look back at the road and experienced the kind of shock you receive when a rubber band snaps in your face and narrowly misses your eye. Mr Chin's Fiesta was passing the church at a walking pace. The driver's window was open and sitting behind the wheel was Shanks. He smiled at me and tooted the horn. As the car moved off down Industry Drive, I looked through the rear window and saw the blade of a chainsaw protruding from the back seat.

I did not have time to consider this alarming turn of events because just then the door to the church opened. Nigel emerged. I shook my head at him and made the international sign for mortal danger by running a finger across my throat. The boy required no further warning and swiftly crossed the car park to where I was waiting. We took off at a run.

A number five bus was approaching as we neared the bus stop. We put on a sprint, frantically waving our arms. The driver's eyes widened and his mouth opened. He jammed on the brakes. As the vehicle skidded past, I took note of the large advertisement along its side. It featured a lookalike of Mobutu Sese Seko, former President of Zaire. The model was dressed in a tasselled military jacket with medals made of chicken clusters. Out of his mouth was a speech bubble: 'I wear my Nack's Chicken Clusters close to my chest. Pure gold.'

'Thanks for the bloody warning,' said the driver as I threw myself on the bus. 'By rights I should charge you for wear and tear on municipal rubber.'

'One adult and one child please,' I said.

'Child?' The driver craned his neck to see Nigel, who had leaped through the door behind me. 'That little bastard better not try any bloody nonsense.'

'I'll take responsibility for him.'

The driver hesitated a moment before pushing the button on the ticket dispenser. As we made our way down the aisle, the recorded message came over the speaker system: 'Closed-circuit television is in service on this bus.' I did not look at the mirror because I knew the driver would be observing us.

Nigel's face was flushed from the run but beneath the rosy glow was a look of disappointment. As we sat down on the back seat I described the flyers I had seen and Chantal Corby's claim to motherhood. 'You're a poster boy for Roger Bottle's election campaign.'

'Whatever.' He shrugged.

'Did you find who you were looking for?'

'Not yet.' He turned away to gaze out of the window.

Nigel did not say another word as the bus made its way down Industry Drive. He remained unresponsive with his face towards the window until the vehicle turned into Cliff Richard Boulevard. It was slowing for a stop when he suddenly sat up straight, his eyes fixed on the pavement. As the bus door opened, he slid down in the seat to hide himself.

The man from the laundrette boarded the bus. In his hand was a racing gazette. His eyes remained on the gazette as he paid for his ticket and limped down the aisle. He reached the middle of the bus and was about to take a seat reserved for the elderly and infirm when the recorded message came over the speaker system. He glanced up from the gazette and searched for the source of the noise, locating the speaker near the driver's cubicle. He raised his arm and shook his fist before sitting down to look at the gazette again.

Nigel nodded as I pressed the red stop button. We stood simultaneously and he stayed close, pressed against my back as I walked to the exit. The man's seat was adjacent to the door. We drew level with him as the bus stopped.

I held my breath and waited but the door did not open. Nigel's chest was pressed against my back and I could feel his heart racing. I glanced up at the driver's mirror and saw him watching us. He raised his eyebrows and must have activated the recorded message because it began to play as the door opened. Nigel's hand landed between my shoulder blades and I found myself propelled out of the bus and on to the pavement with the boy at my heels.

I stumbled and righted myself, spinning around in time to see the gambler jump off his seat and lunge for the open door. But he was too slow for the driver. As the hydraulic mechanism hissed shut,

I could hear him shouting at Nigel, 'That's my T-shirt, you little bastard! I'm going to kill you!'

The bus was pulling away and the man was beating his fists against the door's glass panel when Nigel raised his hand and made a rude gesture with two fingers.

14

The bus was moving off when a familiar shade of fuchsia appeared in the doorway of Jaleel's First Choice Food & Wine. Jocelyn had his head down and was examining the contents of a plastic bag in his hands. He looked forlorn and windswept but raised a smile when he saw us.

'Hello dears,' he said, slipping his purchase into a coat pocket. His movements were shaky and despite eye liner and a layer of pink foundation, he looked tired and drawn. He gestured towards the stage platform in the town square. 'I hope there's not going to be a public hanging of Warren Crumpet.'

'Where's your dog?' asked Nigel.

'Home resting after yesterday's hoopla.' With an unsteady hand, Jocelyn rearranged the mint-green scarf around his neck but did not succeed in completely hiding the scratch marks, which were crimson and looked tender. 'Have you eaten?'

We both shook our heads.

'Then I suggest I treat you both to lunch.'

'Here, take this.' Nigel held out a fabric coin purse to the older man. It was printed in the distinctive D pattern of Christian Dior and trimmed with leather. 'It's five quid short.'

Jocelyn's eyes filled. He was speechless.

'I got hungry.'

'I don't understand,' I said. 'Where did you get it?'

Nigel plucked at his T-shirt. 'Where do you think?'

'From the man on the bus?'

The boy shrugged.

'You know him?'

'Should do. He's wallopered me often enough.'

This was bad news indeed. 'Who is he?'

'Sidney.'

'Who's Sidney?'

'The prick who lives with Foster Cow Corby.' It was clear by Nigel's tone that he was not interested in answering any more questions.

'You are a brave and daring young man,' whispered Jocelyn. His eyes were glistening. 'Thank you.'

Nigel wiped his nose with the back of his hand. 'I'll be a dead one if we don't get out of here. It won't take that prick long to leg it back.'

The boy beckoned us to follow as he cut through a gap between the grocery shop and the boarded-up Christian Joy Fellowship bookshop. This fed into a pedestrian walkway, which in turn led to the steps of a metal footbridge over the railway lines. Halfway across the bridge, my nostrils picked up the smell of fish paste and boiling animal fat. It was an odour that did nothing to arouse my appetite but Nigel had raised his nose in the air like a Labrador tracking the scent of a steak and kidney pie.

We came down off the footbridge and rejoined Harry Secombe Parade beside Chic Timepieces. In its heyday, the shop had sold watches and desk clocks to bank managers and business people. My mother's pride and joy had been a novelty clock from Chic. It had three brass balls that rotated around an axis and made a pleasant whir instead of a tick. The mechanism was encased in a glass dome, which gave it the look of a highly polished scientific specimen. My mother liked to draw attention to the clock whenever a workman or male social worker visited the house. She would tap the glass dome and say, 'I don't have to dust its brass balls,' then laugh in a deep, throaty way. I did not understand what she found so funny about this statement but it never paid to question anything she did.

Chic Timepieces had been closed for several years and its windows were now a pasteboard for notices and advertisements. One of the latest was a campaign poster for Warren Crumpet. I leaned in close to scrutinise his safari shirt but found no hint of feminine mounds. I removed my notebook to copy down the headline: 'Municipal Magic on a Shoestring. Vote Warren Crumpet. Swing the Budget Back to Black.' The word 'Unmanly' had been scrawled in black marker diagonally across the poster. I noted this down as well.

I had to run to catch up with Jocelyn and Nigel, who were waiting for me outside the Sea Breeze. The windows of the fish and chip shop were misted and it was impossible to see inside but the air was heavy with the sweet, fatty odour of its cuisine. The bell tinkled as Jocelyn pushed against the door. It jammed partway across the floor and Nigel had to give it another shove to make it open fully.

The chipman was standing next to the vats stacking fried food into plastic containers and glanced up when we entered. He swallowed something and belched as he sealed a container before turning to press his stomach against the counter. He wiped his tattooed fingers on a grimy tea towel dangling from his belt.

'What can we do you for?' he asked. His manner was efficient but unfriendly, a description often used in guidebooks to describe the German service industry.

'Do you chocolate-dip your bananas?' asked Jocelyn, pointing to a decorative banana hanger that had not been on the counter the previous day. A small handwritten card was taped to its base: 'Today's special. Battered bananas on a stick'.

'We chocolate-dip them, batter them, then double deep-fry them. The trick is getting the timing right. You want your batter crisp on the outside but your banana mouth-wateringly soft on the in.' The chipman wiped his mouth with his C H I P S hand. 'Frying is a form of art. The French would call it a "form of ah". The Frogs don't pronounce the T.'

'Merci pour l'astuce.'

The chipman frowned.

'I take it the banana is fried with the stick à l'intérieur?'

'Compliments of the house.'

Jocelyn nodded and held up a finger to indicate a single banana.

The chipman looked at me. 'We do a lovely deep-fried Ginster pasty.'

'I'd like a plain banana, please,' I said. 'Without chocolate or batter.'

'You've got to be joking.' The chipman gave me an incredulous look. 'No frying?'

'No. I don't need a stick either.'

'Why would you want a plain banana when you can have one of today's specials?'

'I'm a vegetarian. I don't eat food boiled in lard.'

'We use dripping.' He looked offended. 'There's no boiling at the Sea Breeze. All our frying is timed to perfection.'

'I'm afraid dripping would still harden my arteries. It might interest you to know that the heart attack is the biggest killer of British males. It kills more men than lung cancer. That has to be quite a lot when you consider the number of cigarette smokers in this country.'

The chipman raised his hand protectively to his chest. 'At least we don't cook dead cats like those bloody Chinese outfits.' He grunted. 'You'll be paying full price for that banana.'

He turned to Nigel. 'I suppose you want half a bloody head of cabbage on a stick.'

The boy shook his head with a smirk. He ordered a Scotch egg and chips.

'Scotch egg? You were in here yesterday.' The chipman raised his eyebrows. 'I had a lady come in here with a lump, threatening to sue. She claims someone tried to kill her with one of my eggs. I sold only two yesterday. One to you and one to a plumber.'

I saw Nigel's smirk widen into a grin and decided to head him off at the pass, which is a horseback manoeuvre used by a sheriff's posse to block an outlaw's exit from a gulch.

'Ted's café is having problems with plumbers,' I said.

A part of my brain observed me saying this and registered it on the Learning Curve. What I had said was not a lie but neither was it a completely honest response to the chipman's comment. Without any prior thought or preparation, I had applied a method known to politicians and salespeople as 'obscuring the truth'.

The chipman took his eyes off the boy and turned to me with interest. 'What's this about Ted?'

'He did not mention assault but he's very concerned about vandalism.'

'It's the gangs. Out there it's the law of the jungle.' The chipman pointed to the street with a thick and very pink tattooed finger. 'Roger Bottle's going to sort them out. An iron fist is the only thing they understand.'

'Heaven help us,' said Jocelyn, rolling his eyes.

The chipman's head swivelled. He took in Jocelyn's scarf and colourful coat. His eyes narrowed. He looked as if he was about to say something unpleasant when Jocelyn removed the purse from his pocket with a trembling hand and politely requested the bill.

Nigel observed this exchange with a wary smile before leading us over to a plastic table for two. As I was carrying a third chair over, Jocelyn excused himself and headed for the toilet at the back of the shop.

'Did you see how his hands were shaking?' I said as I sat down opposite the boy.

'He needs a drink,' said Nigel.

'But he's given up alcohol.'

The boy shrugged.

'You think he's drinking again?'

'What do you think he's got in his pocket?'

I did not have time to respond to this because the chipman flicked the switch to his ventilation fan and the roar of its motor made conversation impossible. I watched Nigel take a sugar sachet from the bowl on the table and empty it into his mouth. He took another and did the same before removing all the sachets from the bowl and stuffing them into the pockets of his jeans.

The whirring of the fan ceased and the boy sprung from his chair. He was bringing the food to the table when Jocelyn burst out of the toilet. His face looked completely different, alive and enthusiastic.

His cheeks were flushed and his eyes were sparkling. He smiled broadly as he sat down and was handed a paper bag by the boy. He removed the banana by its stick and was about to take a bite when he looked at me.

'What's wrong, dear?' he asked. 'You're frowning.'

I swallowed a mouthful of banana. Telling the truth would have meant confronting Jocelyn about his liver, which seemed unkind when he was recovering from a violent assault. As I struggled to avoid the topic of alcohol, my mind turned to my own problems and I found myself describing the strange events of the past twenty-four hours, the man I had seen in the office from the rail bridge, my encounters with Shanks and the Fiesta with the chainsaw on the back seat.

'I was told on Friday that if I didn't shape up and get normal by Monday, I'd lose my job. Mr Chin warned that he could easily replace me. I'm on the slippery slope.' I paused, aware that Jocelyn was listening attentively to everything I was saying. Even Nigel was paying attention between mouthfuls. It was unsettling to have an audience after a lifetime of being ignored or told to shut up. I pressed on.

'There's another very alarming aspect to all this. I have reason to believe that Shanks is a criminal. He's an associate of Mr Tanderhill, a disreputable hypnotherapist who masquerades as a Hindu.'

'You need to talk to Chin,' said Nigel, pulling up the front of the skull T-shirt to wipe the grease from around his mouth. He had made fast work of the Scotch egg, eating it between two fingers like an apple before stuffing the yolk whole into his mouth.

'I've been banned from the office until Monday.'

Jocelyn coughed politely.

'My dear, a gentleman alcoholic is prone to visions. An occupational hazard, you understand,' he said. 'But the events you've just described appear real and even serious. It seems expedient to take action.'

'Right now I'm not sure that I'm still employed. But if I set foot in the office before tomorrow, I'll most definitely be unemployed.

Mr Chin was very clear on that point. He's a stickler and his word is gold.'

'You need a plan.' Jocelyn pushed himself to his feet. 'Let me pop outside for some air and I'll have a think.'

Nigel raised his eyebrows as Jocelyn left.

'He's very kind,' I said.

'For a pisshead.' Nigel's words were harsh but there was no malice in his manner. 'He's got a nice dog. I'll give him that.'

'Yes.'

'My dad's going to get me a dog.'

'I didn't know you had a father.'

'Of course I have a father!' His face lost its friendliness. He looked down and began rapidly stuffing chips into his mouth.

'I don't.'

His eyes flicked up at me.

'According to my birth certificate, my father is unknown.'

I might never have seen the birth certificate if it had not been required for the passport application. My mother had kept the document in the drawer of her nightstand with all her 'private and personal' papers. The drawer had been out of bounds to me but by the time we were applying for passports, her weight and varicose veins had got the better of her and she rarely climbed the stairs, preferring to spend her days on the worn-out armchair in front of the television or at the window where she could monitor her neighbours. My mother's drawer had contained several other documents related to me. Most of them concerned money and all were from the social services.

The doorbell dinged in an urgent way as the door flew open. Jocelyn burst into the fish and chip shop like a bank robber entering an HSBC. His eyes were uncommonly bright and his smile was even wider than before. He grasped the back of his plastic chair and spun it around with a flourish to straddle it backwards. His movements were energetic, even theatrical.

'I've worked it all out,' he exclaimed in a breathy, excited voice. 'We're going on an adventure!'

Nigel giggled.

'Blow the dust off your magnifying glasses!' Jocelyn held an imaginary magnifying glass to his eye. 'We're going to become sleuths.'

'We?' I had to make sure that I understood correctly. It was rare for people to include me when they used the first person plural. Neither my mother nor Mr Chin had ever extended the umbrella of 'we' to include me.

'*Nous*. We need to investigate your Monsieur Chin.' He looked at Nigel. 'Are you in, *jeune homme*?'

'Depends what's in it for me,' said the boy.

'What do you say to five pounds?'

'And something to eat.'

'*Bien sûr.*'

'And I want to see your dog again.'

'Herb Alpert would be honoured.'

They looked at me.

'It's a very kind proposition,' I said, struggling to contain the competing forces of rising panic, surprise and gratitude. 'But Mr Chin would not appreciate any sort of prying. He's a private man with a volatile temper. I've seen it first hand. It's daunting.'

I then described an incident I had witnessed after the visit of the boy scout. Mr Chin had been unlocking the door to the stairs one morning when a young man in a navy-blue suit had approached, saying that he had just cycled in from a Bible encampment some twenty miles away. He asked if he could have a glass of water and was surprised when Mr Chin said no.

'What do you mean, no?' he asked.

'No water for spy or scout. Policy of company,' replied Mr Chin.

'I am not a spy or a scout, sir. I am a missionary.' He put his palms together in front of his chest. 'Oh happy day!'

'Same, same. Religious spy and scout worst kind. Get on my nerve.'

Mr Chin had turned his back to mount the stairs when the missionary reached out and placed a hand on his sleeve. I heard him say, 'A minute of your time, sir,' before squealing very loudly.

Mr Chin had grabbed the young man's fingers and was bending them back almost perpendicular to his hand.

'Buzz off and desist or Chin call police, have you handcuff for attack.' Mr Chin had then narrowed his eyes and pursed his lips, a clear sign of danger. I stepped back as he released the missionary's fingers.

'But you attacked me.' The young man whimpered and blew on his fingers. There were tears in his eyes.

'You come back private office again, I give you water.' Mr Chin shook a small plump finger in the younger man's face. 'Boiling water from kettle out window on top of head. Buzz off now!'

The missionary had grabbed the bicycle propped against a pillar and cycled off without looking back. After this incident, Mr Chin began locking the lower door at all times. This policy meant I was locked inside once or twice a week when he visited the Jade Dragon or Mandarin restaurants but this was not something that bothered him. Mr Chin only took exception to inconveniences when they cost him money or caused him personal discomfort.

My story did not have the effect I had intended. Jocelyn was looking more enthusiastic than ever and Nigel was laughing.

'What are you laughing about?'

'That missionerary prick's fingers,' said the boy. 'I like the sound of Chin.'

'*Exactement*,' said Jocelyn. 'If it's true he's hired a criminal then surely it's your duty to let him know.'

'But I'm not sure that he has hired one. He might have sold Shanks the Fiesta.' Though as I said this, I knew it was unlikely. Mr Chin took pride in his car. According to him, manual window winders were far superior to the power models. 'When power-window car fall in river, person and occupant trap like rat,' he told me. 'Manual window best policy always. Rotate with hand easy such as pie. Window open. Occupant safety every time.'

Jocelyn raised an eyebrow. 'That's why we must investigate and establish the facts.'

I could not fault his logic but the thought of investigating Mr

Chin gave me 'chicken skin', which is a Hawaiian pidgin expression for goose pimples. I was rubbing the skin on my forearms when Jocelyn asked what Mr Chin did in his spare time.

'He's a very private person. The only places I know him to visit are the Mandarin and Jade Dragon restaurants.'

I was about to add that I had been warned off both of these establishments when Jocelyn clapped his hands together and began outlining a plan of action. First, he announced, we would visit the rail bridge to see if there were any new developments in the office. We would then split up. He would go to the bus stop opposite the Babylon to conduct surveillance while Nigel and I visited the Mandarin to gather information. At two o'clock, we would all meet up at the Jade Dragon.

'What fun!' Jocelyn stood and flapped his hands in an animated way

I did not know how to respond to this enthusiasm. Fun was an alien concept to me, something promised in advertisements for children's adventure parks or camping holidays in Australia. The closest I ever came to experiencing pure enjoyment was when I was opening and shutting the file drawer of my office desk. The thought of giving up the desk, even temporarily, was almost too much to bear.

'I'll just grab some more air,' said Jocelyn. 'Back in a couple of ticks.'

I watched Jocelyn stride over to the door with his coat billowing out behind him and wondered how best to convince him that it was not a good idea to visit the restaurants. Mr Chin was very critical of their proprietors, particularly Mr Ding whom he described as 'worst gossip and trouble-causer'.

When I turned back to the table, Nigel had gone from his chair. On the window behind where he had been sitting was a message written in the condensation: 'Chantelle Corby stinks like horse dungs'.

Before I had time to take the notebook out of my bag, the doorbell tinkled again.

I looked over expecting Jocelyn but was surprised to see the disgruntled gambler from the bus. Sidney glanced at me without interest and entered the fish and chip shop warily, walking up to the counter with a limp. The chipman finished packing a plastic container before greeting him.

'What'll it be?' he asked.

'I'm Roger Bottle's right-hand man,' said Sidney, placing a stack of flyers on the counter. 'We're asking shopkeepers to put these up.'

'It's five quid to put up a notice here.' The chipman was pressing the lid down on the plastic container and did not look at the flyers.

'Five quid!' Sidney whistled through what was left of his teeth. 'It's about a missing kid. Where's your charity?'

'You heard me.' The chipman added the container to a stack next to the vats and returned to the counter, wiping his fingers on his tea towel.

'What if I buy two quids' worth of chips?'

'Then you could tape it to the outside of the window but we take no responsibility.'

Sidney nodded reluctantly.

As the chipman began to fill a basket with his order, Sidney leaned over the counter and spoke in a confidential manner. 'Ever thought about winning the lottery?'

The chipman twisted his head around and seemed to be giving the question serious thought when Sidney spoke again.

'Know what I'd do?'

Without waiting for a reply, he began describing his fantasy about buying a red Ferrari. It was virtually the same story he had told me except this time the women approaching the car were wearing high heels without pantyhose and were attempting to engage him in flirtatious banter. These details seemed to interest the chipman because he plunged the chip basket into the vat without turning on the ventilation fan. He glanced over at the sound of the doorbell but quickly returned his gaze to Sidney.

Jocelyn tripped as he entered the shop and had to grab the table to steady himself. His face was flushed and his eyes were blazing. 'Where's our young associate?' he asked.

'He's hiding,' I whispered, pointing to the toilet. 'That's Sidney at the counter.'

'*Le villain!*' Jocelyn's eyes widened. A wild smile appeared on his lips. 'You create a distraction while I spirit our boy away to safety.'

His plan was reckless and I would have preferred to discuss alternatives but he was already striding towards the back of the shop, his fuchsia coat once again flapping behind him.

My head was whirring as I stood and approached the counter.

Sidney was describing how 'she devils' were begging him for a ride in his Ferrari when I tapped him on the shoulder. He stopped mid-sentence, shrugging my hand away in an aggressive manner.

'I've got some information that might interest you,' I said, addressing both men.

The chipman and Sidney glanced at each other, their expressions hovering between confusion and irritation.

'The Babylon theatre was built in 1933 by an architect called Emile Toot. It might interest you to know that 1933 was the worst year of the Great Depression.' I nodded to make sure they understood the gravity of this historical period. 'Many people believe that 1929 was the worst year but they are incorrect.'

'You're interrupting a perfectly good story,' whined Sidney. His voice was high but not loud enough to block out the tapping of Jocelyn's knuckles on the toilet door.

I raised my voice to a shout. 'The Babylon is a landmark and historic relic!'

The men jumped.

'King George V himself opened the theatre! He had a full beard and moustache and enjoyed popularity as a monarch until his untimely death from influenza!'

The knocking ceased. I stopped shouting and spoke at the volume of regular conversation.

'Roger Bottle wants to pull the cinema down.'

'For Christ's sake!' Sidney's voice was a snarl. 'Tell it to someone who cares.'

'A Chinese gang's moved into that place,' said the chipman. He spoke quietly. His tone was serious. 'The only way to get rid of that lot is to pull it down. They're a law unto themselves.'

'Who?' I asked.

'The Chinese gangs. They call themselves triads but they're your garden-variety criminals and murderers. I have it on good authority.'

'Whose authority?'

'A businessman.' The chipman raised an eyebrow in a confidential way. 'He came in here asking all sorts of questions. Apparently, the gang's kingpin has set up shop above the cinema.'

'What did the businessman look like?'

'Oy!' said Sidney.

The chipman ignored him. 'Tall and English. Very pleasant. He bought two dozen battered oysters.'

'Did he have prominent eyes?'

'Like golf balls.'

'Oy!' Sidney was waving his arms about.

The chipman frowned and was in the middle of telling him to pipe down when Nigel burst out of the toilet. He bolted across the shop and out of the door with Jocelyn flying after him like a greying superhero.

'Hey!' The chipman flipped back the hinged countertop, and shoved Sidney aside. He rushed for the door but before he could make it through the doorway, Sidney shouted again.

'Oy!'

The chipman glanced back. His eyes widened.

'Oy! My chips are on fire!'

A cloud of blue smoke was gathering under the hood of the ventilation fan. The vat was foaming and gurgling in a dangerous way. The chip basket was clanking against the metal sides.

The chipman gave a cry of alarm and launched himself back towards the counter.

I grabbed the door and slipped out of the shop. I hit the pavement running and did not stop until I had reached the rail bridge. There I squeezed under the broken gate and mounted the stone steps to the top of the bridge.

My heart was pounding as I eased myself down on to the ledge and made my way over to Jocelyn who was leaning against the side of the bridge, gasping for breath. In between gasps he was laughing. Nigel was sitting cross-legged on the electrical box with an amused expression.

'I can't believe I let a *rongeur* like Sidney take me from behind,' wheezed Jocelyn. He laughed again.

'He takes everyone from behind,' said Nigel. 'He's a muggerer.'

'He should never have hit a minor,' I said.

'My dad's going to sort him out.' The boy's expression was fierce. He turned his face away.

Jocelyn was still catching his breath as I returned to my vantage point of the previous day. Standing on the same piece of wood, I hooked my hands over the side and pulled myself up to peer over the edge.

The office lights were still on but Mr Chin's chair was now turned towards the window. It was empty. There was no movement in the room, which looked strangely lifeless as if abandoned. I lowered myself on to my heels and walked back to Jocelyn and Nigel.

'It looks empty,' I said.

I then proceeded to tell them what the chipman had said about the businessman with prominent eyes.

I knew only one person who fitted this description. The thought of Mr Tanderhill sent a shiver up my spine.

15

Jocelyn stopped outside the door of the Mandarin restaurant and removed the purse from his coat pocket.

'Your salary,' he said, handing Nigel five pounds. He then winked at me and gave an exaggerated salute. 'Jade Dragon, fourteen hundred hours. Alpha beefeater foxtrot.'

I watched him stagger off down the street. 'Do you think he'll be alright?' I asked.

Nigel shrugged. 'He's pissed.'

'It's not safe to walk the streets without all your faculties.' I resisted the urge to quote the council's handbook on the dangers of public inebriation.

'Half the pricks in this town don't have them.' The boy smirked. 'He wasn't pissed when he got muggered yesterday.'

Nigel was right but it did not make me feel any less concerned. Even if Jocelyn did avoid an accident or another attack, his liver had to be under serious strain. The liver is a large and unattractive organ and while it is not as popular as the brain or the heart, it is a power-house of vital functions that are compromised when alcohol is consumed. Chronic drinking can lead to cirrhosis and even cancer as many former footballers know only too well.

In his seminal book, *Fear and Forgetting – How Addictions Are Taking the Edge off Britain*, B.S. Pappenheimer states that people consume alcohol and drugs to feel happy but what they are really doing is dulling their fears: 'Take away the Tia Maria and Prozac and you'll have a nation of Britishers shaking in their boots.'

The consumption of alcohol certainly made Jocelyn bolder if not reckless. There was another effect, too, one that I was more reluctant to admit. He was obviously happier and more confident when he drank.

I nodded to Nigel. 'Shall we go in?'

The Mandarin was the size of two large living rooms and laid out on two levels. The raised area at the rear was furnished with three metal and Formica tables. Around these were seated twelve men. They were making a lot of noise when we opened the door but fell silent as we entered. All the men were Chinese and all seemed about Mr Chin's age. I did not know exactly what this age was but I estimated it to be somewhere between forty-five and sixty.

In the middle of each table were plastic chips, tiles and dice. I recognised these as the accoutrements of mah-jong, a popular gambling game in the Far East. I also recognised the bottles on the tables. They were the same brand of plum liquor that Mr Chin had been drinking on Friday when he sent me off to get normal.

The only ornamentation in the restaurant apart from plastic plants, a large mirror and lattice screen was the Mandarin calendar pinned to the wall above the reception desk. When the door jingled closed behind us, a man materialised from an alcove next to the cash register. He was short with a wide, oily face and dressed in a white polo shirt, black trousers and scuffed rubber-soled shoes. He held up his palms and shook his head.

'Restaurant closed,' he said.

'But you have customers,' I replied.

'Here meeting of Chinese Friendship Society. Private and exclusive. End of story.'

'Your friends are playing mah-jong. I recognise the tiles.' I did not bother mentioning the piles of money in the middle of each table. 'Mah-jong is an ancient game that originated in China. Confucius is said to have enjoyed it. He was an esteemed philosopher who lived five hundred years before Christ, which is quite a long time ago when you think about it.'

'Of course ancient game. Chinese history oldest and best in world.

Mah-jong number one. Better than football.' He pursed his lips proudly.

'I would prefer mah-jong to football but I have no experience in either game. Both require a number of players and I am lacking in the people department.'

'What you want?'

'Some information. Are you Mr Ding?'

'You inspector of health and safety?'

'No.'

'Then no information here.' He folded his arms over his chest. 'Now leave restaurant.'

The mah-jong players seemed to take this as a cue and recommenced throwing dice and stacking tiles. They were loud and wild, more like revellers at a Mexican fiesta than board-game enthusiasts.

'Hoy!'

Mr Ding's shout rang out over the restaurant. The mah-jong players stopped moving, hands frozen in mid-air. Silence fell.

'Control brother!'

Nigel had slipped out from behind me and was standing in front of the tables.

'He's not my brother.'

'All look same-same.' Mr Ding herded the boy towards me. 'Now must vacate immediately. Chinese Friendship Society private affair.'

'Please.' I held up my hands to prevent Nigel being thrown against me. 'I need information about one of your customers, a Mr Chin.'

Mr Ding stopped shoving. 'You say Chin?'

'Yes, Augustus Randolph Chin.'

'Ha! Chicken Chin!' His lips parted to reveal dangerous-looking teeth. They were remarkably long, like the teeth of a donkey, an animal known for its stubbornness and vicious bite. Mr Ding's laughter set off the mah-jong players, who began laughing in a high and irreverent manner.

'Why are you laughing?' I did not understand. There was nothing funny or chicken about Mr Chin. He was neither a comedian nor a coward as he himself had pointed out.

155

Mr Ding was too busy laughing to answer my question.

'Earlier this year, Mr Chin presented me with one of your restaurant's calendars. He described it as magnificent and attractive. Apparently, it improves *feng shui*.'

'Chin say calendar magnificent and attractive?' Mr Ding stopped laughing. His face showed interest.

I nodded but did not bother to add that Mr Chin found the Jade Dragon's calendar superior. 'Why did you call him Chicken Chin?'

'Because he run too fast.' Mr Ding raised his eyebrows at the players seated around the tables and did a comical imitation of a runner. The men laughed.

'Mr Chin doesn't run. He walks or drives a car.'

'He run from man with stick and knife. Leave small brother in Macao for torture or death. Chin love money and collect gold too much for saving family. Traitor and coward, like I say.'

Mr Ding's story did not make sense. Mr Chin was from Hong Kong not Macao. He had never mentioned a brother and even if he did have one, I could not imagine him leaving a family member in jeopardy. The Mr Chin I knew was a fierce yet principled man who never acted in a contradictory or dishonest way. If he said he was not a coward then I was inclined to believe him. Indeed, my future depended on it. If I lost faith in Mr Chin, I would lose faith in all that was important to me.

'Mr Chin is no coward. I've seen him physically challenge a much taller and younger man with his bare hands. His opponent was a cyclist with a tenacious manner and robust health.' I paused before delivering my next item of proof. 'Mr Chin has a length of green bamboo and is not afraid to use it.'

'Green bamboo? Ha. Chin never dare beat even fly of mosquito with bamboo.' Mr Ding did a comic pantomime of taking swipes in the air with something.

The men at the tables hooted.

'He says he'd like to use his bamboo to beat the so-called Chinese who make the chicken chow mein in this country.'

Mr Ding stopped laughing. 'Mandarin restaurant have finest chicken chow mein.'

'Mr Chin says it's slop and a disgrace.'

'Chinese Friendship Society club private. You not welcome.' He glowered at me and gave Nigel a shove. 'Clear off and take little bastard.'

'Keep your hands off me, you prick,' said Nigel. 'I'll have you done for man-handlering a minor.'

Mr Ding was about to give him another shove but thought better of it.

'Some friendship society you have here.' Nigel pointed to the tables.

'Best friendship of Chinese gentlemen.' Mr Ding avoided the boy and grabbed my shoulder. He pushed me towards the door.

'If you're all friends, why is everyone cheating?' Nigel laughed.

'What cheating?' Mr Ding let go of my shoulder and looked over at the mah-jong tables.

'They're stuffing their pockets with those white blocks.'

Nigel's words triggered a volley of shouting. One man stood and slapped another's face. The slap set off another slap and soon the men were wrestling each other and grabbing money off the tables. Mr Ding hurried across as a table overturned, scattering coins and tiles across the restaurant.

Nigel was laughing as he nudged me out of the restaurant and slammed the door behind us. He was clearly pleased with himself and stood for a moment at the window to observe the activity inside the restaurant. I stuck my hand out and felt the beginning of drizzle. The rain did not warrant an umbrella or raincoat but it was enough to dampen the spirits of people with eyeglasses or hair extensions. It did nothing to ease the anxiety I was feeling about investigating Mr Chin.

The Jade Dragon restaurant was located next to Slawek's delicatessen, a place I had often visited with my mother when it was still Da Silva's butcher's shop. At one time there had been a substantial Portuguese population in the town, particularly during the period of Portugal's dictatorship. The largest number of immigrants had arrived during the Maverick Years when factory cogs and conveyor belts were still turning on Industry Drive. These newcomers had been given an enthusiastic welcome by the mayor. Jim Snick had dubbed the influx the 'Port Wine Revolution' and even hired a Portuguese chauffeur to drive the mayoral Vauxhall Firenza.

Sadly, this 'Brothers in Arms' policy and other such initiatives were abandoned during the oil crisis when council conservatives used a loophole in the town's electoral bylaw to force Jim Snick out of office. The infamous 'Putsch of 1973' is a dark moment in the town's history. Many of the progressive aspects of the council vanished overnight. Portuguese families lost their preference for council housing and translators were sacked from the council. Even the mayoral chauffeur lost his job. The Firenza and all other council property bearing Snick's distinctive yellow and orange stripes abruptly disappeared from the local landscape.

I had not visited this part of town for some time and was surprised to find the Polish delicatessen closed with a large notice stuck to the inside of the window: 'Liquidation sale. Every sausage and pickle must go'. The sale had been and gone. The shelves of the shop were bare and the door was chained shut. A campaign poster for Warren Crumpet had been taped to the glass but someone had already defaced it with crude breasts over the pockets of his safari shirt. 'Bean lover' was scrawled across his face but the headline had been left untouched: 'Crumpet for Mayor. The Penny Pincher with a Conscience.' I wanted to note everything down but Nigel was already pushing open the door of the Jade Dragon.

The familiar sound of an oxygenator greeted me as I entered the restaurant. The fish tank was long and wide, and functioned as a partition between the entrance and seating area. Unlike the tank in the office, this one was populated with fish of various shapes and sizes. Nigel tapped the glass and a red fish darted out from behind a rock. It was shiny and narrow like a herring but was gone before I could examine it more closely.

'*Willkommen*,' said a voice from a row of plastic rubber trees next to the tank. 'Table for two?'

The foliage parted and a tall, elegant Chinese man appeared. He was dressed formally in a black suit and white shirt with a wine-coloured cravat around his neck. The cravat was anchored in place by a gold tiepin in the shape of the British pound.

'We've not come to dine,' I said, aware that my purse contained only six pounds ninety.

'This not zoo.' The restaurateur rapped the tank with one of his elegant knuckles. The red fish darted out from the behind a rock before disappearing again. 'Viewing of water scene for paying customer only. All fish here for eating purpose.'

I glanced at the tank again. The fish were like condemned prisoners awaiting a lethal injection. I looked away.

'*Bitte*, follow me.'

The elegant man had misinterpreted my interest in the fish tank. Beckoning us to follow, he led us around the plastic plants and into the seating area. The restaurant was bigger than the Mandarin and furnished with carved wooden tables and chairs. There were no customers but all the tables were set with white tablecloths, white porcelain plates, several sets of cutlery and cloth serviettes folded into crowns. The man pulled out the chair of a table for two and gestured for me to sit down as Nigel took the seat opposite.

'Today afternoon is yum cha specialty at magnificent Jade Dragon.'

'I think you misunderstand.' I felt the man's hand on my shoulder and found myself being pushed into the chair. 'Are you Mr Lung?'

'Winston Archibald Lung here at your service. Archie Lung for short purpose.' He placed a hand on his chest and took a bow, fluttering his other hand like a marquis from the court of Louis XIV.

'Mr Lung, I've come here to ask you some questions.'

'Halt horses. Don't say word. Lung know what you want.' He barred his lips with a finger and, before I could stop him, had disappeared through a swing door at the rear of the restaurant. A decorative clock above the door caught my eye. It was a pendulum clock in the shape of a Swiss chalet. As I watched, the minute hand moved to twelve and the clock struck two. A tiny wooden man in lederhosen popped out of a tiny door, and bowed twice to the chiming of the clock before snapping back inside.

Nigel smiled at the clock as he unfolded the cloth crown of his serviette.

'I think it might be difficult to get information out of Mr Lung,' I said.

'Money talks with that sort of prick,' he replied, tucking the serviette into the neck of his T-shirt. He then removed a pair of chopsticks from their paper sleeve and began to drum on his plate.

'But I've virtually no money left.'

No sooner had I spoken than Mr Lung appeared with two round bamboo steamers. He uttered a high-pitched hum like someone tuning a harmonica before placing them on the plates in front of us.

'Dim sum delicacy,' he said, opening the lids with obvious pride. I pulled my head back as pork-scented vapour rose from steamer. Inside were three small dumplings resembling miniature bleached Christmas puddings. Each was topped with a green pea.

'I think there's been a mistake,' I said. 'I didn't order dim sum.'

Mr Lung narrowed his eyes. 'What information you want?'

'About Mr Chin, Augustus Chin.'

'Ha.' Mr Lung rocked back on his heels and shook his head. 'Why everybody ask for Chin?'

'Everybody?' My hands gripped the seat of my chair. 'Have you been approached by a tall man with large, bulging eyes?'

'Natürlich. Bulge-eye with lip like famous man of Africa.' Mr Lung used a thumb and forefinger to indicate a large area between the nose and mouth. 'Bulge-eye order nothing, ask question. Ha!'

'You gave him information?'

'You think Lung foolish?'

'No.'

'Of course give information! He finally take Peking duck. Succulent house speciality with dipping sauce and other luxury. Bulge-eye leave very satisfy.' The restaurateur patted his stomach to indicate culinary satisfaction.

'Did he come here with another man wearing a hat?'

'Peking duck for two.'

'It was not a good idea to give them information.'

'Of course good idea! Peking duck very high cost. Delicious like hell.' Mr Lung pointed to a chalkboard affixed to the wall over the reception desk. Below the words, 'Payment of All Kind Kindly Accepted' was a list of exchange rates for the euro, American dollar and Japanese yen against the British pound. At the very bottom was an asterisk with the price of gold. The rate was at least twenty per cent lower than that offered by the pawn shop, which was already at least half the official market rate.

'Bulge-eye pay British pound sterling cash. Next time, he say, he pay gold.'

'Did he say he's working for Mr Chin?'

'Archie Lung recommend Jade Dragon wonton and deep-fry pork ball. Very best and delicious. Deep-fry prawn and spicy dipping sauce. Fragrant rice. For follow-up, baby radish on stick. Help for digestion.'

I shook my head but Mr Lung ignored me and vanished once again behind the swing door. I glanced at the clock and felt my armpits prickle. It was twenty past two and Jocelyn was nowhere in sight.

'You want them?' asked Nigel, pointing to my steamer.

I shook my head and slid it towards him. He speared all three dim sum with the pointed end of his chopstick and crammed them all in his mouth, chewing rapidly with his cheeks full.

'I don't trust Mr Tanderhill or Shanks.'

Nigel raised his eyebrows and swallowed. He wiped his mouth with the serviette dangling from the collar of his T-shirt.

'And Mr Lung makes me nervous. He's a forceful entrepreneur.'

'He's a tight-arse prick.' The boy burped loudly and grinned.

The kitchen door swung open and Mr Lung reappeared with a large tray bearing several dishes. Working quickly, he arranged the food in the middle of the table, placing finger bowls of water beside each of our plates. He nodded in a satisfied way as Nigel speared a fried wonton.

'Where does Chin live?' asked the boy, before shoving the wonton into his mouth.

'He just move house,' said Mr Lung, nudging the finger bowl closer to Nigel. 'Lucky number *acht*. Doonican Terrace.'

'Do you mean number eight Val Doonican Terrace?' I asked.

'Like I say.' His eyes flashed at me. '*Acht* Doonican Terrace.'

Mr Lung was clearly sensitive about his diction. I did not want to upset him, especially when I did not have money to pay for the food he had served us. Jocelyn had sent us on an investigation and in the absence of any alternative this seemed the most practical course of action to take.

'I was just talking to Mr Ding at the Mandarin restaurant.'

'Ding gossip like hell.'

'He said something strange about Mr Chin.'

'Of course strange. Mandarin price cheap. Quality bad. Cockroach and mouse. Toilet block every time. No water bowl for washing finger. Dirty like hell.' Mr Lung's voice had got higher and higher until he was almost shouting.

'We didn't eat.'

'Best idea.'

'We went there to gather information.'

'Information?' His manner changed. He rubbed his elegant hands together. 'Lung recommend Peking duck with dipping sauce.'

'Oh!'

Again he refused to listen as I tried to protest. I looked at the clock as he disappeared into kitchen and felt my pulse increase. It was a quarter to three. Where was Jocelyn?

'Quack, quack,' said Nigel, filling his mouth with a shrimp and scoop of rice.

I took a deep breath and tried not to look horrified when Mr Lung arrived ten minutes later with a plate of pancakes and a very dark and oily cooked duck. Its head and beak were still attached but its neck was tucked to the side as if the bird had decided to take a nap after being scalded, boiled and roasted. Mr Lung began removing the skin and dark flesh with a double-bladed electrical knife. I looked away and saw Nigel stuff a pancake loaded with two wontons and several shrimps into his mouth. Mr Lung continued to strip the duck of its skin and flesh, his face rigid with concentration.

'Is it true that Mr Chin abandoned his brother to armed men in Macao?'

'Gangster for gamble debt.' Mr Lung pressed a button on the handle of the knife and stopped carving. He held up the greasy blade and scoffed. 'Chicken Chin see such knife. Run like hell.'

'I don't understand.'

'What *kein* understand? His brother Cornelius Chin love gamble too much!' Mr Lung tonged a pile of duck skin and flesh on to the plate at my elbow. 'Small brother make huge debt. Gangster angry like hell. Big brother must pay debt that is family obligation and duty. But Big Chin traitor and coward. He run like hell.'

'But Mr Chin is not a coward. I've seen him confront an athletic missionary with his bare hands. Neither can I believe that he would betray someone or leave a debt unpaid. He's a very honourable man.' I realised what I was saying and stopped. 'I need to confess something.'

Mr Lung frowned. 'Catholic?'

'I don't have the money to pay for all of this food.'

'What? *Kein geld?*' His metal tongs flashed across the table and removed the duck skin from my plate.

'Not enough. I might be able to pay for the dim sum and fragrant rice but that's probably the limit of my funds.'

'No moving!' He began snatching plates and bowls from the table and stacking them on a tray. 'You must leave valuable watch and jewellery trinket or Lung give trouble like hell.'

I did not have a watch or anything of value on me. I looked over at Nigel but he was grabbing food off the plates as fast as they were being removed and did not seem to understand the gravity of the situation.

The Swiss chalet clicked and the tiny wooden man appeared and bowed three times. Simultaneously, the front door opened and a familiar voice called out from beyond the plastic hedge.

'Daddy's back!'

Jocelyn's face poked through the foliage. It was red and very shiny. His eyes were glassy and bloodshot.

'I should have brought my jungle machete.' He laughed, forcing his way through the plants and weaving over to our table. 'Please excuse my tardiness. Apparently, I fell asleep in a bus shelter.'

'I'm very glad to see you,' I said.

Jocelyn hiccupped and grabbed the edge of the table to steady himself. 'No sign of Chin, I'm afraid.'

'Oh.'

'But I did see a Buffalo Bill character.'

'A man in a cowboy hat?'

'Very Village People.' Jocelyn nodded. 'He had a lasso over his shoulder as if he'd just ridden in from a muster.'

'Who you?' asked Mr Lung, pointing his greasy tongs at Jocelyn's chest.

'A gentleman friend.'

'You friend! You pay bill!' Mr Lung pulled a piece of paper from his pocket and shoved it under Jocelyn's nose. 'Fifteen per cent service tip. Regular and correct.'

I opened my mouth to explain but Jocelyn quieted me with an unsteady wave of a hand. Mr Lung's eyes widened as he removed his coin purse and pressed a wad of notes into his hand.

'Your décor is charming,' said Jocelyn. 'The jungle theme is simply delightful.'

'*Vielen Dank.*' Mr Lung flushed with pride and made a contented harmonica sound. With a bow, he disappeared through the plastic rubber plants and was waiting for us with a tray as we reached the door. On it was a bottle of plum liquor and a shot glass. He filled the glass and handed it to Jocelyn.

'House compliment,' he said. 'Come back many time, sir and good customer. *Auf wiedersehen* soon.'

Jocelyn emptied the glass before I could protest, shaking his head as it went down. He blinked a couple of times before letting out a high-pitched 'Whoopee!' to the amusement of Nigel. Before Mr Lung could refill the glass, I led them both out of the restaurant.

'Thank you very much for your generosity,' I said, prompting Nigel with a nod.

'Yeah,' said the boy.

'*De rien,*' said Jocelyn. 'Any new leads, my dears?'

I shook my head. 'Just a lot of confusing information.'

'We got Chin's address.' Nigel stopped picking his teeth with a toothpick. 'Val Doonican Terrace.'

'You're not proposing we visit his house?' I tried to catch Nigel's eye but he was looking at Jocelyn. 'Mr Chin is a very private man.'

'But my dear, that's precisely what you *must* do!' Jocelyn clapped his hands. 'You haven't been banned from his home, have you?'

'No, but then I've never suggested a visit.'

'Perfect. It'll be a surprise.'

'Mr Chin doesn't like surprises.' I thought of the day I had moved his desk and felt my armpits prickle.

'But surely if we're going to help him, we need to get our facts straight.'

Again, I could not fault Jocelyn's logic but he did not know Mr Chin and had not witnessed his fiery temper.

'Think of it as a fact-finding mission, my dear.' Jocelyn removed a five-pound note from his purse and handed it to Nigel. 'I'm sure this young man will go with you for moral support.'

The boy trousered the money with a shrug.

'What about you, Jocelyn?'

'The polling station awaits, my dear. Warren Crumpet needs every vote he can get.' He glanced at the lady's silver watch on his wrist. 'Let's rendez-vous *chez moi* at six thirty.'

He made to salute but his hand missed his temple. I watched him walk off unsteadily and worried.

16

Nigel nudged me as the number two bus approached the stop. Along its side was a large banner advertisement with the head and shoulders of someone resembling Ringo Starr. The model was holding up two crumbed chicken drumsticks and smiling. Out of his mouth was a speech bubble: 'Nothing beats Nack's drumsticks. A solid gold hit every time.'

The driver frowned as I boarded the bus. 'Not you a-bloody-gain,' he said.

'One adult and one child, please,' I said, placing three pounds on the plastic tray.

'By rights, I shouldn't let that little bastard on the bus.' He shot Nigel a look. 'I'm sick of cleaning up after the likes of him.'

The boy took a step towards the driver but I held him back with my arm.

'You must be busy with voters today.'

'What a bloody headache.' The driver exhaled noisily. 'They're all heading to the high street where they'll all buy their bloody crisps and chocolate.'

'You don't eat crisps or chocolate?'

'Of course I do. I'm English.' He frowned and took the coins off the tray. 'But I don't go leaving litter behind for others to clean up.'

'I am not a litterbug and we don't have any litter to leave.'

'I'll be keeping my eye on you.' The driver shot Nigel another look and issued two tickets.

'Closed-circuit television is in service on this bus,' droned the loudspeaker as we walked down the aisle to the back seat. I turned to face the window to avoid the driver's eyes and found myself looking at the boarded-up Woolworths. On the pavement in front of the building was a large message scrawled in blue chalk: 'POWER AND GOOD TIDINGS TO THE PEOPLE.' The shop had been closed for a long time but a metal grille had prevented people from putting up posters and writing on the windows. In the recessed shop entrance, someone had built an elaborate construction out of old boxes. It was a cardboard cabin with a cardboard door and a window sealed with see-through plastic. The door of the cabin was open and inside I glimpsed a teapot and mug sitting on a cardboard table.

This scene stayed on my mind and it was not until we reached our destination that I realised I had forgotten to note down the latest chalk message. I added it to the other mental notes and hoped I would not forget them all before I had a chance to update my notebook and OBSERVATIONS ring binder.

Val Doonican Terrace is one of at least ten streets of identical rows of houses that were built during the Industrial Revolution to accommodate the town's working population. The streets had begun life with names such as 'Cartwheel Place' and 'Coal Shuttle Road' but were later given more contemporary and popular names by Jim Snick. The terraces are two stories high and have no gardens or ornamentation apart from cast-iron spiked railings. You can see what urban life was like for the town's early workers and their families at the council display. The photos are sepia and blurred but it is obvious that dirt played a major role in the lives of people during this era. The skies are dark and heavy with industrial smoke and a film of grime covers everything from trees and horse carts to the clothes on washing lines. Even the children playing in the streets look as if they have been dipped in coal dust.

I had never visited Val Doonican Terrace and was pleasantly surprised to find it lined with trees. They were mature birches and judging by the thickness of their trunks, they had been planted either during the Benevolent or Maverick years. The birch is an attractive deciduous tree with small leaves and flexible whip-like branches.

These branches were once favoured by headmasters and prison warders and used to inflict punishment on the backs and buttocks of their charges. It is a surprising fact that corporal punishment was not fully outlawed in British schools until 2003. I have never been beaten with a birch branch or green bamboo for that matter but I have been slapped repeatedly in the face with an open palm and that was unpleasant enough.

Nigel had run on ahead and was peering through the open doorway of number eight when I reached the gate. I should have been paying attention to the boy but I was distracted by the fact that Mr Chin had left his door open. Before I could stop him, Nigel entered the house, jumping over a cardboard box to disappear down the hallway.

My pulse rate increased and my heart seemed to surge upwards inside my chest. I could feel it pumping along my collarbone as I rapidly scanned the street for any sign of Mr Chin or his Fiesta. I hurried up the steps and called through the open doorway, half expecting my enraged employer to fly out of the house waving a length of bamboo.

'Hello?' I pushed the top half of my body through the doorway. 'Nigel? Mr Chin?'

No one answered.

I called out again and when I got no reply, I stepped inside. I had to find Nigel and get him out of there. Invading the home of Mr Chin not only went against his personal policies of privacy and security but it was also highly illegal.

I stepped over the cardboard box and discovered several shoes scattered over the floor. I bent down to pick up a familiar black leather boot. It was a size-seven ankle boot and heavy despite its small dimensions. I turned it over and recognised the 'Secret Boot Made in Japan' imprint on its rubber sole. To the untrained eye, it looked like a regular man's boot. However, inside its sole was an ingenious foam insert that raised the height of the wearer by two inches. I had read this information on a shoebox I once discovered while emptying Mr Chin's dustbin. The unusual Japanese-style

English on the box had caught my eye: 'Enjoy Bigger Height With Miracle Technology. Your Secret Safe With Secret Boot.' There was truth to this claim because I had known nothing of Mr Chin's secret until I discovered the box.

From my reading at the public library I knew that short men are often sensitive about their height and can suffer from a mental ailment called the 'Short Man Syndrome'. This psychological complex puts enormous pressure on the sufferer, driving him to great heights of achievement or compelling him to engage in daring or aggressive behaviour. Napoleon is a case in point. He invaded much of Continental Europe in the early part of the nineteenth century and earned renown for his cunning and surprise tactics. He is often portrayed in paintings wearing very tight trousers with a hand over his small intestine.

'Take a look at this!'

I put the boot down and followed Nigel's voice to a room off the hall where I found him sprawled on a huge rocker-recliner chair upholstered in brown leather. The floor was scattered with belongings and cardboard boxes as if Mr Chin was in the middle of unpacking and was not being very methodical about it. The chair was the only upright thing in the room and rose out of the chaos like the throne of a deposed king. The boy grinned at me, working a mahogany lever to demonstrate its footrest function.

'Dad would love one of these,' he laughed.

'We shouldn't be in here,' I replied, glancing behind me to make sure Mr Chin was not standing in the hallway.

'Keep your hair on.' The enthusiasm went out of the boy's voice. His face lost its joy. 'Nobody's here.'

I looked away and spotted a small jade monkey on the floor next to the chair. Mr Chin had once told me that people born in the year of the monkey were superior. 'Tricky and wise,' he said. 'Best person for all business. Personality good and adorable. Excellent for television show.' When I had asked him about the year of the sheep, he had frowned. 'So-so. Sheep foolish but good for worker. Follow boss and leader.'

I glanced back to the boy. 'It looks like Mr Chin is still unpacking.'

'Whatever.' Nigel let the footrest fall and pushed himself off the chair. He shouldered me out of the way as he made for the door. 'I'm having a look round.'

'I don't think that's a good idea.'

The boy ignored me and made for the stairs.

I did not want to remain inside the house but neither did I want to abandon Nigel. There was no knowing what Mr Chin might do if he discovered an intruder. The only sensible thing to do was to wait outside and keep a vigil for incoming trouble.

I crossed the road and made for a large birch tree. Its trunk was not wide enough to hide me but I felt less vulnerable standing next to something taller than myself. The house opposite Mr Chin's was identical except for its iron railing, which had been augmented with coils of barbed wire. The gate was locked and bore a white plastic plaque: 'Alarmed & Monitored by Globcom.' I looked up and found the CCTV camera mounted on a lamppost. It had not been masked.

The door of the house opened and to my surprise, Roger Bottle appeared in the porch. Even more surprising was the smile he flashed as he approached me, buttoning up his tweed jacket. My immediate impulse was to turn to check on Mr Chin's house but I suppressed this desire and looked down, my eyes falling on Roger Bottle's shoes. They were brown leather loafers with tassels over the toes, a popular footwear choice for bankers and American men with MBAs.

'I'm preparing myself for victory,' said the mayoral candidate. 'You must be the reporter from the *Cockerel.*'

'No,' I replied, positioning myself between Roger Bottle's eye line and Mr Chin's porch.

'I'll be heading down shortly with my assistant to cast my own vote. Every vote counts. Ha, ha.' He showed no indication of having heard me let alone recognising me. 'You may as well come along for the ride. You'll enjoy the fanfare.'

'I'm afraid that's impossible.'

'Unbiased journalism and all that.' He tapped his nose and laughed again in a false way, prompting his large Adam's apple to bob up and down. 'You must have questions for me.'

I did have questions. I also wanted to keep him occupied and distracted.

'Fire away.' He cleared his throat in the manner of a priest about to give Mass.

'Have you seen the man who lives across the road in the last twenty-four hours?'

Roger Bottle looked disappointed by the question. 'The Jap?'

'He's Chinese. He was born in Hong Kong.'

'Same thing.' He raised himself up and ran a finger over his moustache. 'They come over here hidden inside the backs of lorries and then have the gall to call themselves refugees. They live off the state while stuffing their furniture with money and valuables.'

'Mr Chin flew into Heathrow on Cathay Pacific.' I knew this because he had complained about the meals. 'He's a British national and claims no benefits.'

'The worst kind.'

'Sorry?'

'You heard me.'

Talking with Roger Bottle was like conversing with my mother. Neither of them was particularly informed but both had very strong opinions, especially about non-Anglo-Saxons. When my mother had not been criticising immigrants, she was accusing Arabs of kidnapping young English women for the white slave trade: 'A blonde English virgin with a good figure fetches a fortune in Saudi Arabia. Attractive girls as young as fourteen are being snatched off our streets in broad daylight and smuggled out in barrels.' My mother had always ended such statements by running a critical eye over me before adding, 'You have nothing to worry about.'

'Have you seen anything suspicious going on?'

'As a matter of fact.' Roger Bottle narrowed his eyes and lowered his voice in a confidential manner. 'The Jap turned up this morning in a Ford Fiesta with a driver and bodyguard. Two white men. They were inside the house for less than an hour. When they left, the Jap was sitting up in the back with his bodyguard like King Farouk.'

'Mr Chin does not have a chauffeur or a bodyguard.'

'I know what I saw.' He filled his lungs and pushed out his chest. 'If I wasn't so busy with the election I would've reported him.'

'For what? It's his house.'

'Probably a squatter.' He frowned. 'You'll see changes around here when I'm elected.'

'Is it true you want to introduce English tests for foreign residents?'

'If you're going to live in an English town you should speak the Queen's English.'

'Most locally born residents do not speak the Queen's English.'

'*Genuine* locals would not be tested.'

'That doesn't seem fair.'

'Fair? Don't be ridiculous!' His eyes slid to one side. He tilted his head to look over my shoulder.

I followed his gaze to Mr Chin's porch where Nigel was now standing with a coil of blue rope in his hands. He waved, unaware of the mayoral candidate behind me.

Roger Bottle cleared his throat and lowered his voice. 'I've been looking for that little bastard.'

I discreetly raised my hand and tried to signal Nigel to leave.

The boy waved back.

'My phone's inside the house.' Roger Bottle's voice was now a harsh whisper. 'Go over there while I call for backup. Don't let that little bastard leave! Put him under citizen's arrest if necessary.'

'Citizen's arrest is a form of vigilantism.' I pulled a face at Nigel and made a shooing motion with my hand. 'It dates back to the Middle Ages.'

'Just shut up and do as I tell you!'

Without warning, Roger Bottle pushed me from behind. It was a violent thrust that propelled me forwards and caused me to stumble over the pavement. My head was thrown back and my eye caught the CCTV camera that had just recorded the mayoral candidate's shove.

I crossed the street at a gallop, leaping up the steps to where Nigel was standing.

'You've got to get out of here!' I said. 'That's Roger Bottle and he's in a violent mood.'

'Look what I found,' said the boy.

He held up the blue nylon rope. It was knotted with a sheepshank, a rope-shortening knot popular with mountain climbers and boy scouts.

'Roger Bottle said he's calling for backup.'

'I found this next to the rope.'

Nigel pressed a small metallic object into my hand before leaping down the steps and dashing out of the gate. I waited until he had disappeared from sight before opening my hand.

A shiver travelled up my spine.

The object was a chain bearing a small medallion of St Christopher, a charm worn by travellers and bookbinders and a talisman against pestilence and epilepsy. It was the medallion Mr Tanderhill had used to mesmerise me.

Wa-oh, wa-oh, wa-oh!

I jumped at the sound of the security alarm and saw a blue light flashing above the door of Roger Bottle's house. Slipping the medallion in my pocket, I pulled Mr Chin's door closed and waited for the alarm to stop before re-crossing the road. I did not want to resume conversation with the mayoral candidate but Nigel needed a head start.

Roger Bottle stormed out of his house, shouting. 'You fool, you let him go!'

'I had no legal right to hold him,' I replied.

'Idiot!' His eyes narrowed. 'You're not from the *Cockerel*, are you?'

'Correct.'

He looked me up and down, his eyes fixing on my trousers. His expression became a sneer. 'Tartan.'

'Correct. This is the tartan of Clan of MacDonald. A clan is a place to hang your hat.'

'Clan McDowdy more like it. Ha, ha. You should stick to the burgers.'

'The MacDonald clan has an unfortunate history. Over three hundred years ago the MacDonalds were betrayed by the Campbells in Glencoe and brutally massacred. Many people in Scotland still feel very strongly about this seventeenth-century tragedy. It doesn't pay to visit the area if you're a Campbell.'

'You play golf?'

'No.'

'Only golfers and lesbians wear tartan trousers.' He *ha-ha*'d in an unfriendly way and patted his jacket pocket. Removing a mobile phone, he turned his back on me to concentrate on its keypad.

For Nigel's sake, I held steady and reined in an urgent desire to flee. Roger Bottle repelled me like the smell of ammonia or the sound of heavy metal music. He was impolite and belligerent, an ideal candidate for the B.S. Pappenheimer Litmus Test.

This psychological exercise should not be confused with the water-soluble dye method for gauging the acidity of materials. No chemicals are required for the B.S. Pappenheimer test, which is a convenient tool for determining a person's depth of feeling for another human being. It involves asking yourself a simple question: 'Would I give the person in front of me one of my kidneys?'

I focused on Roger Bottle's tweed-covered back and imagined him plugged into a dialysis machine, desperate for a kidney. In my mind's eye I saw him bring his hands together to plead his case. As he did this, the plastic hospital identity bracelet slid down his arm, which was thin and yellow. The skin on his face was tight over his cheekbones and his teeth looked enormous behind his sparse moustache and shrunken lips. Roger Bottle was going to die and I had a compatible blood type. The doctors had just informed me that I was the ideal donor. Would I save his life and go through the rest of mine with a dent in my back?

'You've got to break a few eggs to make an omelette,' he hissed into his mobile. 'Do whatever you have to. Black and blue if necessary.'

He slipped the phone back into his jacket pocket and turned, fixing his eyes on me.

'You still hanging around?' He waved me away. 'Get lost or I'll call the men in white coats.'

'You're telling me to leave?'

'Piss off.'

'And not come back?'

'Or else.'

'Thank you.'

My response seemed to surprise Roger Bottle. He frowned in a confused way and stepped back from the gate.

As I power-walked away, I felt light and unburdened. Something very decisive had just occurred in my psychology and I chalked up yet another high point on the Learning Curve. I now knew without a shadow of a doubt that I would never give Roger Bottle a kidney. I did not like him and would feel no loss if he died of organ failure.

My lungs were pleasantly burning by the time I reached the bus stop. The timetable was screwed to a metal pole and while the bus schedule had not been defaced, the pole itself was covered with graffiti neatly written in gold marker. I recognised the handwriting of the large message at eye level, 'CONQUERING LION OF THE TRIBE OF JUDAH', and of the others repeated down its length, 'KING OF KINGS' and 'ELECT OF GOD.' A final message had been scribbled near the base of the pole: 'ROOT OF DAVID.'

I looked around for more graffiti but the author had limited his efforts to the timetable pole. Attached to the lamppost beside the bus shelter was a CCTV camera. I was not surprised to find its lens masked with duct tape.

17

I circled the pole several times and came to the conclusion that it was an object of worship, like a totem pole or statue of the Virgin Mary. The messages had been penned on the metal with care and the choice of gold marker gave them a devotional if not sacred air. Someone was very taken with the bus timetable and whoever this was had a lot of respect for Haile Selassie. I had recognised the titles of the former Emperor of Ethiopia. The conquering lion of the tribe of Judah died in 1962 but is still revered in many parts of the world, particularly in the Caribbean.

In 1936, Haile Selassie was chosen as Man of the Year by *Time* magazine. It was unusual for the publication to put an Ethiopian on its cover but Haile Selassie was an unusual man. In the aftermath of the Armenian genocide in the early part of the twentieth century, he adopted forty Armenian orphans and had them educated as musicians. As adults, these musical orphans formed the imperial brass band. When he travelled through Europe in 1924, he took with him a pride of lions to give away as gifts. One of the recipients was President Poincaré of France. The president must have been surprised to receive a lion but the French are known for their courtesy. I can imagine his elegant response: '*Merci beaucoup*, Monsieur Selassie. I shall treasure it.'

After noting down the Selassie graffiti in my notebook, I checked the Sunday schedule. Buses on the Val Doonican route followed a loop from the town centre to the Municipal Baths, which were constructed during the Maverick Years under Jim Snick. The mayor had convinced the council to build an Olympic-sized pool complex under his 'Staying Afloat' campaign and promised to have every citizen 'swimming like an otter' within five years. The swimming pool is still a favourite of schoolchildren and pensioners but the more controversial elements of the complex, such as the mixed naturist sauna and jet bath, were closed almost immediately after the conservatives took control of the council.

The next bus was due in twenty minutes, time enough to note down all the messages I had committed to memory and consider what to do next. The bus shelter had been fitted with glass panels against rain and wind but instead of a regular seat it was furnished with an angled metal bar. This provided support for the buttocks but was not comfortable enough to offer rest for a homeless person or loiterer. As I propped my weight against it, I noticed a campaign poster for Warren Crumpet taped to a side panel: 'Warren Crumpet, Number Cruncher Extraordinaire. Putting Municipal Money to Work'. My spirits lifted at the message, which referred to Mr Crumpet's proposal to offer low-interest loans to innovative business projects. The message was encouraging but I was even more pleased that the poster had not been defaced. I glanced down and realised I had stepped over graffiti on the pavement, a single word in white chalk: 'VOTE'.

I had been writing in my notebook for several minutes when I became aware of the sound of a bus decelerating. The vehicle appeared from around the corner and I watched as it stopped across the road. The doors hissed open and shut, the brakes released and as it pulled away in the direction of the Municipal Baths it left Sidney behind on the pavement. His hands were twitching and his expression was grim. He appeared to be muttering.

Pushing myself to my feet, I slipped out of the bus shelter to flatten myself against a tall yew hedge. The council handbook does not mention bus shelters but it does go into great detail about the dangers of being cornered by known aggressors in doorways, cubicles, toilet stalls and stairwells. This scenario is called 'The Dead End' and is outlined in the book's red section.

Sidney was still muttering as he began to circle a large, scruffy birch tree. I watched as he glanced up and down its trunk, examining its limbs. Without warning, his hand darted out and grabbed a branch, wrenching it from the tree with a loud *crack*.

My first impulse was to protest but I managed to resist this urge and remain flattened against the hedge. Sidney now had a weapon and it did not seem wise to confront or inflame him. He swished the branch several times as he crossed the road and was passing the bus shelter when he stopped to frown at Warren Crumpet's campaign poster. His hand slipped into his pocket and removed a black marker. As he lifted it to the poster, my sense of civic responsibility got the better of me. I cleared my throat. His head swivelled in my direction.

'It's a crime to deface a political poster,' I said.

Sidney slipped the marker back into his pocket. He raised his eyebrows and puckered his lips into a pout. It was not a French pout, which in reality is more like a shrug. It was a British pout and, according to my reading on cross-Channel cultures, this pout can indicate one of two things: self-pity or guilt. Sidney did not appear to suffer from self-pity.

'So is soliciting,' he said finally, moving out from the bus shelter to examine me more closely. His eyes flicked over my face but showed no sign of recognition.

'I'm waiting for a bus.'

Sidney swished the birch branch idly a few times. His eyes took on a faraway look. 'Ever wondered what you'd do if you won the lottery?'

'No.'

'Know what I'd do?'

'Yes.'

Ignoring me, he began to repeat his fantasy of winning a Ferrari. It was an abridged version of the scenario he had told the chipman and did not include details about the women's chests or their use of mascara. He had just reached the point where he was refusing rides to a 'bevy of young beauties' when the sound of Roger Bottle's security alarm cut through the air. His head jerked and a wild look came into his eyes. Without another word he broke into a run, holding the birch branch in front of him like an Olympic flame.

I returned to the bus shelter and re-examined the undamaged campaign poster. Warren Crumpet did not have a particularly striking face but his eyes looked directly at the camera as if he had nothing to hide. His glasses and safari shirt were not fashionable or even attractive. Neither were the pens in his pocket. I raised my eyes to his neck. It was long and clean-shaven. His Adam's apple was a discreet bump of thyroid cartilage.

My ears pricked up. Nearby someone was singing. It was a melodious voice, the rich baritone of a professional singer.

> *The seahorse told the octopus*
> *Your arms are strong and true*
> *But don't cling to me so tightly, dear*
> *Give me room to love you, too*

The singing stopped and a man appeared from between the branches of the hedge like a performer parting stage curtains. I recognised the foamy hairstyle and antenna of the Rastafarian. He was dressed in loose clothes of various colours and vaguely nodded as he passed me on his way to the decorated timetable pole. There he spread his hands outwards like the wings of a bird until two of his long fingers rested on the words 'CONQUERING LION.'

'Lo and behold,' he said.

The man's gesture and words did not invite conversation but his proximity left me free to examine the elaborate way in which his dreadlocks had been twisted on top of his head. The hair fanned out from the base of his neck to form an isosceles triangle and stood taller than a busby. He turned and addressed me.

'Lady, lady, lady,' he said, nodding several times.

'You have a very nice singing voice,' I replied, reaching into my handbag. 'Would you like a multigrain cereal bar?'

The man's presence was calming and in this calm I realised I was hungry. I had not eaten since the banana in the chip shop and was feeling light-headed, which is a classic symptom of hypoglycaemia. This condition occurs when the level of glucose drops in the bloodstream and the brain does not receive adequate fuel to function properly. Light-headedness is unpleasant but if left unchecked, hypoglycaemia can cause fainting or even seizures. In the worst-case scenario, it can lead to death.

'Thanking thee muchly.' The man slid the bar into the pocket of his rainbow trousers.

'You came to my aid at the cinema. I would like to thank you.' I peeled back the wrapper of my own muesli bar. 'I do not know what would have happened if you had not appeared.'

'We must join hands as neighbours. Rise up as one.' He formed a bird with his hands, fluttering them in the direction of the taped-over CCTV camera. 'You have been relieved of the evil eye.'

I glanced at the roll of duct tape around his wrist. 'I noticed.'

'He that hasteth to be rich hath an evil eye, and considereth not that poverty shall come upon him.' He let his hands fall. 'The seeing-eye is a curse on the private and personal workings of citizens.'

'I have counted one hundred and seventy-seven CCTV cameras in the town centre, which is quite a lot when you think about it. We would be constantly monitored and recorded without your handi-work. Many believe that public surveillance is an invasion of privacy and a form of state control.'

'Ho, ho, ho.'

'Surveillance and state control are not necessarily good things. The former Socialist Republic of Romania is a case in point.'

'Too true, lady girl. Too true.' He moved away from the pole to stand before the campaign poster of Warren Crumpet, gently pressing his finger between the mayoral candidate's eyebrows. 'Hail Man Crumpet! The reign of the savage carnivore must end. Let Crumpet turn this town into a Garden of Eden. The way of the future is the root vegetable.'

'I eat a lot of root vegetables.'

He turned to face me. 'What is your favourite root?'

'I do not have a favourite but the carrot is a very versatile tap root. A raw carrot is good for the teeth and gums but a carrot cooked with a little oil is an excellent source of beta-carotene.'

'Let the trumpets toot and sound!' The Rastafarian looked at the sky for a moment before dropping his chin to focus his large brown eyes on me. 'Lovers of the carrot will link arms with Man Crumpet and till the soil together. But first we must vanquish the bristled beast.'

'Roger Bottle wants to build a public surveillance centre. He's an advocate of weapons.'

'Dastardly doings. Dastardly doings.' He reached up and adjusted the aerial on the top of his head. 'This town is a box of worms. If the people do not awaken, the bristled ginger thief will come in the night and steal the very future from their children.'

'People are disgruntled and restless.'

'Their weapon is the vote!' He tilted his head to one side and looked at me. 'Are you disgruntled, lady bird?'

'Me?' I was taken aback. I was not accustomed to being asked about my well-being. 'I would not describe my state as disgruntled. It's more like confusion and loss, with a good dose of anxiety.'

The Rastafarian did not say anything. I continued.

'I've just come from Val Doonican Terrace where I was making investigations into the personal life of my employer. I went there with a boy who had to flee unexpectedly. His name is Nigel but people tend to call him "the little bastard".'

'Ho! The little bastard.' The Rastafarian rolled his eyes and whistled. 'Jesus, the holy lord, was a little bastard in the manger.'

'But Joseph married Mary.'

'And I put it to you, was old Joe the father?' He shook his head slowly and whistled. The wire on top of his hair twitched. 'Do not begrudge the little bastard.'

'By all accounts, Jesus Christ was kind to lepers and taught compassion, mercy and tolerance. Nigel has been very helpful.'

'The she wolf and the lamb shall feed together.'

'You speak in a very Biblical manner.'

'I read the King James and the Holy Piby.' He made a rapid bird gesture in the air. 'The H. Piby is the true man's bible: "And when the chariot appeared unto Elijah, He ascended and returned to his throne in heaven where he reigned from the beginning and shall unto the end, King of kings and God of gods".'

'That's a very triumphant scene.'

'Wise man's wisdom, lady bird.' He whistled appreciatively and adjusted his antenna. 'My wisdom wire.'

'I wondered about its function.'

'Many receive the BBC World Service through the fillings of their very teeth and that's a fact.' He fingered it again.

'Gold crowns would be better conductors than amalgam. I know something about teeth and dental fillers.' I thought of the office and let out a deep sigh.

'I sense a nub of tension.' He ran his palms downwards through the air as if he were feeling a Perspex wall between us. 'The cap of the knee is a receptacle of stresses. The cage of rib bones heaves. What ails you, lady bird?'

'I'm abnormal.'

'The abnormal should rightly inherit the earth. It is the normal who are making problems for the forests and fishes.'

'But I'm worried about my job and career plans. My employer instructed me to get normal by Monday. He gave me a lump sum and said my job was on the line. I consulted several experts but none of them was helpful. Now the money has gone and I've learned things about Mr Chin I do not understand.' I took another deep breath, aware that the Rastafarian was giving me his full attention. 'In a nutshell, my quest for normality has been derailed and instead I find myself entangled in the private affairs of Mr Chin. Certain people say he left the Far East under a cloud. It now appears he's consorting with criminals. I've seen things I can't explain like a chainsaw and cardboard boxes, and a talisman belonging to a disreputable hypnotherapist who masquerades as a Hindu.'

'You fear losing your pigeon hole.'

'My current job and plans for the future. I also fear for Mr Chin's welfare.'

'Fear not. All is not lost. All is never lost. It is just moved.' He placed a hand on his chest as a way of introduction and presented the other for a handshake. 'Dutty.'

'Pleased to meet you, Mr Dutty. You are very attentive.' I held out my hand for the shake but received a palm rub instead of a grasp. It was a smooth and rapid gesture that did not involve the competitive grip of a regular British handshake.

'*The* Dutty.' He bowed slightly.

'My name is Sherry.'

'Lo and behold the beverage.' He tweaked his antenna. 'That is some bad man's drink.'

'My mother chose the name.'

What I did not say was that she held a bottle of Spanish sherry responsible for my conception. Alcohol had a stimulating effect on her personality and tended to arouse the social side of her nature. When I was a child it was not uncommon to find a complete stranger sitting at the breakfast table after one of her evenings at the pub. These strangers were always men and always in a hurry to leave. Sometimes they would leave before breakfast. I would hear the front door slam and look out the window to see a man walking briskly from the house tucking in a shirt or putting on a jacket. My mother's socialising added an unpredictable element to my childhood. I would not know whether she was in a good humour in the morning or whether there was any bread left for toast. I never saw her drinking sherry but there was always a bottle of port in the cupboard under the sink. This she drank out of a beer glass while watching television and eating the chocolate she kept under the cushion of her armchair.

'Your eyes are covered with scales, lady bird. You cannot see the truth in front of your person. You have lost your way.' He made a bird again and fluttered his fingers close to my face. 'Close the lids.'

It did not make sense to close my eyes in front of a tall male stranger on a deserted street but I found myself doing as instructed. There was something genuine and intrinsically kind about the

Dutty that overrode any sense of caution. He placed his thumbs on my eyelids and wrapped his hands around the sides of my head.

'In the holy names of old King Solomon and lady Queen Sheba, release this girl child from confusion.'

He then pressed his thumbs against my eyelids once, fast and quite hard. My vision flashed neon pink. He removed his hands and released me.

I opened my eyes and felt a wave of dizziness. When this passed I realised something strange had happened to my perception as if my field of vision had expanded by twenty-five per cent. The bus shelter and hedge looked newer and shinier. The colours of the Dutty's trousers were brighter. I tilted my head back and looked up. The clouds parted over the bus shelter, exposing a patch of vivid blue sky and illuminating its transparent panels in a pool of light.

The Dutty waved a finger in front of my face like a windscreen wiper. On its tip were the remnants of pink chalk dust.

'The scales have fallen.'

'I'm experiencing something very unusual.' This was an understatement. I felt as if a dart had been fired into my chest and warm liquid was being pumped into the cavity, buoying my internal organs and loosening the tension holding them together. It was a release from pressure that had been there for as long as I could remember, like the habitual discomfort of underwear elastic. I was overcome by a sense of relief, and something else, too, a very positive feeling that I had never experienced before. It made me feel like singing or laughing or both. I looked at the Dutty and realised I was smiling. He smiled back.

'Now the Dutty will tune into the reverie for you.' He adjusted his antenna and turned around three times. Rocking on the balls of his feet, he made a deep rumbling noise as if clearing his throat.

'When you have the thirst, you must go to the wellspring. When you seek illumination, you must speak to the makers of music. When the time comes to join the people, you must take up the pen and make your mark. When you need direction, you must visit the gentle and wise man. And when you do the work of the holy saviour, you must bide by the rivers of Babylon.' He stopped speaking and shook his head. 'But beware, lady bird, beware!'

'Your message is very Biblical.' It was also incomprehensible but I did not want to upset the Dutty by questioning his wisdom, especially when I was feeling so positive. He had helped me in my hour of need under the cinema awning and for that I was extremely grateful.

'Hark!' He cupped a hand around his ear. 'The motorised plague is upon us. I must take my leaving.' He made a move towards the hedge.

'Can we meet again?'

He glanced back and created a bird with his hands. 'I am busy this day of all days but when the good work is done, the pleasure of your attendance awaits at this holy place.'

Without saying goodbye, he turned and parted the hedge, singing in his deep baritone as he slipped gracefully between its branches.

> *The dog and cat were fighting*
> *The dog it grabbed the bone*
> *The cat it left, the dog it howled*
> *Come home, sweet thing, come home*

The sound of an engine drew near and a police car appeared from around the corner. Behind the wheel was the policewoman from the chip shop. Big Trish spotted me and slowed. Her indicator was flashing and she was pulling up to the kerb when the sound of Roger Bottle's security alarm cut through the air. She shot me a warning look and mouthed, 'You'll keep,' before accelerating away. Her car had no sooner turned into Val Doonican Terrace than I heard the comforting growl of a municipal bus engine.

Along the side of the number two bus was a banner advertisement with a lookalike of Mao Zedong, the former leader of the People's Republic of China. The model was dressed in a simple peasant tunic buttoned up at the neck and was holding a round fried object between chopsticks. Out of his mouth was a speech bubble: 'Fuel your revolution on Nack's Potato Puffs. The power of gold.'

185

The driver frowned as I entered the bus, raising an eyebrow when I asked for one adult.

'So you've woken up and come to your bloody senses,' he said.

'You are very perceptive,' I said.

'That little bastard was nothing but bloody trouble. You're better off without him.'

'He was no trouble at all.'

'The little sod flashed me the V's when he got off the bus.'

I had not seen Nigel do this but knew from experience that he was quite capable of such behaviour. 'You must get a lot of that.'

The driver's face hardened. 'What do you bloody-well mean by that?'

'People are disgruntled and restless. You're a natural target.'

His expression changed. He tapped the Perspex barrier. 'I'd be a lot happier if this was bulletproof glass.'

'I think you do not have to worry. Perspex can withstand considerable force. It's a protective polymer.'

The driver gave me a hesitant smile and issued a ticket. He did not play the recorded message as I made my way down the aisle and when I reached the back seat I found him observing me with benign interest in the mirror. I smiled before turning my face to the window.

The bus was passing a school and along its brick wall was scrawled the word 'VOTE' in enormous chalk letters. Next, I saw chalk graffiti on the wall of a medical centre. Then along the front of an empty building and then on another. It was scribbled over and over, on walls, the pavement and the tar-sealed surface of the road.

The Dutty had indeed been busy, on this day of all days.

18

As the bus reached the centre of town, I pushed the red stop button and rose to my feet. The door opened and I turned to call out, 'Thank you.'

The driver twisted in his seat and tapped the Perspex. He smiled and nodded in a friendly way.

The town hall square had burst into life while I had been away and was now throbbing with the expectant atmosphere of a car-boot sale. I had not seen so many people in the square since the disastrous weekend of the vintage car show. The *Cockerel* had described the event as 'Old Bangers and Mash' after one of the cars had backfired and someone had shouted, 'Run! He's got a gun!' The ensuing panic had caused a stampede. Several people had been crushed in the fracas and taken away in an ambulance.

The drizzle had ceased and the afternoon sun was now a vague glow in the grey mass overhead. The clock on the town hall tower bonged five times. As if on cue, I thought of Ted's café and immediately felt a desire for one of his rehydrating coffees. I was suddenly thirsty, very thirsty.

The last time I had seen Ted he had told me to 'piss off'. What he had not added was 'and never come back.' From experience I knew the latter constituted a lifetime ban while 'piss off' could mean anything from 'You've got to be joking' to 'Go away before I punch you on the nose.' Ted had never shown any inclination towards pugilism. I decided to try my luck.

I was halfway around the square when a cheer went up and a

man dressed in a red jacket and striped trousers appeared from behind a row of portable toilets. He was walking on stilts and juggling white skittles. His face was painted like a clown's and he was wearing a wig of yellow curls. As he turned unsteadily on his stilts, I noticed a cardboard sign attached to his back: 'Roger Bottle, a Man To Look Up To.' I glanced down at the juggler's trousers and realised why people were cheering and pointing. The satiny fabric had split along the seam and the juggler did not appear to be wearing underpants.

'Battered sausages on a stick,' called out a familiar voice. 'Pre-fried to perfection and served at room temperature. Lovely.'

The chipman was standing with his back to me, waving a sausage in the air. He had created a makeshift stall from one of his plastic tables and had laid out containers of deep-fried food next to a stack of canned drinks.

The chipman was not the only one displaying a sense of enterprise. Several other vendors had set up shop and were selling snacks, drinks, hats and children's toys. I stopped to observe a short blonde woman fashion a Dachshund out of a flesh-coloured balloon. She was wearing one of her creations on her head, a long purple balloon, inflated and twisted to resemble a padded crown. Her cheeks were pink and swollen from inflating balloons, which gave her freckles a three-dimensional look as if a mud bomb had exploded in her face. She saw me and called out in a friendly voice, 'Your star sign in a novelty balloon, love?' I apologised and explained that I did not have the money for a personalised balloon. The friendliness disappeared from her manner and, muttering something incomprehensible, she turned her back to me.

I left the square and as I crossed the high street, I noticed that I was walking rapidly with a sense of urgency. I was now extremely thirsty, the sort of hysterical thirst sportswomen must experience after playing power netball on a sunny day. The brick wall opposite Ted's café had been spray-painted with new graffiti, 'Chantelle Corby is a thiever', but I did not stop to note it down.

Ted was standing behind the counter when I entered his café.

There were no customers at his tables and the air smelled of old shoes and bad drains. He looked up from the counter and scowled.

'I thought I gave you your marching orders,' he said, closing a magazine and sliding it towards a stack of dirty plates and cutlery. The magazine was called *Duck* and its cover featured a photograph of a man kneeling beside a lake. He was wearing hunting clothes and leaning on a rifle, holding up a dead mallard duck by its webbed feet. The vivid blue of the bird's wing looked unreal against the brown camouflage of its assailant's jacket.

'Are you a hunter?' I asked, making the conscious and unusual decision not to respond to Ted's statement. This is called 'being evasive' and is used effectively by politicians and footballers to avoid penetrating questions by members of the press. My thirst was now almost uncontrollable and I did not want anything to come between my dehydrated digestive system and one of his thirst-quenching coffees.

'I'm a fan of the sport.' Ted started to smile but got no further than unfolding his lips before thinking better of it. He refolded them into an even harder line. 'You're not one of them animal rights fanatics?'

'You have to be actively dedicated to a cause to be a fanatic. I'm still at the information-gathering stage.'

'I'll tell you what you are.' Ted shook his head. 'Abnormal.'

'Correct.'

My response seemed to throw Ted. He shook his head again.

'I'd like to purchase one of your famous coffees.' Merely stating what I wanted seemed to make me thirstier.

'That would be a coffee *and* a cake.' This was a statement rather than a suggestion. 'You're on probation.'

'How much are those?' I pointed to the fairy cakes in the display case. On Friday there had been four, of which I had purchased one for Nigel. Three cakes still remained. 'I've only got one pound ninety.'

Ted scratched his scalp, which was grey and oily under his thinning hair. 'Coffee and a cake would be two pounds.'

'What if you cut a cake in half and sold me a half?'

Ted pondered this proposal for a moment before inputting one pound ninety on the cash register. He held out his hand for the money and told me to sit down at a table for one. 'I don't want your sort lounging while I've got work to do.'

I settled at a table near the window and had just recorded the latest Chantal Corby graffiti in my notebook when Ted slammed a polystyrene cup and half a cake on the table.

'Don't expect a serviette for that price.'

'No mug either?' I did not bother adding that Ted had not provided a plate with the cake. Neither had he used tongs. The fairy cake had been brought to the table in his fingers and simply dumped on the plastic tablecloth.

'Dishwasher's out.' He gave me a fierce look. 'Drain's blocked and the plumber's refusing to come back here. Reckons I tried to poison him.'

I nodded and waited for him to return to the counter before gulping down the tepid brown liquid. Relief washed through me as the coffee descended my oesophagus, soothing my digestive system with liquid warmth.

After emptying the cup, I picked up the wedge of cake and turned it over in my hand, scrutinising its rough hard surface. Its texture was like pumice, a porous volcanic rock used for removing the dry, horny skin off the heels of barefoot enthusiasts and pensioners. I tapped it against the table as Nigel had done and was examining it for dents when a shadow passed in front of the window.

The door opened and I stopped tapping. It was Big Trish and she did not look pleased. Her eyes focused on my open notebook before flicking to the cake in my hand, narrowing as they travelled up the arm of my cardigan to fix on my face. I sat perfectly still, trying to maintain a blank expression and struggling not to be the first to blink. The policewoman expelled a jet of air through the gap between her front teeth before making a move towards the table.

'Is there a problem?' called Ted from the counter. He looked from the policewoman to me.

Big Trish stopped mid-step, swivelling her head in his direction. She exhaled again before striding over to where he was standing.

'I'm making a round-robin of local commercial enterprises,' she said. 'Asking shopkeepers for assistance.'

'It's the shopkeepers that need assistance. Where are the cops when we need them?' Ted puffed out his chest. 'Someone's been urinating in my entry. It's unhygienic.'

The policewoman straightened her spine and squared her shoulders. Exhaling loudly, she tilted her head to make a study of the display cabinet before leaning over the counter to examine the floor and benches behind Ted. 'Would you like me to call a health and safety inspector?'

Ted pursed his lips.

'They've just closed down the kitchen over at the primary school. Dirty floors.' She sniffed. 'Blocked drains will put a place out of business for months.'

'How can I assist you?' Ted's smile looked uncomfortable.

'A boy's gone missing.' The policewoman removed a photo from her pocket and showed it to him.

'That little bastard looks familiar.'

'Tone down your language!'

Big Trish threw her hands on her hips, spreading her fingers over the tool pouches of her utility belt. Her pelvis was broad but her buttocks had the bulk of someone who did gym work and drank protein shakes. Their solid mass was encased in very tight trousers, which seemed impractical given the active nature of her profession. I wondered how fast she could move as I slipped the notebook into my handbag. The door was three steps from where I was sitting. I was pushing my chair back when she turned and gave me a warning look. I picked up the cake again and began re-examining it.

'Pardon my French.' Ted *ha-ha*'d in apology and offered the police-woman a complimentary coffee. When she did not respond, he added the word, 'Free,' and then, 'Milk and sugar on the house.'

'I'm not thirsty.' She shoved the photo back in her pocket and hitched up her trousers, which were already sitting very high on her powerful waist. 'The boy's name is Nigel Coote. He was last seen in Val Doonican Terrace, heading towards the centre of town. We're asking people with information to come forward.'

Ted was still nodding when Big Trish turned away from the counter. Her eyes fell on me again and narrowed. She ran a large hand up the front of her stab vest to her shirt collar, pulling it away from her neck, which was thick and strong. Tightening her mouth in a no-nonsense way, she launched herself in my direction, covering the distance to my table in less than a second to position herself in front of the door.

'I recognise you.' Her voice was low. 'I've seen you on the streets, power-walking.'

Ted froze behind the counter, cocking his head and straining to hear what was being said.

I nodded.

'The tartan's a dead giveaway.'

'I have an affinity.' Under other circumstances, I might have provided historical background on the tartan I was wearing but Big Trish was an imposing authority figure and I was aware that I had engaged in illegal activity. Her gaze was penetrating.

'I want to talk to you.'

I nodded again but remained silent, wary of incriminating Nigel or myself.

Her radio crackled. She threw a hand to her chest, pushing it up to her mouth to speak. 'Big T here.'

The radio made a loud screech. A voice spoke but I caught only one word: 'Corby'.

'I'm on my way.' Big Trish was already at the door. She turned and gave me a fierce look before disappearing.

'What was all that about street-walking and a tart?' Ted was leaning over the counter. His look was accusing.

I was about to explain his error when the door opened.

Shanks turned to toss a cigarette butt into the street before entering. Tipping his hat at Ted, he strode over to the counter, the metal plates on his cowboy boots clacking loudly on the linoleum. I twisted in my seat to observe him and noticed something black dangling from the back pocket of his jeans. It was long and thick. At first glance it looked like a chunk of the velvet rope used inside banks to keep queues orderly. I took a closer look and recognised the faded fake fur of Nastassja Kinski's panther tail. Strange!

'Howdy tooty,' he said, throwing something heavy on the counter in front of Ted. It was flesh-coloured and resembled a skinned American possum.

'Afternoon, son,' Ted replied, flashing an open, friendly smile I had never seen before. 'What can I do for you?'

'Know what Japs eat?'

Ted stopped smiling and gave Shanks the same look he'd given Nigel when the boy had tried his jokes. 'No.'

'Then just give me three all-day breakfasts. To take away.' Shanks slipped his hand into the pink thing and removed a twenty-pound note. He handed it to Ted. 'Keep the change, pal.'

Ted's smile returned in an even bigger, friendlier way. His lips parted and rolled back to expose his gums. They were swollen and completely overshadowed his teeth. 'I'll open a fresh can of beans for that.'

'There's plenty more where that came from, my friend. I'm working on a big project, making serious do-re-mi.'

Shanks picked up the pink thing and held it up for Ted to see. It was not a wallet or a skinned American possum. It was a money belt and I knew only one like it in Great Britain. In my seven months as Mr Chin's employee, I had never seen him remove it from his waist let alone entrust it to anyone. The only money he had ever given me apart from my salary and the one hundred pounds was the ten pounds petty cash that I kept in my file drawer. Mr Chin handled all major purchases from his money belt, which he kept hidden under his shirt. It was a unique accessory, tailor-made in Hong Kong by a man called Minty Patel. Mr Chin told me he had insisted on 'nude beige' after the colour of skin foundation. 'Natural colour like belly skin,' he had explained. 'Hide against body like tricky soldier clothes in storm of desert. Chin lift shirt. Robber see skin only. Trick criminal and thief every time.'

Shanks turned and noticed me. He flashed a crooked smile. 'Whoa!'

His cowboy boots clacked as he crossed the floor to my table. Without waiting to be asked or rejected, he grabbed a chair and sat down, pulling Nastassja Kinski's tail between his thighs in a provocative manner. He threw the money belt on the table and winked.

'That's full of cash, darling,' he said. 'A lot of the bills in there are twenties.'

I looked at the money belt and reminded myself that I was on an investigation. I knew from my reading in the 'Crime' section of the public library that police often began an interrogation with a neutral and unrelated subject. This is called 'breaking the ice' and is helpful for putting a suspect at ease.

'Nude beige is an unusual colour for a money belt.'

'There's no beating around the bush with you, is there!' Shanks threw his head back and laughed in an energetic way. It was an unpleasant and forceful sound like a dog scratching at a door.

I now had to move to the second phase of the interrogation process, which is called 'cutting to the chase'.

'You must have an interesting job.'

He stopped laughing and raised an eyebrow. 'I'm doing business with a powerful man.'

'What kind of business?'

'Making money.' He leaned forwards, bringing his face to within a hand's width of mine and overwhelming me with the smell of pickled onions and bicycle grease. 'You know the game, darling.'

'Here you go, son!'

Ted's voice was loud and aggressive. I sat up and found him standing very close. He glared at me before handing Shanks a plastic bag of polystyrene containers.

Shanks stood, flicking the tail behind him and wedging the money belt in the front pocket of his jeans. He winked at me. 'No monkey business this time, darling. Duty calls.'

He gave Ted a manly nod before swaggering out of the café.

I was on my feet preparing to follow when Ted gripped the top of my arm. 'This is a café. Not a pickup joint.'

'Correct.' I tried to pull my arm out of his grip but he held on tight. I did not want to let Shanks out of my sight until I knew where he was going.

'It's all a game of cat and mouse for you, isn't it?'

I did not know what he was talking about but it did not seem the right moment to ask. His face had flushed the colour of his gums and I did not want to inflame him any further. I wanted him to take his hand off my arm so I could follow Shanks.

'You're sick.' His face showed disgust.

'No, I'm abnormal. There's nothing wrong with my health.'

I knew this because in my first week of work, I had undergone a full medical check. Mr Chin had insisted on a lung X-ray and blood and urine tests. Tuberculosis was making a comeback and he did not want to take any chances. 'Office like incubator of germ. Microbe and other dirt fly in air from employee mouth, trap in lung of Chin. You want excellent job with kind and generous boss, you take full and complete test of health.'

Ted dug his fingers into my biceps. 'I don't want you plying your trade in here again.'

'Are you banning me for life?' I reached over and grabbed my handbag from the table.

'I'm saying get out.'

'And never come back?'

He nodded.

'Then can I leave now? I don't want that customer to get away.'

'You're shameless.' Ted let go of my arm as if it were radioactive and stepped away from me.

'I have enjoyed your coffee, Ted. It's weak and virtually never hot. Your cakes, however, are inedible.'

Ted flinched.

'I can think of only one use for them.' I tucked my handbag under my arm. 'Horny skin.'

This information seemed to surprise Ted. His mouth opened and his tongue twitched but no sound came out.

As I stepped around him, I realised I did not care what he thought or did any more. He had banned me from his café and it did not make sense to waste any more time in his company. Nigel had been right about Ted's character. He was not a nice man and in accordance with the B.S. Pappenheimer Litmus Test, I would not be giving him one of my organs.

I made it to the pavement just as Shanks reached the corner of the street. He stopped, hesitated and then disappeared inside the betting shop.

I waited a moment before making my move.

19

I felt strangely invigorated as I strode away from the café. Swinging my arms to chest height, I imagined myself with a busby strapped to my head like a Grenadier Guard. I slowed as I neared the corner and out of habit glanced up at the CCTV camera mounted on the brick wall across the road. Its lens had been masked with duct tape and the word 'VOTE' was written below it in green chalk. I thought of the Dutty and felt a surge of optimism.

I stopped at the window of the betting shop and spotted Shanks standing in a queue in front of the teller. The panther tail was still dangling from his pocket. The plastic bag of food was on the floor between his feet. His body was facing the teller but his head was twisted around to a large flat-screen television on the wall. The screen was blue and displaying a list of racing information in white lettering.

The man at the front of the queue moved away with a stub in his hand and Shanks took his place, skidding the bag across the floor with the toe of his cowboy boot. He placed Mr Chin's money belt on the counter and licked his fingers before peeling off five twenty-pound notes. He must have shared a joke with the teller because when he turned away from the window he was laughing. With a swagger, he walked over to join a cluster of men standing in front of the television.

He was still looking at the screen when someone familiar entered the betting shop. It was Sidney and his expression was pinched and nervous, his movements furtive. With his head pulled low on his shoulders, he scuttled over to the teller to dump a handful of coins on the counter. A moment later, he turned away smiling and headed for the group in front of the screen to stand beside Shanks.

No one gave me a second look as I entered the shop or noticed me slip behind the television viewers. Everyone was too engrossed in the odds displayed on the screen. I saw Sidney nudge Shanks and I leaned closer to listen. Neither of them took his eyes off the screen.

'Which horse you riding, cowboy?' asked Sidney, rounding off his question with a weak laugh. It was a laugh I had heard other men use in male company and it had nothing to do with humour. Sidney's laugh was a verbal white flag, a noise made to convey 'I come in peace'.

Shanks glanced at him and then back to the screen. 'Got a hundred clams riding on Gold Fever,' he said.

'A hundred quid?' Sidney ran a hand over his greasy hair and shook his head in amazement. 'I've just put a fiver on Karma Sutra.'

'Should've backed Gold Fever. Ha, ha.' Shanks's laugh was free and easy. There was nothing ingratiating about it.

The screen changed. The shop fell silent. Horses bearing jockeys were being led into stalls. The camera moved to the stands where it panned across women with impractical hats and men peering through binoculars.

In the silence, I became aware of the hot, oppressive air in the betting shop. The plastic bag between Shanks's feet was giving off the sweet, heavy odour of baked beans and fried eggs and I could smell nervous sweat and unwashed clothes on the men in front of me. On the screen, a palomino reared up as it was being led into a stall. The word 'Karma' flashed across the bottom of the screen. I thought of Mr Chin.

On my first day of work, Mr Chin had explained his religion, making it clear that Buddhism was superior to Christianity. 'Buddhist religion best in world. Politician and thief criminal get recycle as cockroach and mosquito. Kind and generous boss that is Chin get recycle as king or even large eagle that is bald. Superior system. Justice and goodness every time.' He had ended this explanation with a lecture on the office policy of what he called the 'Three E's': honesty, secrecy and security. I was forbidden to call dentists outside of work hours or discuss the details of my work with anyone outside the office. 'Chin is oyster man. Lip seal tight like oyster. You kind of barnacle. Must keep lid shut. Policy clear and crystal. What go in office, stay in office.'

How could Mr Chin have such convictions yet consort with people like Shanks and Mr Tanderhill? It did not make sense. Neither did the accusations of Mr Ding and Mr Lung.

The screen switched back to racing information and everyone relaxed. Sidney turned to Shanks and elbowed him again. 'Couldn't help noticing your tail,' he said with another small laugh.

'The ladies love it.' Shanks reached behind and stroked it.

Sidney scowled and shook his head. 'Women like only one thing. Money.'

'You obviously don't know female psychology.' Shanks tapped his temple under the brim of his cowboy hat. 'You've got to understand how they think. I've learned a thing or two about manipulating the brain from my business partner. A highly educated professional. Hypnotherapist.'

'How do you know he's not hypnotising you and manipulating your brain?'

Shanks's head jerked in Sidney's direction. His mouth opened and shut. He turned back to the screen and ran a hand up under his hat, rubbing the back of his head in an irritated way.

Sidney noticed his agitation. 'You were saying, the ladies like your tail.'

'They love it.' Shanks stopped rubbing. 'I was just propositioned by a saucepot in a café. Straight off she started talking nude this, nude that. Bold as brass.' He patted his pocket. 'Right now I'm too busy for the china dolls. Got a big project cooking. We're talking real money. Moolah.'

'Ever dreamed about winning the lottery?'

'Probably every day of my life, if not every hour.'

'Know what I would do if I won?'

'How could I?' Shanks frowned. 'I've just met you.'

'I'd buy a Ferrari.'

'You'd want to buy a Porsche, friend. Can't beat the Germans for technology. They got it all worked out in the war with their tanks and submarines.' Shanks leaned in close. 'They don't broadcast it but there's V2 rocket technology in a Porsche. That's why the motor's in the back. Jet propulsion. Those Krauts are clever bastards.'

Sidney waited for Shanks to finish and then carried on as if he had not spoken. 'I'd buy the latest, in red. Testarossini.'

He then began to describe his fantasy of parking the Ferrari on the high street. By the time he got to 'page three girls with large bosoms' he had Shanks's full attention.

I surveyed the other gamblers. All of them were male and none appeared to be rich or lucky. The screen changed once again. A tense silence descended. Seconds later, a shrill sound shattered it.

'Sihhh-diney!'

The voice was female and had the pitch and force of a circular saw cutting through the body of a Honda Civic. I knew exactly what this sounded like because I had witnessed Mrs Da Silva being cut out of her car after she rammed it into the front wall of my mother's house and ended up trapped in the garden.

'I'm talking to you!' Chantal Corby was standing in the doorway. Her face was lavender except for the bruise on her forehead, which was bright yellow like a speleologist's lamp.

Her shriek reverberated through the betting shop but the only person affected by it was Sidney, who managed to look up and shrink down at the same time.

I flattened myself against the window as Chantal Corby launched herself forwards, heading straight for Sidney with the force of a cork released from a warm bottle of homemade Jamaican ginger beer. Her hand darted out of the sling to grab him by the neck while her undamaged arm swung towards him. Her fleshy palm connected with Sidney's ear with a loud *smack*. The men in the betting shop jumped but no one took his eyes off the screen, which now showed horses galloping around a track.

'I knew you'd be here, you useless sack of dirt,' she shouted, shaking him by the scruff of his neck. 'I'm trying to make us a living and you won't even answer your phone.'

'You can stop shouting in that ear. I can't hear a bloody thing,' said Sidney, cupping a hand over the ear. With a whimper, he wrenched himself out of her grasp. 'You've probably buggered my ear drum.'

'I'll bugger them both if you don't get out and do what you're told.' She raised her hand again but let it hang in the air like a threat. 'Where've you been?'

'With Rog.'

'Liar. You left there an hour ago.' The hand swished downwards, landing on Sidney's cheek with another loud *smack*.

'Ouch!' He covered his cheek. Tears sprang to his eyes.

'That jailbird's knocking on doors, asking questions. The bloody cops are on my tail.'

Shanks's head swivelled at the mention of 'cops', lingering for a moment on Chantal Corby before returning to the TV screen.

'Get out there and do your job!' She gripped Sidney under the arm, bundling him across the shop and out the door.

'But I've got five quid on Karma Sutra.' Sidney had grabbed hold of the doorframe. He flashed the racing stub.

'Find that little bastard!' She snatched the stub and sent him flying with a shove. 'Or we'll be cut off!'

The horses were thundering towards the finish line as she pushed her way back through the gamblers with the point of her elbow. The first two horses crossed the finish line neck and neck followed by another clump and then a horse on its own. Shanks cursed. His eyes were still on the screen when Chantal Corby spoke.

'Did Karma Sutra come in?' she asked.

'Slowest pony on the track,' he said, turning to glance at the stub in her hand. 'Never mind, darling. At least you didn't just lose a hundred crisp ones.'

'You bet a hundred quid on a horse?'

'Peanuts.' He shrugged and removed the money belt from his

pocket, pulling it open to show her its contents. 'Plenty of twenties in there, darling.'

'You must be a very successful man.'

'Tycoon, more like it.' He tipped his cowboy hat in a gentlemanly way.

Chantal Corby let out a squeal of delight and turned her body to face him, running a hand over her sandy hair, which was pulled back tight off her face. Her ponytail twitched as she thrust her chest upwards and forwards, presenting her breasts to Shanks like a tray of vol-au-vents.

I had seen my mother do the same thing whenever she set foot in Mr Da Silva's butcher's shop. Her breasts, she liked to say, were her 'best asset'. When mine failed to develop beyond an A cup, she had blamed my father's genes. But when I asked who that might have been, she snapped, 'I don't remember and it doesn't matter.' Her response had not been very helpful. I had no idea whether my genes carried a predisposition for heart disease or bowel cancer or whether abnormality was an aberration or predetermined by my DNA.

Chantal Corby's best asset clearly impressed Shanks who whistled loudly. His eyes moved upwards to her face, taking in the bump on her head.

'How did you get that shiner, darling? Some man been treating you bad?'

'Real bad, cowboy.' Her voice was soft and baby-like. Her chest heaved.

'Daddy'll make it better.' Shanks removed a ten-pound note from Mr Chin's money belt, folded it lengthways and slipped it down the front of her synthetic T-shirt. 'Buy yourself something nice.'

'That won't go far, Daddy.' She inched closer. 'Baby needs a lot of aspirin.'

He took out twenty pounds and was poking it in beside the first note when a shadow passed in front of the shop window. Shanks's mouth dropped open.

I heard the sound of air being expelled and knew it was Big Trish even before I turned. Her boot made a thud as she threw it inside the betting shop. The gamblers parted to let her through with a rustle of nylon sports clothes. Her eyes, like heat-seeking missiles, sought me out and narrowed.

'Sorry, love, gotta go,' whispered Shanks. He pushed his cowboy hat low over his eyes and grabbed the bag of food, skirting the gamblers to avoid the policewoman as he made for the door.

Disappointed by his abrupt departure, Chantal Corby let out a loud squeal. The policewoman looked over and did a double take. Veering away from me, she made a beeline for Chantal Corby.

'Mrs Corby!' she said in a loud voice.

Chantal Corby turned. Her eyes widened. She opened and shut her mouth before hastily rearranging her face into a smile and pushing out her chest. 'Miss.'

'We've been looking for you. A word, if you don't mind.'

'Of course, officer.' She flicked her ponytail. 'Anything for a lady in uniform.'

I did not wait to hear what Big Trish had to say. Squashing my handbag under my arm, I slipped out of the betting shop and power-walked away, swiftly crossing the high street to plunge into the relative safety of the crowd gathered in front of the town hall.

The square was now busier than ever and pulsing with the chaotic excitement of a carnival. Several men in overalls were setting up a sound system on the stage platform but rock music was already blaring from speakers perched on the roof of a white van parked nearby. A few of the bolder townspeople were moving their hips in a self-conscious way to the music while others stood by, watching with their arms folded and their lips pressed together. A hairy man with a rotating tub was doing swift business selling balls of candy-floss. So was a long-necked teenager who was waving packets of crisps in the air and calling out 'Cheese and onion, alive, alive oh.'

Those who had purchased snacks were eating on their feet because the square did not have any benches. Public seating had been removed from the town centre under Jerry Clench's 'Cleanup Drive'. The campaign had promised to rid the streets of 'riffraff' and eradicate vandalism but had failed on both counts. The one group it did successfully clean off the streets was pensioners who found it difficult to cover distances on foot without the comfort of rest stops.

I had an hour before my rendezvous with Jocelyn and did not want to upset him by arriving too early. I have found that most people prefer visitors to arrive late rather than early, which is something I do not understand.

Out of habit, I headed towards the council annexe building. The photo display had been closed all week but I felt a desire to at least view the building to reassure myself of its existence.

As I made my way around the stage platform, I noticed a group of men seated on folding chairs behind the wheelchair ramp. They were dressed in matching dark blue suits and each was holding a stringed instrument.

'You're abnormal!'

I froze.

'That's what you are.'

I sought out the source of the accusation and was relieved to find a banjo player pointing at a violinist.

'Abnormal!'

The violinist rose to his feet and bowed. Slipping his instrument under his chin, he played a few bars of music. It was dramatic, the sort played in a film when a woman is thrown into the snow with a baby in her arms.

This musical response seemed to amuse the two guitarists, who turned to face each other and exchange a 'high five', which is a congratulatory slapping of palms commonly performed by competitive sportspeople and stockbrokers.

The violinist bowed again and as he sat down, I scrutinised him for signs of abnormality. He was of average height with a regular face, small eyes, nose and mouth. He was not wearing glasses or jewellery and from what I could see had no body piercing or tattoos. His suit was pressed and his shoes polished. The only unusual thing about him was the violin. Classical instruments were not popular in the town. Most local people preferred music from the latter half of the twentieth century and tended to play it on a stereo or car radio.

'Can I help you, love?' called out the banjo player.

The musicians turned in my direction. I felt heat rise in my cheeks.

'I beg your pardon,' I said.

'You're pardoned.' He laughed.

'I was passing when I overheard you call your musical colleague abnormal.'

'You heard right.' He laughed again. The others joined in, even the violinist, who seemed to laugh the loudest.

'Normality is a hard nut to crack.'

The men seemed to find this even funnier.

Encouraged by their friendliness, I turned to the violinist. 'I would appreciate your personal insights into the condition. I've been seeking relief from my own abnormality and am at the end of my tether.'

The men laughed again but with less enthusiasm. The violinist raised his eyebrows. I took this as a cue to continue.

'Do you ever feel as if you're suspended over human society in a Perspex pod?'

The musicians stopped laughing. They looked at me as if I had just announced that an asteroid was about to hit the earth and they had two minutes to tie up loose ends.

The violinist pursed his lips. He gave my question some thought before answering. 'Funny you should ask me that.'

I nodded. He glanced at his band mates before continuing.

'When I was a kid, I imagined I had a bulletproof cone over my bicycle. I was convinced someone was going to shoot me in the back with a pistol, a small one with a pearl handle.'

'Do you still experience the cone?'

'I don't ride a bike any more.' The violinist shrugged. 'I drive a Toyota.'

'Your car doesn't have a cone?'

He smiled sheepishly.

'Do you think there's a cause and effect relationship between abnormality and the cone?'

The violinist turned to his colleagues for help but caught no one's eye. Their heads were down and they appeared to be deep in thought. When someone finally spoke it was the banjo player.

'A cone's not so bad,' he said. 'Try a Plexiglass pup tent for size. It descends on me every night when I go to bed. My wife doesn't hear a thing I say.'

The guitarists shifted in their seats. The banjo player stole a look at the violinist, who was running a hand over his stringed instrument.

'Mine's a fish tank,' said one of the guitarists, folding his lips nervously. 'It started the year I was sent to boarding school.'

'Astronaut's helmet,' said the other. 'Buzz Aldrin was an inspiration.'

They fell silent again and in the stillness I realised that I was feeling lightheaded, as if a tight hat had been removed and my skull was expanding outwards. My awareness was expanding with it, flowing towards the musicians and then further to the people in the square and out over the town at large. As my rational mind caught up with what was happening, the awareness dimmed and I found myself back at the wheelchair ramp, my handbag tucked under my arm and four musicians looking at me expectantly.

'I've just had an experience,' I said.

They nodded for me to continue but I could not explain what had just happened. The word 'epiphany' had sprung to mind and I was grappling with its significance. Epiphanies are moments of heightened clarity and insight that can strike a person at any time. I had read about people discovering the meaning of life or God while eating a cheese sandwich and I wondered whether this was what had just happened. I sensed the experience had something to do with the Dutty but it was the openness and generosity of the musicians that had allowed my awareness to move beyond the confines of my body.

I turned to the banjo player. 'Why did you call your colleague abnormal?' I asked.

'He breeds pigeons,' he replied.

'Why does that make him abnormal?'

'It's an obsession. He's trying to breed a pigeon with blue eyes.' He smiled and gently elbowed the violinist in the ribs. 'He wants to call it Frank Sinatra and teach it to croon.'

'But he seems normal.' I scanned the members of the musical ensemble. 'You all do.'

'Normal is a lot more abnormal than you think.' He laughed.

The others joined in.

I found myself smiling with them but inside my head, my brain was struggling to make sense of this new insight. If a normal person could also be abnormal, then there was hope for my condition.

I waited for them to stop laughing.

'You've just said something insightful and very helpful,' I said. 'I was between a rock and a hard place but you've given me hope and that has to be a good thing.'

'We can only live in hope.' The banjo player shrugged. 'That's all some of us have got.'

I thanked him and as I bid the musicians goodbye I imagined the Learning Curve as the jagged snow-covered peak of Mount Everest. I pictured Sir Edmund Hillary pushing the pole of the British flag into the snow. He then turned to throw his arm around the shoulders of Tenzing Norgay. The two hugged but did not kiss each other, taking care not to tangle the oxygen equipment they were wearing.

The annexe building was closed and I found a council worker slouched against its door smoking a cigarette. His name was Gary and he was a short, bald man with a large waist and small feet. He ignored me when I said hello but did not prevent me from reading a handwritten notice taped to the door: 'Closed for vote counting.' Gary filled his lungs with smoke and flicked the cigarette butt on to the pavement near my feet. With a grunt, he went back inside, shutting the door behind him.

I did not mind being ignored by a council worker. It was a lot more pleasant than being called a kook or shouted at for suggesting improvements to the photo display. No new photos had been added to the display since Jerry Clench had cut funding to civic cultural programmes over a decade before. The room was rarely dusted and never updated. It did not make sense to let a local cultural legacy go to ruin.

As I turned to leave, I noticed a chalk message on the side of the building. The words stopped me in my tracks: 'THE TIDE IS TURNING.'

20

I looked around but saw no sign of the Dutty. The only other person near the annexe was a woman. She was standing with her back to me, gazing up at a masked CCTV camera. I recognised the broad shoulders and wide flat buttocks. Her torso was a perfect rectangle, like a compact fridge with a freezer compartment.

Bijou Poulet looked shorter and less significant without the couch and diplomas of her therapeutic chambers. Her blonde hair was either uncombed or artfully back-combed and sat high on her head. The two-tone effect created by the dark roots gave it the look of an unruly clump of pampas grass. She was wearing a tight green synthetic dress that revealed the indents of her bra line and the Y of her G-string. Over her arm was a complicated brown handbag with tassels and gold buckles. She was shoving a packet of Marlboro Lights into the bag when I approached. Her fingernails were now silver-pink and had lengthened even more overnight.

'Hello,' I said. 'I've just had an enlightening experience with four musicians.'

'A woman's brass band, I take it,' she said, removing an unlit cigarette from her silver-pink lips. She looked at me critically, taking in the twinset and tartan trousers. 'Do I know you?'

'Yes.'

'I don't *think* so.'

'You're Bijou Poulet.'

'I know who I am.' She exhaled impatiently. 'You're the unknown factor.'

'I had therapy with you yesterday.' I was accustomed to people not recognising me on the street but Bijou Poulet had spoken at length to me and was privy to certain intimate details of my life. 'You don't remember me?'

'Ho-kay.' She raised an eyebrow. 'Are you trying to pick me up?'

'No.'

'Hnihhh.'

I hesitated. It was my mother's habit to snort whenever she was frustrated or did not agree with the content of a conversation. Her 'hnihhh' worked as an alarm, a warning that something unpleasant was about to follow. I did not want conflict with Bijou Poulet and decided to change the subject. I pointed to the CCTV camera.

'I noticed you were looking at the camera. It might interest you to know that there are at least one hundred and seventy-seven CCTV cameras in the centre of this town. They tend to be located at hotspots, outside public bars and betting shops. Children's playgrounds are another favourite.'

Her mouth softened from a hard line into the hard V of a smile. She glanced in the direction of the town hall. 'Roger Bottle's promised more funding for the visual arts.'

'I'm quite familiar with Roger Bottle's campaign. I've heard no mention of the arts.'

'He's going to build a state-of-the-art video imaging centre.'

'I think you're mistaken.'

Bijou Poulet looked at me in an unfriendly way.

'He's proposing something a lot more controversial, a monitoring and surveillance centre. Many believe CCTV surveillance is an invasion of human rights, that it contributes to a climate of fear while actually doing nothing to protect people. It's a known fact that fearful people are easier to control. Former East Germany is a case in point.'

'I'm a professional. I don't make mistakes.'

She put the cigarette back in her mouth and lit it with a dented gold lighter. As her lips puckered over the filter, my eyes were drawn to a moustache of tiny bristle-like hairs. They were blonde at the ends and dark near the follicles like her hair. The tip of the cigarette flared.

She inhaled deeply, holding the smoke in her lungs until her eyes began to water before abruptly forcing it out through her nostrils. She frowned at me.

'You still here?'

'Yes.' But I was debating whether to leave or ask her the question that had been on my mind since the previous day.

'Get one thing straight, I'm not on the meat market.'

'You told me yesterday that I suffered from a Joan of Arc complex.'

'A doctor does not discuss a case outside the four walls of a professional practice.'

'You're a doctor?'

'More or less.'

Her answer was ambiguous but I took it as a negative. I had not scrutinised the certificates on her wall but I now suspected that Bijou Poulet was not suited to the rigours of prolonged academic study. Her aggressive personality and quick temper were more suited to operating heavy machinery or guarding an industrial warehouse. It was not difficult to imagine her in lace-up boots with a Taser strapped to her belt.

'Could you kindly explain what you meant by a Joan of Arc complex?'

'Use your imagination.'

'Joan of the Arc was burned at the stake.'

Bijou Poulet shrugged.

'A martyr?'

She shrugged again, this time with a smirk.

'A Christian?'

'Try dyke for size.'

'I don't understand.'

'I'm not talking about the ditches of Holland.' Bijou Poulet snorted and ran her fingers through the clump of hair. 'You're not the first crazy fan to fall in love with me.'

'I'm not a fan and I didn't fall in love with you.'

'Sure you didn't.' She pointed to her face. 'You know who I am?'

'Bijou Poulet, Psy Dram?'

'Britain's answer to Jodie Foster.'

I examined her features as she drew on her cigarette but could find no resemblance to the Hollywood star. I knew something about Ms Foster from my reading in the 'Pop Culture' section of the public library. She was American and a popular actress, director and lesbian. As far as I knew, Bijou Poulet was neither an actress nor a director. That left one thing.

'Are you a lesbian?'

Bijou Poulet's face tightened. She spluttered and then coughed seven times without covering her mouth. When she finally raised her hand it was to slap herself between the breasts.

I raised my arms and took a step towards her. I had just witnessed someone almost choke to death and did not want to repeat the experience. 'Can I give you a Heimlich?'

Her eyes widened. She stepped back, shaking her head violently.

'It's a therapeutic hug applied with force.'

'Get away from me!' Bijou Poulet spat out the words between coughs and threw up a hand as a barrier to intervention. The skin of her palm was vivid pink, a condition that can indicate problems with certain vital organs. I might have mentioned this if I had not been distracted by a message scribbled on her mount of Venus, the large fleshy area at the base of the thumb. According to palmistry enthusiasts, the mount of Venus is the home of emotions and sensuality. The scribble was a note written in ballpoint pen: 'Nudity clause, YWCA fight scene.'

Her coughing eased and she dropped her cigarette, grinding it out angrily with the toe of her gold sandal. Her feet were small but her sandals were even smaller and hugged her bunions in a painful way.

'Go away.'

'Alright.'

My response seemed to surprise Bijou Poulet who pulled in her chin and stepped back further. I turned and as I walked away, I ran her profile through the B.S. Pappenheimer Litmus Test. Once again, I found myself deciding against a kidney donation. I rounded the corner of the annexe and immediately stopped thinking about her.

A group of townspeople was gathered near the steps of the town hall below a large 'Polling Station' banner. I was considering whether to approach the group for observation purposes when a familiar headpiece caught my eye. Its owner was kneeling below one of the hall windows, scrubbing the wall with a large nylon-bristle brush and bottle of kitchen detergent. The turban now sat impossibly high on her head, like a plum balanced on top of an egg. She had replaced the jumpsuit with black Lycra bicycle leggings and a red poncho-style top with a gold star motif. The wall in front of her was covered with foam but the spray-painted message was clearly visible: 'Chantelle Corby is a pubic newsants.'

'Hello, Mrs Corby,' I said.

The fortune-teller stood up noisily and pushed back the turban, which was now anchored under her chin by a length of hat elastic. The jewel was missing.

'Who the hell are you?' she asked.

'Sherry Cracker.'

'Don't know you. Don't care.'

She turned back to the wall and resumed scrubbing. As she raised her arm towards 'Corby', the poncho top gaped and I found myself staring at a moist armpit with a patch of dark stubble. I looked away and noticed a card table draped with a crocheted tablecloth. Pinned to this was a handwritten paper sign: 'What will the next decade bring? Lady Luck reveals all. Pensioner discounts.'

I was walking over to examine the stack of cards on the table, when Mrs Corby shouted, 'Don't touch anything!' Her knees cracked as she pushed herself to her feet again. Her eyes narrowed and her manner changed. As she approached, her face took on the sly look of a vegetable-stall owner eyeing a potential customer with a bunch of bananas.

'I'd like to talk to you.'

'I do discounts.'

'I haven't come for a reading.'

'You're not one of them Jeehoover's Witnesses?' Her brow concertinaed.

'No. I'd like to ask you something.'

'You're not getting any money.'

Her response made me think of my mother who assumed everyone was 'on the take' and had a policy of being rude whenever she was approached on the street. 'Every man for himself' was her personal motto, something she pursued with enthusiasm and even force. She did not believe in giving to others and did not see the point in volunteer work or charity. 'You never help panhandlers when you give,' she told me. 'You only take away their motivation to work. They know only too well that if they sit on a street corner with a bad leg, some fool will throw coins at them.' My mother lived off government benefits but she was not referring to herself. 'A so-called cripple will drive himself to a handicapped parking spot and then strap on a calliper under the dashboard,' she said. 'Giving them money does more harm than good.' Her convictions were not supported by fact but she was hardly alone in this.

I doubted Mrs Corby paid much attention to facts. Neither did she seem particularly concerned about the welfare of others.

'I was at your house last night.'

'You're not that cop?'

I pointed to her turban to prod her memory. 'You said I had the cards of Mahatma Gandhi. I was puzzled by this assessment.'

'Some bitch called the cops.' She frowned and eyed me suspiciously. 'My Chantal had to evacuate out the bathroom window.'

'It wasn't me.' I shook my head to emphasise this fact. 'I don't have a mobile phone and there are virtually no working public phones left in this town. The red public phone booth is disappearing from the British landscape.'

'What the hell are you talking about?'

'Red public phone booths. They're being uprooted and sold off. I've read that the Germans are snapping them up for garden novelties.'

'For God's sake!'

I looked into the tiny fierce eyes of Mrs Corby's wrinkled face and thought of a bonobo monkey, one of the smaller members of the chimpanzee family. The bonobos are social, peace-loving apes and share at least ninety-eight per cent of the same DNA as human beings. Their wrinkled faces are expressive and reflect the deep intelligence that enables them to communicate with humans through gestures and symbols. I smiled as an image arose in my mind of a friendly bonobo using sign language to compliment a zookeeper on his uniform. 'Epaulettes suit you,' signalled the bonobo. The zookeeper flushed with pride and gave the monkey a coconut.

Mrs Corby ground her teeth. The image disappeared.

'What the hell are you smirking at?' She curled her lip, severing all connection with the peace-loving primate.

I imagined her being wheeled into a renal clinic and did not need to complete the scenario to know what I felt about her.

'I've just seen your daughter.' I had not known that I was going to say this until the words were out of my mouth.

'My Chantal would have nothing to do with the likes of you.'

'Correct.'

The fortune-teller seemed surprised by this response. 'Where did you see her?'

'In the betting shop.'

'Chantal doesn't gamble.'

'She was talking to a policewoman.'

'What?'

'She was talking to a policewoman.'

'I heard you the first time!'

Mrs Corby threw down the scrubbing brush and tore the turban off her head, tossing it to the ground and kicking it away as if it were an active hive of wasps. A wad of newspaper flew out as it bounced off the side of the building and rolled into the gutter.

She swivelled away from me with a curse and as she took off across the square I recognised the waddle of Chantal Corby in her gait. It was an inefficient way to move a human body over terrain and had nothing in common with Mr Chin's streamlined method of walking.

I turned and found myself looking at the town hall clock.

Something clicked inside my chest as if the teeth of two factory cogs had found each other and begun to turn in unison. It was almost six, the time when 'Cocks take slumber and voting must cease', according the town's electoral bylaw.

I began moving forwards as if pushed by a hand on my back, the powerful hand of someone large and insistent like a nightclub bouncer or primary-school teacher. At the foot of the stairs, a newspaper boy had set up a stand and was handing out a special issue of the *Cockerel*. He saw me and called out 'Bottle Making Toast of Crumpet.' I shook my head but glanced at the newspaper headline as I climbed the steps: 'New Maverick vs Globcom Goliath.'

Inside, the reception area was bustling with people and smelled of damp wool and pine-scented cleaner. Along the wall near the door to the hall was a table with trays of voting papers. I recognised the beefy council worker seated behind the table. Her name was Shelly and the corners of her mouth were curled downwards in the way of the permanently disgruntled. She was wearing a 'Poll Clerk, Your Questions Answered' badge but looked unapproachable, which is how she always looked whenever I visited the photo display.

A voice called out, 'Voting is about to close, ladies and gentlemen,' and someone shoved me from behind. I stumbled several paces and ended up in front of Shelly who was reading a magazine feature on the cabbage diet. Without looking up, she thrust a voting paper into my hands and waved me away.

A familiar male voice behind me said 'Move it,' and I found myself being jostled towards the hall where a man I recognised was seated on a stool by the door. His name was Colin and he was the most difficult of all the council staff. It was Colin who had first branded me a kook and removed the suggestion box from the council annexe building. He saw me and made a face.

'Last vote!'

The call was met with squawks and a frenzy of activity.

I gasped as someone drove the point of an elbow into the side of my ribcage. It was a fast, cunning jab, the sort of disabling attack inflicted on a wing defender in a competitive game of netball. I leaped forwards, covering the distance to the doorway as if fired out of a cannon. Colin screeched and threw up his hands to protect his face but I was able to grab the doorframe to avoid a collision.

'Hello, Colin,' I said, rubbing my side.

He lowered his hands. His face was flushed and angry.

'I've come to vote.' A thrill went through me. The smiling face of Sir Edmund Hillary flashed through my mind.

Colin's eyes narrowed. He glanced over my shoulder.

'That gentleman is the last voter today,' he said, smiling at someone behind me. 'Hello, Mounty. We were wondering when you'd show up.'

I turned to find Andromeda Mountjoy standing in a bold way with his hands on his hips. He had changed his T-shirt but was still wearing the shiny jeans, which now bore a vague brown stain over the groin. He smiled smugly at Colin and tried to push past me but I found myself resisting. My elbows fanned out of their own accord like the arms of a wing defender guarding a hotly contested ball.

'I was here first.' My own protest startled me. It was as if part of my personality had broken away and was taking the law into its own hands.

'She's a troublemaker.' Colin spoke over me to Mr Mountjoy. 'I'll have her ejected.'

'You'll do nothing of the sort!' said a female voice from the door to the hall. As its source emerged from the shadows, I recognised the fortune-teller's customer from the previous evening. Her nose was now covered by a large bandage and pinned to her breast was an official-looking badge: 'ELECTION MONITOR.' She pointed to me. 'That young woman was here first.'

Mr Mountjoy began to protest but Colin quieted him and held up the town's electoral roll. 'She's not eligible to vote.'

'I'm on the roll and I've got proof of identity,' I said, rummaging in my handbag for my passport.

My heart was racing as I handed it over.

'She's known to us.' Colin glanced at the passport and shook his head at the election monitor. He tapped his temple. 'A kook and a mental case.'

217

Colin's assessment left me speechless. I was wondering how to defend myself without looking like a kook when the election monitor spoke up again.

'I know this young woman.' She glanced at me. 'She's perfectly normal.'

I looked around to make sure she was not referring to someone else.

'If you don't allow her to vote, I'll call the authorities. I've already noted several discrepancies and will be making a report when this show is over.'

Colin took a deep breath. His face tightened and his eyes moved from the woman to me. He worked his jaw several times and shook his head. Raising a hand, he reluctantly waved me through.

I turned to the election monitor as I entered the hall. 'Thank you,' I said.

'I should thank you. I would've wasted thirty quid last night if it wasn't for you.' She pointed to the nose bandage. 'That big woman with the sling knocked me out cold. When I finally managed to crawl out of out there, I called the police.'

She led me over to a row of makeshift wooden booths and told me to wait until one became available. Within seconds a large man backed out of one of the narrow enclosures. He was wearing overalls with 'Paradise Plumbing' embroidered over the pocket. He stopped and looked at me.

'I know you,' he said, his eyes narrowing. 'You were at Ted's on Friday.'

'Yes,' I replied, preparing myself for something unpleasant.

'I wouldn't go back there if I were you. I was as sick as a dog the other day. Reported him to health and safety.' He smiled and beckoned me into the booth. 'It's all yours, love.'

The cubicle was warm and smelled of peppery men's cologne. A woman coughed in the adjoining booth. On the other side, a man sighed. I placed the voting paper on the ledge provided and picked up a pen dangling from a piece of string. I read the instructions and reread them to make sure I understood, surprised by the simplicity of the voting procedure. There were only two candidates: Roger Vivien Bottle and Warren Desmond Crumpet.

I raised the pen above the paper and made a cross, taking care not to go over the edges of the square next to Crumpet. Just to make sure, I reapplied the pen, pressing hard as I re-crossed the box.

The words 'Citizen Cracker' glowed in my mind's eye as I chalked up yet another high point on the Learning Curve. My mind leaped ahead to Monday morning and I saw myself reporting to Mr Chin. He was sitting behind his desk and as I described my personal progress, he flashed me one of his rare smiles. He then held out a box of sweet sesame biscuits and told me to take one, assuring me that my job was safe; I would get a promotion and time off to study criminology. 'Make big teapot,' he said. 'Use two tea bag.'

The election monitor had gone when I exited the booth but Colin was waiting for me. He followed me over to the ballot box and watched as I slipped the voting paper inside, poking my finger into the slot to make sure it was securely inserted.

'The council's going to close the photo display,' he said. 'Bottle agrees it's a waste of money.'

Colin smiled with his teeth closed as if presenting them for inspection. They were small with a thick residue of tartar. He had the vivid gums of a gingivitis sufferer.

I turned away without replying but my chest had tightened and the joy of the Mr Chin scenario had disappeared. As I passed through the reception area, I was gripped by feelings of futility and despair, the same profound sense of loss I had experienced when the public library was closed.

'Oy!'

Nigel was standing in the shadows next to a stack of metal beer kegs.

'Hello, Nigel,' I said, my spirits lifting at the sight of the boy. 'It's good to see you.'

'Thought I'd find you here,' he said, wiping his nose with the back of his hand.

'Why?'

He did not reply. Neither did he tell me where he had been or ask what I had been doing. His restless eyes darted from left to right. He beckoned for me to follow, leading me down the side of the building and along a narrow path. This fed into a street that skirted the rear of the rose gardens.

We did not meet anyone as we made our way through a network of backstreets to Des O'Connor Crescent. Jocelyn's house was closed up and looked as if its owner had gone on holiday. All the curtains were drawn and I could see no hint of light behind them.

I took hold of the brass hand of the ornamental doorknocker and knocked twice. When no one answered, I knocked again. A full minute later we were still standing on the doorstep. Nigel nudged me out of the way and, lifting out the metal hand perpendicularly, he rapped it hard against its brass plate several times.

A vague cry came from within.

The dog started barking.

'Now we're talking,' said Nigel with a smile.

21

I put my ear to the door and heard a thud like a sack of potatoes being thrown onto a wooden parquet floor. The dog barked again and a voice called out, 'Coming!'

The stairs creaked. Nigel and I looked at each other as someone began descending the staircase in a cautious manner.

The door opened. The dog shot out and made straight for the boy, who laughed with delight as he gathered it in his arms.

'Oh!' My hand flew to my mouth.

Jocelyn's face was dull matt grey. His lips were colourless and his eyes were puffy and bloodshot. The scratches on his neck were crimson.

'You don't look well,' I said.

'I haven't got my face on, my dear,' he croaked. A tremor passed through his shoulders. His hand trembled against the doorpost. 'I was taking a beauty nap.'

I glanced at his rose-coloured nightgown. 'Your sleepwear is very striking.'

He smiled and adjusted its satin neckline. The nightgown was cut low over his chest, which was speckled with the distinctive red star-burst marks of spider angioma. The spots themselves were benign but their presence indicated liver problems.

With a gracious wave, he beckoned us inside and led us into the parlour where we were invited to sit on the brocade chairs. The boy placed the dog on his knee, laughing as it jumped up to lick him on the chin.

Jocelyn flopped on the sofa and closed his eyes. His hands twitched on his knees. I noted the involuntary shaking of his legs and wondered about delirium tremens, a condition experienced by alcoholics after withdrawal from excessive drinking. Delirium tremens is always unpleasant but in the worst-case scenario it can kill. Symptoms include shaking, disorientation, racing pulse and hypertension. The sufferer can also experience hallucinations.

'I've had a vision.' His eyes flicked open. They were red and watery.

'Is your heart racing?'

'How astute.'

'I think I might know the reason.'

'My mother.' Jocelyn's face lit up. 'She came to me in Givenchy, matching handbag and shoes. Not a hair out of place. She was radiant, an angel.'

'But I thought your mother had passed away.'

Jocelyn's eyes took on a distant look. '*Ravissante.*'

'Are you feeling alright, Jocelyn?'

He looked at me and blinked. 'Excuse me, I was being rude.'

'Not at all. You're probably the most polite person I've ever met. I know what I'm talking about because I meet a lot of impolite people.'

'You're too kind.' He smiled and ran a hand through his hair. 'How did you fare with your detective work?'

I looked over at Nigel but he was occupied with the dog and showed no interest in contributing to the discussion. I began describing our visit to Mr Chin's house, the open door, the cardboard boxes and belongings scattered over the floor. Jocelyn's hands danced on his knees at the mention of Roger Bottle but he clasped them together and stilled the shake as I recounted the mayoral candidate's description of the two men and the Fiesta.

I paused when I got to the part about Mr Tanderhill's medallion, removing it from my pocket and dropping it on the coffee table. Nigel glanced at it but did not say anything. I pushed on, describing Shanks's purchase of three meals with Mr Chin's money belt. 'Mr Chin had it tailor-made in Hong Kong. He is quite particular about it.'

Jocelyn coughed politely. I continued.

'Shanks kept talking about a big project, saying that he was coming into money.'

'You didn't mention the rope,' said Nigel. He stopped stroking the dog.

'Nigel found a rope inside Mr Chin's house.'

'It was wound around a kitchen chair.'

'Oh!' This was news to me.

'That prick at the Chinese resteraurant said someone was asking about Chin. So did that prize prick at the chippie.' Nigel narrowed his eyes at me. 'It was that hypnotiser prick, wasn't it?'

'Correct.'

'You said you don't believe the story about the Chinese gangsterers. You reckon Chin's straight.'

'Mr Chin grew up on the mean streets of Hong Kong. He's severe but a stickler for rules. I've never seen him do anything cowardly or dishonest.'

'So why would he knock around with two crooks, invite them to his house, let them drive his Fiestera and then give them his money?' The features of Nigel's face were compressed. His eyes were fixed on mine. 'Well?'

I could not answer because with each of his questions, I had felt panic rising in my chest like a cistern filling with water. The cistern had now reached maximum capacity and felt as if it were about to burst its siphon-flush valve.

Jocelyn, too, had become increasingly agitated as Nigel spoke. His hands were twitching on his knees and his breathing was heavy. Without warning, he pushed himself to his feet and walked over to a large mahogany china cabinet. He picked up a photo in a silver frame and turned his face to the ceiling.

'*Maman, tu es belle,*' he said.

Nigel and I glanced at each other and then back to Jocelyn, who was pressing the photo to the left side of his chest.

'Don't go.' He scooped the air with his free hand before letting his head drop forwards in a disappointed way. When he turned, tears were running down his cheeks. He looked from me to Nigel in a confused manner. 'Where were we?'

Nigel shrugged.

Jocelyn's gaze returned to me.

'I think Mr Chin's in trouble,' I said, unable to say more. My imagination had hit a roadblock with flashing lights and refused to venture any further.

'Oh, dear.' A tremor passed through Jocelyn's body. He grabbed the edge of the china cabinet to steady himself. 'Perhaps it's time to pay a visit to your office.'

I shook my head but could not muster a 'No.'

'My dear, sometimes you reach a point when you have nothing left to lose. Your job is in jeopardy whether you go or don't go.' He paused. 'Naturally, I'm not suggesting you go alone. I will accompany you.'

I was once again struck by Jocelyn's kindness. Before meeting him and the Rastafarian, no one had ever offered to help me, not even when the hem of my skirt had got caught in the chain of my bicycle and was yanked off in front of a crowded pedestrian crossing. Most of the help I had received in my life had been in exchange for some kind of payment. Even my mother had received special needs benefits and allowances as my carer. These were stopped on my eighteenth birthday when a new social worker called Mrs Marjorie Bean had been appointed to reassess my case. Her name was spelled like the *legume* but pronounced *Bane*. My mother had immediately taken a dislike to the woman and referred to her as 'that bitch Mrs Brussels Sprout' after the benefits were cut.

Jocelyn turned to the boy. 'What do you say, *jeune homme*? Are you in?'

Nigel raised an eyebrow.

'Five pounds?'

The boy nodded in an offhand way but quickly pocketed the money that was placed on the coffee table. 'Got any grub?'

'Help yourself.' Jocelyn pointed to the kitchen. He then turned to me and excused himself, saying he needed to freshen up.

Nigel was on his feet before Jocelyn had left the room, quickly disappearing through the kitchen door with Herb Alpert under his arm. I could hear him opening cupboards and removing tins as Jocelyn climbed the stairs. About halfway up the staircase his footsteps stopped. He exclaimed, '*Mais, Maman, je suis prêt à tout,*' before resuming his climb.

I thought of my own mother and the events that had been set in motion by Mrs Bean's decision: the whirlwind courtship of Barry Bunker, the passport applications and the sale of virtually everything in the house except for her armchair. No one had wanted the rickety piece of furniture despite its 'knock-down price'. The springs had gone and the upholstery was worn and stained from years of constant use. Until the eve of my mother's departure, I had thought I was going with her. I was not looking forward to moving to New Zealand but I had not been presented with an alternative. As I had never been permitted to make decisions, I had gone along with my mother's plans without comment. I do not know when she changed these plans but she did not notify me until I was packing. I was in my bedroom putting what was left of my belongings after the sale into a suitcase when she stuck her head in the doorway. There was no furniture in the room and I was squatting on the floor. The bed and nightstand had been sold along with most of my clothes. 'You're staying here,' she said. 'Barry doesn't want extra baggage.' I did not bother to unpack my suitcase because there was nowhere left to put anything.

Nigel returned with a stack of biscuits and the dog at his heel. He sat down and broke off a corner of a digestive to entice Herb Alpert on to his lap.

'Did you find your father?' I asked.

The boy looked at me. The smile disappeared from his lips. 'Not yet,' he said.

'He's been asking after you.' I did not bother adding that I had overhead this from Chantal Corby.

His face lit up. 'He said he'd come and get me when he got out.'

'You said he's going to buy you a dog.'

The boy frowned, unsure of whether he was being teased.

'Sir Edmund Hillary had dogs.'

'Who the hell was Edmund Hillerary?'

'He was probably the greatest adventurer of the twentieth century. He climbed the world's highest mountain and crossed the Antarctic with dog teams and two Ferguson farm tractors.'

Nigel tried not to smile but his cheeks glowed pink. The glow highlighted the furry circle of his birthmark. He pulled his cap lower and stuffed two biscuits in his mouth.

Pipes rattled above our heads as a tap was turned off upstairs. Floorboards squeaked and Jocelyn's footfalls could be heard on the stairs. They were light and rapid. The parlour door flew open and he burst through the doorway with his arms outstretched and a loud 'Tah dah!'

Nigel choked and sent a spray of biscuit crumbs over the dog.

Jocelyn was dressed in full Scottish regalia with a kilt, sporran, short-sleeved white shirt, tartan tie and white knee socks with tartan tabs. The ensemble was flawless and would have looked impressive on the field of the Edinburgh Tattoo if not for his footwear. Instead of lacing himself into the gillies of a highlander, Jocelyn had slipped on a pair of women's mules with kitten heels. These were made of black patent leather and had novelty tartan bows over the toes.

My eyes moved back up the ensemble to his face, which had shed its dull matt grey for glowing Ibiza bronze with vivid pink circles on each cheek. His lips were now shiny pink and his hair had been styled into the tucked wings of Princess Diana on her wedding day. His eyelashes were lush and his eyes were sparkling. He looked like a different person, more woman than man, and a lot more alive than fifteen minutes previously.

'That's a very handsome tartan,' I said.

'The McDermott,' he replied, removing a lace-edged handkerchief from his sporran and patting his forehead. His hand had lost its shake and patted with confidence.

'Are we making tracks or talking tartan?' Nigel carefully placed the dog on the floor and stood, brushing crumbs off his T-shirt.

'Don't look so worried, my dear,' said Jocelyn, eyeing me. 'What's the worst that can happen?'

I dared not imagine.

'If we've made a mistake, I'll simply explain everything. *Je dirai que c'était ma faute.*' Jocelyn splayed his fingers over his heart. 'If, however, there's trouble, we have Herb Alpert.'

I glanced at the tiny dog hoovering crumbs off the carpet and tried to suppress the feeling that the events of the past two days were gathering dangerous momentum like a gigantic snowball hurtling down a mountainside towards a family picnic. I had left the office on Friday with a feeling that something big was about to happen. Now it had been set in motion and there was no way to push the killer snowball back up the mountainside.

Floral eau de toilette wafted my way as Jocelyn ushered us out of the front door. It was gardenia mingled with another fresher smell. I recognised the tang of juniper berries and hint of quinine.

Once outside, Herb Alpert began barking and running in frantic circles. A wind had come up and dark cumulus clouds were gathering in the direction of the Babylon. An urgent, unsafe feeling took hold of me. An image of the office glinted in my mind's eye like a piece of anthracite coal. It was dark and full of burning potential. As we set off, I willed myself to stay calm and keep pace with Jocelyn, whose kitten heels slowed him down to the pace of a window shopper.

Nigel ran on ahead and was in the rose gardens when we caught up with him, chasing the dog around the floral clock. The gardens were empty but the Dutty had recently visited. 'VOTE FOR MAN CRUMPET' was scrawled in chalk over the pavement and walls. I thought of Warren Crumpet's earnest face looking out of his campaign posters and wondered how the vote counting was going.

Herb Alpert suddenly stopped running and started barking. Nigel stood still. Jocelyn's hand moved to his throat as a figure emerged from the French urinal.

'Oy! Come here, you little bastard!'

Sidney was glaring at the boy. He shouted again before leaping off the urinal's concrete pad and sprinting towards us.

Nigel scooped up the dog, thrust it into Jocelyn's arms and made a dash for the gate. He was already out of the gardens when Sidney flew past, rustling loudly as his arms pumped against the nylon of his shell suit. He was fast despite his damaged ankles and might have caught the boy if another person had not been entering the gardens as he was exiting. The newcomer was carrying a tall stack of plastic containers and did not see Sidney before he was rammed. The containers seemed to explode on impact, making a popping sound like a string of firecrackers and sending their contents flying over the path. A cylindrical object bounced over the asphalt like a skipping stone and came to rest against the toe of my air-cushion sports shoe. Its stick was missing but the battered sausage had survived impact intact.

The chipman lay sprawled, groaning on the path but Sidney had already leaped to his feet. He lifted a Doc Marten boot over the chipman's F I S H & fingers and brought it down with a rubbery *thud*. The chipman yelped and struck out with his C H I P S hand but Sidney sprang out of reach. With a parting curse, he bolted out of the gate.

'Let me help you up,' said Jocelyn. He put down Herb Alpert and held out his hand.

The chipman frowned and ignored the hand. Propping himself on to his elbow, he sneered at the patent-leather mules. The sneer remained as his eyes travelled up Jocelyn's clothes to fix on his face.

'Must have banged my head,' he said. 'I'm seeing fairies.'

Jocelyn's smile wilted. He dropped his hand.

I moved forwards, as he stepped back, my foot narrowly missing an overturned plastic container. Battered fish and deep-fried pies lay scattered over the path.

'Oy! Careful with the merchandise. Watch where you put your bloody feet!' The chipman pushed his large body into a sitting position and blew on his fingers.

'But this food is contaminated,' I said. 'The paths of these rose gardens see a lot of foot traffic and as you must know, the sole of the shoe is a vehicle of pollutants and micro-organisms. Droppings, cigarette butts, chemical residues. The list is long.'

'You don't know what you're talking about.' The chipman scooped up a handful of sausages. 'Deep-frying kills germs. The vat has the power to heal.'

'Not when you merely reheat food. Reheating a precooked sausage will not kill E. coli or salmonella. You'll be putting people's lives at risk.'

'The world would be better off without some of them.' He gave Jocelyn a meaningful look and went back to picking up his wares.

Jocelyn moved further away. Out of the corner of my eye, I saw him remove a silver flask from his sporran and put it to his lips.

'I was at Ted's café today.'

'Why don't you and Lady Godiva just piss off.'

'A policewoman came in while I was there.'

The chipman stopped, a pair of sausages in his hand.

'Things became quite heated at the mention of a health and safety inspection. Apparently, inspectors have been closing down kitchens.'

With the toe of my sports shoe I nudged a battered Scotch egg.

The chipman's eyes fixed on my foot. His lip-less mouth hardened into a flat line.

I did not think that Sidney's earlier behaviour was exemplary but the chipman had been unkind to Jocelyn and was clearly prepared to risk people's lives. The situation called for decisive action. I lifted my foot and brought it down on to the Scotch egg, crushing it flat to expose the dull yellow of its yolk. Herb Alpert darted forth for a sniff but quickly pulled away with *yap*. The dog started barking and did not stop until I had looped my arm through Jocelyn's and led him out of the gardens.

Our arms remained linked as we made our way down Harry Secombe Parade. Jocelyn was silent and I was too preoccupied to start conversation. An urgent, unsafe feeling had taken hold of me and I felt myself being drawn towards the office like a car body pulled over a wrecker's yard by a large industrial magnet. I wanted to hurry, to sprint or do something reckless such as leap on the back of a moving motorcycle, but Jocelyn was wobbly on his mules and a weight on my arm.

The rain that had been threatening started to pelt down as we reached Mr Chin's lime-green Fiesta, parked at an awkward angle outside the cinema. Its driver's window was open and the panther tail was lying on the seat. The car door was slightly ajar.

I released Jocelyn's arm and wound up the window with the manual winder. I shut the door securely before joining him under the shelter of the awning where broken glass still lay scattered over the ground. Near the door to the stairs, I picked up the faint odour of menthol. I tried the handle of the door and felt a flutter in my chest as it turned.

'My mother's film played here,' came Jocelyn's voice from behind me. '*Love's Diabolical Mistress*. A cinematic triumph.'

He was gazing at the sagging metal of the awning and showed no intention of moving.

'*Ma bien aimée.*'

'Jocelyn?' I gently tugged his arm. 'I'd like to go up now.'

He shivered and looked at me. His eyes had taken on the lost, frantic look of a dog separated from its master in a public park. He removed the flask from his sporran and drank greedily, shaking it empty before putting it back inside the pouch.

His eyes flashed and he smiled. '*Après moi.*' He grabbed the door and yanked it open, squinting into the dim stairwell.

I rushed to his side. 'The lights don't work. Let me show you the way.'

'Nonsense, my dear.' With a shake of the head, he gallantly stepped inside.

Herb Alpert scuttled between our feet and the door snap-closed behind us on its spring hinge, plunging the stairwell into total darkness. I could not see Jocelyn but I could hear his laboured breathing and the sound of his kitten heels just above me as he slowly made his way up.

He reached the landing at the top of the stairs and let out a loud sigh. Herb Alpert began scratching at the metal door of the office.

Without warning, the door flew open.

'*Maman!*'

I saw Jocelyn lift his arm as if to embrace or ward off someone before disappearing through the doorway.

22

Herb Alpert's barks were reverberating inside the stairwell as I leaped the last three steps to the landing and stuck my head in the office. What I saw looked nothing like my workplace. Before I could make sense of it, Jocelyn reappeared in front of me with his arms outstretched like a cartoon sleepwalker. He was moaning and staggering, and let out a shriek as a hairy arm snaked around his neck and yanked him backwards. He stumbled and was dragged back inside.

I lunged but instead of moving in a forward direction, I found myself thrown backwards as a man in a balaclava drove his head into my chest like a battering ram. My back hit the wall at the top of the stairs. Air rushed from my lungs and my chest exploded with pain.

Page fifteen of the council handbook flashed through my mind as I gasped for breath. I raised my arms above my head and began windmilling them, pelting my assailant on the back with repeated blows of my fists and forcing him to his hands and knees. The stairwell echoed with the thuds and gasps of vigorous struggle and the insistent barks of the Chihuahua.

'*Au secours!*'

I looked up at the sound of Jocelyn's cry in time to see him crumple to the floor. His hands were over his eyes. He twitched as his assailant threw a large sandaled foot on to his chest. The man's face was hidden behind a balaclava but the abundant hair on his toes was unmistakable.

'Don't hurt him!' I shouted and dropped my arms to my sides.

Herb Alpert seemed to take this as a signal and stopped barking.

Mr Tanderhill pulled his foot off Jocelyn's chest. His enormous eyes blinked at me from the slit of his hood.

My assailant scrambled to his feet and grabbed me around the neck. I put up no resistance as he wrenched my arm up my back in a half-Nelson, one of the most effective grappling holds known to professional wrestlers. The balaclava had hidden the face of my opponent but I had already recognised the country and western clothes of Shanks.

I remained focused on Jocelyn as Mr Tanderhill seized an arm of his limp body. Jocelyn's eyes were closed and his mouth was open. With a grunt, the hypnotherapist began dragging him away from the doorway. Jocelyn's shirt came untucked from his kilt. His mules slid off his feet.

Herb Alpert was nowhere to be seen. The dog had disappeared into the tangle of telephone cables and piles of papers strewn across the linoleum. The office was in chaos. Chairs were overturned and desks and filing cabinets had been ransacked. Computers and telephones were lying on the floor. Anything made of wood had been sawn into pieces. The fish tank was still standing but propped against one of its legs was a chainsaw with a 'Husqvarna' stamp along its metal arm. I glanced over at my desk and was surprised to find it upright. My eyes flicked to the window.

I stiffened and would have gasped if the arm around my neck had not been compressing my windpipe.

Mr Chin's small eyes fixed on me and flashed with anger. His mouth was gagged with a tea towel but his face was red and looked like it was about to burst. He bucked against the blue nylon rope tied around his chest. His Komfort King lurched forwards and hit the desk in front of him. Despite the gag, he was making considerable noise, rumbling and whistling like a Mongolian throat singer. His bucking became wilder as Mr Tanderhill dumped Jocelyn on the floor beside him.

Shanks tightened his grip around my throat and pushed me from behind, forcing me to move forwards. Mr Chin whistled loudly as a chair was flipped upright and rolled next to Jocelyn. I was pushed down on to its seat by the hypnotherapist and held in place while Shanks shortened a length of rope with a sheepshank before winding it around my body and attaching it to the chair with frapping turns. His knots were sophisticated, the sort of rope skills used by adventure scouts to scale rock faces or lash mountain goats to carrying poles. He smiled in a satisfied way as he secured the rope under my ribcage with a clove hitch.

The hypnotherapist flipped another chair upright and rolled it between Mr Chin and me. The two men grabbed Jocelyn under the arms and lifted him on to its seat. His body slumped forwards as a rope was wound around his torso. The Diana hairstyle had collapsed and his makeup was smeared.

'What the hell's this?'

The sound of Mr Tanderhill's voice made my scalp prickle. He had pulled his hands away from Jocelyn and was holding out his palms for Shanks to view. They were dirty, smeared with an oily orange substance. Shanks examined his own hands and then glanced at Jocelyn.

'It's the fag's war paint,' he said, wiping his hands on the sides of his jeans. 'It's like chicken grease.'

Mr Chin whistled under the tea towel.

Jocelyn's arms were mottled Ibiza bronze and white-grey. They had been bound tightly to the sides of his body and his fingers were already showing signs of swelling.

'Mr Tanderhill,' I said.

He gave a start.

'I know you.'

'No, you don't.' His voice was high and defensive. His eyes bulged out of the balaclava. They were fissured with tiny veins. His pupils were dilated.

'I recognise your voice and the distinctive hair on your toes. You're a hypnotist.'

'Hypnotherapist, Royal Academy!' His voice was even higher and more defensive. He tore off his hood. 'Master Chakraologist, Imperial Grade A!'

'Could you untie me now?'

'Not before you tell me where the gold is!'

I was about to explain that there was no gold on the premises when Mr Chin let out a muffled screech. I leaned forwards but could not see him for Jocelyn, whose head was dangling from his neck at an awkward angle.

Mr Tanderhill moved in close and before I could think of a defensive manoeuvre, jabbed me between the eyebrows with his index finger. I felt a jolt, as if someone had fed an electrical wire into the centre of my brain and turned on the juice. I imagined the tiny pine cone of my pineal gland light up like a diode.

'Hello, anybody home?'

His words made my fingers tingle. My ears cleared with a pop. I sought out his eyes and locked on to their dilated pupils. Several seconds must have passed because Mr Chin became quiet. The hypnotherapist blinked and shuffled his feet. He shook his head and took a step backwards.

'Here, let me have a go,' said Shanks, shunting Mr Tanderhill out of the way. 'You'd better start talking, girlie, or you'll get the gully knife.'

He lifted the leg of his jeans to reveal a knife strapped to an ankle holster. It was a safari knife with a curved serrated edge, a versatile blade for hacking a path through dense jungle or removing the pelt from a dead goat. He yanked it from its sheath and slashed it through the air in an arc before bringing it up short at my throat. The tip of his nose was almost touching mine and he was breathing directly into my face. I pushed myself back against the chair. His breath smelled of fermented potatoes.

'Shanks,' I said.

He nodded automatically at the sound of his name and then cursed when he realised what he had done. Frowning through the slit of the balaclava, he removed the serrated blade from my throat.

'You've been drinking vodka.'

His eyes slid towards Mr Tanderhill and then back to me. 'What's it to you?'

'Knives and alcohol don't mix.' Neither did cars, guns or heavy machinery, according to the council handbook, but Shanks did not need to know this.

'That's rich advice coming from a tart.' He pulled off the balaclava and rubbed his face vigorously. His cheeks were pink and irritated from the synthetic material. 'You're a fine one to tell me what to do.'

I was surprised. Shanks appeared to recognise me. 'You know me?'

'Know you?' He laughed. 'What do you expect when you keep throwing yourself at me?'

'How did you find this office?'

He tapped his nose. 'Once a scout, always a scout.'

Mr Chin whistled again.

'Scouts don't steal from people.'

'Shut up!' shouted Mr Tanderhill. 'This isn't a bloody jamboree!'

He shoved Shanks out of the way and, avoiding my eyes, slapped me across the cheek.

'Where's the frigging gold?' His eyes were inflamed and enormous.

The violence inflicted on my cheek found an echo in my chest and triggered a vivid memory. My mother was standing over me, waving the letter from Mrs Bean and slapping me repeatedly across the face.

'Is someone roasting chestnuts?' Jocelyn's voice was whisper soft. He'd come to and was blinking in a confused way. 'I hear crackling.'

The hypnotherapist turned to him and was raising his hand again when I spoke up.

'I think I can help you.'

He swivelled back to me, his arm above his head.

'Mr Chin handles inventory. He has the information you need.'

Mr Chin shrieked from under his gag.

'You think I haven't asked him already?' Mr Tanderhill slapped my cheek again, harder this time. 'The Chink's had plenty of slappy-slappy but the bastard's made of iron.'

'*Maman?*' Jocelyn's voice was weaker, less sure. He raised his head to stare at the ceiling.

'Let me try asking Mr Chin.' My cheek was burning but my mind was crystal clear. 'I work for him. We have a boss–employee relationship.'

Mr Tanderhill narrowed his bulging eyes at me.

'I need you to remove his gag so he can respond.'

The hypnotherapist's nostrils flared. He filled his lungs and gave a cautious nod to Shanks, who stumbled forwards waving the knife. The blade passed over Jocelyn's head, ruffling his hair.

'For God's sake, you drunk idiot! Stop waving that thing about!' shouted the hypnotherapist. 'Someone's going to lose an eye!'

He snatched the knife from Shanks and approached Mr Chin, slipping the tip of its blade under the tape holding the gag in place. As he sliced upwards, the towel loosened and fell away.

Mr Chin's eyes narrowed and without losing a second, he threw his head forwards. His mouth opened swiftly like the lid of a rubbish tin responding to pressure on a foot pedal. It snapped shut just as fast to clamp down on Mr Tanderhill's hand.

The hypnotherapist yelped and dropped the knife with a *clatter*. Slapping his free hand against Mr Chin's chest, he pulled backwards.

Mr Chin held on, his jaws locked like the beak of a snapping turtle.

Mr Tanderhill let out another yelp as Herb Alpert appeared from under a tangle of cables and began nipping ferociously at his ankles. Hopping from one foot to another, the hypnotherapist gave his arm a powerful yank.

The unpleasant sound of teeth raking over sinew and bone accompanied yet another yelp as he pulled his hand free. Clutching it to his chest, he danced around the Chihuahua. 'My golden fingers, my golden fingers.'

Herb Alpert was barking, Mr Chin was screeching and Mr Tanderhill was whimpering when Shanks swooped on the knife.

'No one try anything or I'll gut you like—' He stopped shouting and frowned, trying to think of something to say.

'—red herrings?' I offered.

'Shut up!' Brandishing the knife in front of him like a sword, he backed his way towards the door. His bottom was almost against the heavy rectangle of reinforced steel when it suddenly sprung open on its powerful German hinge. His buttocks were hit full force and he was thrown forwards like a projectile from a catapult. He fell with his knife-arm raised and his head unprotected. His temple hit the corner of a metal filing cabinet with a loud *clang* and his body collapsed to the floor.

Mr Chin stopped screeching.

The dog scuttled under the desk.

Mr Tanderhill blinked at the knife that had landed at his feet. He grabbed it and shook his head. His eyes flicked to Shanks, who was lying face down on the linoleum with his arms outstretched like the wings of an aeroplane.

The room was silent except for a strange rasping sound. I twisted my head to look at Jocelyn. His chin was sitting awkwardly on his chest, restricting his breathing. A line of saliva dangled from his open mouth. My chest tightened as I realised he had fainted again. I strained against the rope around my torso but I was bound tightly to the chair.

'A tea party!'

The voice from the doorway made me stop twisting in my seat and sit up straight.

23

Nigel poked his head in the office and looked around the room. His eyes avoided mine as they skimmed over the three of us tied to chairs before returning to the knife in Mr Tanderhill's hand. The boy's cap had gone and his short blonde hair was flat to his scalp. He looked tougher and older, like one of the men I occasionally saw outside pubs selling electronic goods from the back of a white van.

He raised his eyebrows and stepped over Shanks as if it were perfectly natural to encounter a body upon entering a ransacked office. There was a strange smile on his lips but his face showed no surprise or fear.

'Who the hell are you?' shouted the hypnotherapist.

'Either your business partnerer or your worstest enemy,' said the boy with a smirk.

'Get out!' Mr Tanderhill was standing several steps from the boy. He lunged, knife first.

'Olé!' Nigel nimbly stepped aside and kept moving.

'Little bastard!' Mr Tanderhill lunged again and missed. He leaped over an upturned chair, crying out as his knee caught on its wheel.

Nigel danced away, his light body avoiding a filing cabinet and springing over a sawn-up desk with ease. He reached the far wall smiling and grabbed the standard lamp to steady himself.

With a roar, the hypnotherapist rushed him.

The boy laughed and threw the lamp in his path, agilely stepping over the chainsaw and out of his reach.

As Mr Tanderhill dodged to the side to avoid the lamp, his foot caught the blade of the Husqvarna. He lost his balance and tipped to one side. His shoulder hit the fish tank with the dull *boof* of a controlled detonation. The glass shattered and caved inwards. Water exploded from the tank, sending spray as far as the window. I closed my eyes as fine droplets hit my cheek. When I opened them again, water was lapping at my feet.

Mr Tanderhill looked down at his sodden clothes and cursed. He was breathing hard. His face had lost its colour.

'Wet enough for you?' Nigel laughed from behind the safety of my upright desk.

The hypnotherapist looked up and narrowed his eyes only to glance down again as a yellow projectile darted out from under the desk. The dog leaped high and sank its small teeth into the hand with the knife, twisting in the air like a great white shark trying to tear a chunk from a tuna. The hypnotherapist cried out and dropped the knife, which bounced out of reach under a pile of telephone cables. Herb Alpert let go and scuttled off.

Mr Tanderhill crossed his arms over his chest like an effigy of Tutankhamen. His face was creased in pain. Turning his back on the boy, he squelched over to where Shanks lay. Sticking the toe of his boot into his accomplice's shoulder, he nudged him but got no response. He cursed and kicked him hard in the ribs. A weak moan escaped Shanks's lips but his body did not move.

'Bloody amateur!' He kicked him again and let out a shriek of frustration.

'I think it's a football match, *Maman*.'

Jocelyn was gazing at the ceiling again. His face was two-tone, ghostly white and bronzer orange. He was shaking so much that his knees were vibrating like active mobile phones switched to silent. His arms were twitching at his sides. The veins on his hands were thick and cord-like but his fingernails were pale and bloodless.

On the other side of him, Mr Chin was ominously silent, his eyes on the hypnotherapist. His hands were tightly bound to the arms of his Komfort King and his fingers were red and swollen. I did not know how long he had been tied to the chair or whether he had been given a toilet break. But from my experience inside the broom cupboard I knew that a full bladder was a very uncomfortable condition.

Nigel had not moved from behind my desk. He was watching the hypnotherapist with the intensity of a border terrier eyeing a rabbit hole or the leg of a gas meter reader.

I coughed.

Mr Tanderhill looked at me. His eyes were fierce, blazing red.

'Untie me please,' I said. 'I'll show you where Mr Chin keeps his valuables.'

Mr Chin's screech made the hair on my arms stand on end. Jocelyn jumped. Out of the corner of my eye, I saw him turn his head towards my employer and say something. Mr Chin fell silent.

'This better not be a trick.' The hypnotherapist shot me a warning look.

'She's too thick for that,' said Nigel.

'I didn't ask for your opinion.' He glared at the boy. 'Do something useful and untie her.'

'So we're business partnerers then.'

'Just shut up and do as I say.'

Nigel did not look at me or say anything as he undid the rope around my chest, backing away as Mr Tanderhill squelched over to stand behind my chair.

'Get up.' He drove the point of his elbow into my back. 'I'm right behind you so don't try anything.'

'I need to get into my desk.' As I stood, he increased the pressure of his elbow on my spine. I knew only too well about the dangerous potential of an elbow. The council handbook describes it as a violent weapon and single woman's best friend. A well-aimed elbow chop to the underside of the jaw can cause a mandibular fracture. As any boxer knows, a broken jaw will put hard caramels and rump steak off the menu for life.

'Nice and easy.' Mr Tanderhill removed the elbow and hooked an arm around my neck. He pushed me forwards.

'I need to go over there.' I pointed to my desk, which was now standing in a puddle of water like a Pacific atoll.

'Get on with it.' He pushed me towards it, his arm uncomfortably tight around my neck.

'Please let me sit down.'

He released me but stayed close as I flipped my damp chair upright and settled my buttocks on the familiar comfort of its neoprene padding. Mr Tanderhill dug his fingers painfully into my armpit. He moved from behind my chair to stand at my side. His long legs were bent and he was leaning over the desk. I felt his breath on my ear and could smell menthol.

'Hurry up, for God's sake!' He increased the pressure of his fingers on the soft glandular tissue of my armpit.

The first page of the council handbook bears a quote: 'When you find yourself cornered by a Class A assailant, drive your fingers into his eyes, smash his nose with your elbow and knee him in the testicles. There is no such thing as mercy when your life is on the line. Gerald Fack, Editor.'

I took a deep breath and leaned down to grasp the handle of my file drawer. It was wide and heavy and contained the office cash box. With an expert jerk of my arm, I yanked it open at high speed and heard the familiar *whoosh* of its tiny plastic wheels along the metal rails. Its hard, reinforced frame made a sickening crunch as it caught Mr Tanderhill under the kneecaps to penetrate the vulnerable area between the tibiae and patellae with terrific force.

His arms flew up in the air and he emitted an ear-piercing scream. I twisted in my seat as he fell backwards and saw him land hard on his buttocks with a *splash*. Hugging his knees to his chest, he rocked on to his back, whimpering.

The Australian salt-water crocodile can float like a log for days in wait for prey to approach and then attacks with shocking speed and ferocity. Using its tail for propulsion, it can leap vertically from the water like a dolphin to seize a low-flying bird out of the air. People who have witnessed this phenomenon describe the crocodile's action as an explosion. It was a crocodile that I imagined as I exploded out of my chair.

Mr Tanderhill was still on his back with his arms wrapped protectively around his kneecaps, leaving the delicate fleshy interior between his thighs conveniently exposed. He was wailing in pain with his eyes closed and did not see me retract my leg and drive my sports shoe into his groin. He opened his mouth wide to scream as the spongy buffer of his testicles gave against my foot. I saw the uvula at the back of his throat, but no sound came out of his mouth. His damaged hands flew to his groin. With a shudder, he curled into a foetal position on his side.

Despite the tension of the moment and the rapidity of my gestures, I had gauged the velocity of my kick to wound without permanent damage. As the council handbook states: 'The testicles are highly sensitive organs and excessive force can cause mortal injury'. Mr Tanderhill merited punishment and would certainly not be receiving one of my kidneys, but he did not deserve to die. His silent scream gave way to strangled gurgling. He was alive and damp, but effectively disabled.

The room came into focus again.

Mr Chin was screeching and bucking in his chair, throwing his chest against the rope. Shanks was out cold. Nigel had enticed the Chihuahua from under the desk and was holding the dog against his chest, nuzzling it with the side of his face.

Only Jocelyn was still. He caught my eye and tried to say something. It was impossible to hear him over Mr Chin's screeches. I stepped around Mr Tanderhill and went over to kneel at his side.

'Unleash your employer, my dear,' he wheezed.

Mr Chin ignored me as I tried to slip my hand under the rope around his chest. He continued screeching and straining at his bonds, making it impossible to undo the knot under his ribcage. With a strange boldness I did not recognise in myself, I placed a palm on his chest and shoved him back in the chair. The screeching stopped. Mr Chin looked up in surprise. I loosened the sheepshank and untied the knot near his breastbone. The rope uncoiled and fell to the floor.

I had pictured a crocodile when I went for my prey but it was a boar I now saw in Mr Chin. The wild pig is renowned for the speed with which it takes off and the violence of its tusk thrusts. Mr Chin shot out of the chair and made for the film room, leaping over puddles and furniture like a much younger man. A split second later he emerged with a thick length of green bamboo and immediately began thrashing Mr Tanderhill. The injured man yelped and writhed in pain but Mr Chin showed no mercy, bringing the stick down on him over and over again. With every *thwack*, the cries diminished until the hypnotherapist lay whimpering in a tight ball.

Mr Chin stopped abruptly. His head spun in the direction of the door.

Nigel had crept around the furniture and was making for the stairwell with the dog tucked safely under his arm. But he was too slow for Mr Chin who launched himself from a crouch to hurdle my desk and block his exit. The bamboo slashed downwards at lightning speed to stop just above the shoulders of the boy.

'No, Mr Chin!' I shouted, jumping to my feet and hurrying over. 'He's with us.'

Mr Chin lifted the bamboo away from the boy's head. He frowned at me.

In the silence, car horns became audible. People were shouting and whistling in the street. It sounded like a convoy of Italians on their way to a wedding or returning from a football match.

'The election,' said Nigel. 'Results must be in.'

Mr Chin turned back to the boy. 'Who you? Delinquent and so on?'

'He's a friend.' As I said the word 'friend', a shiver passed through my body. 'He can go get help.'

'You friend?' Mr Chin lowered the tip of the bamboo to the floor. Nigel shrugged.

'These men are criminals.' I pointed to Mr Tanderhill, who was still curled in a ball, whimpering. 'We need to alert the authorities.'

'No authority yet.' Mr Chin held up his hand. He eyed the boy. 'You alert authority and police but must give Chin thirty minute. Follow rule, get bonus. Understand?'

Nigel raised an eyebrow. 'How much?'

'Five pound cash.'

'Thirty.'

'Most Chin can afford is ten pound.'

The boy raised an eyebrow.

'Chin do you favour.'

I nodded to Nigel, who nodded to Mr Chin. The boy pocketed the money and winked at me. He gave the dog a farewell kiss and put it down before disappearing into the dark stairwell.

'Be so kind as to untie me, my dear,' said Jocelyn. His voice was whisper-soft and without urgency, as if he were asking me to button up the back of a blouse.

'I apologise!' I said, running over to his chair. 'I was distracted by the melee.'

Jocelyn looked exhausted. The patches of his face showing through the bronzer had gone from white to pale blue. I untied him quickly, catching him as he fell forwards to prevent him from hitting the floor. Herb Alpert scuttled over to his master and began pawing his ankle.

'You don't look well, Jocelyn.'

'I could do with a pick-me-up.' He ran a shaky hand through his hair and straightened his kilt before reaching under the desk to remove a bottle of plum liquor. 'I couldn't help noticing this decanter during the hubbub.'

Mr Chin glanced at the bottle and looked away, his attention focused on Shanks.

'Aghhh.'

Shanks groaned and raised his upper body, looking around in a dazed manner. On the side of his head was an enormous lump shaped like the volcanic cone of Mount Fuji, the highest mountain in Japan. He was struggling to push himself on to his hands and knees when Mr Chin brought the green bamboo down across his back with a hearty *whack*.

Shanks cried out and fell forwards as the blows began to beat down on him. Crawling on his elbows like a commando, he headed for the cover of my desk but Mr Chin was faster, seizing him by the ankles and dragging him back out into open terrain. He then recommenced the beating, striking the cowboy over the shoulder blades again and again.

'I think the filet mignon is sufficiently tenderised,' said Jocelyn, replacing the cap on the bottle.

Mr Chin stopped beating. His head swivelled towards Jocelyn, who was pushing himself up on shaky legs. He grabbed the back of the Komfort King for support.

'Hit with punishment stick never enough for robber and crook!' Mr Chin's voice was high and wild. He strode over to Jocelyn, waving the bamboo. 'Who you?'

I hurried over to throw myself between them. 'He's another *friend*,' I said.

Mr Chin's eyes flicked to me. He shook his head in disbelief. 'What now? Suddenly friend this, friend that.'

'*Amis*.' Jocelyn had retrieved his shoes and assumed his full height in kitten heels. 'We are indeed friends.'

Mr Chin narrowed his eyes and looked him up and down critically. His gaze fell on the sporran and lingered. His face softened and lost its suspicion. 'Hairy purse very nice and good. You lady man.'

'I've been called many things.' Jocelyn smiled politely.

'Lady man of Hong Kong highest quality. Look like real and genuine lady. Very charming and kind. Never steal wallet.'

'I've never stolen a thing in my life.'

'Best policy.'

Mr Chin pursed his lips into a point. He gave Jocelyn a curt nod. I recognised the gesture. It was same nod of approval he gave me whenever I made a significant purchase of gold crowns.

'Lady man now help Chin with important business. Understand?'

Jocelyn smiled and gave a graceful nod.

Mr Chin motioned for me to pick up the ropes. 'You tie up crook with string. Make powerful knot. Tight and painful is best.'

When I did not immediately move, he waved at me with the back of his hand. 'Hurry and fast before authority come!'

I turned away and quickly began doing as I had been instructed, happy to be following Mr Chin's orders again. Shanks was conscious but lacked the strength to protest as I tied his hands behind his back and bound his feet together. I secured the rope in place with a simple reef knot from *Rope Skills of the Nautical World*, an illustrated book I had rescued from the library skip. I then moved on to Mr Tanderhill and did the same. The hypnotherapist was barely conscious after the beating and put up no resistance. I made sure the ropes were secure without trying to inflict pain. I did not agree that painful was best. They had both experienced considerable pain already.

Tying up criminals is physically demanding work. By the time I had finished, I was hot and perspiring freely. I glanced over at Mr Chin's desk and did a double take. My heart leaped as if I had stuck a dining fork into a wall socket.

The spot where Mr Chin's desk and chair usually sat was now a gaping hole. Jocelyn was standing above the hole, holding open a trapdoor. The desk and chair had been moved to one side. The damp square of Chinese carpet was rolled back.

Mr Chin poked his head out of the hole like a Swiss marmot in an alpine meadow. In his hand was a small brick wrapped in the colourful red and gold paper of the Chinese New Year. He saw me staring and gave me a sharp look.

'You cover eye of crook?' he asked.

'You want me to blindfold them?' I replied.

'Wrapping eye is key and crucial. Also must plug crook ear with tissue that is paper. Crook see nothing. Hear nothing. Like wise monkey that is actually stupid and lazy.' He gestured again for me to hurry. 'Tight and painful. Best policy.'

I did not agree that binding the eyes tightly was the best policy and was very careful not to do this. The eye is a delicate gel-filled vessel and is very sensitive to pressure. People with glaucoma know this only too well. But I did not have any reservations about the ears, which I tightly stuffed with tissue. I then pulled their balaclavas over their eyes and, leaving the breathing passages free of obstruction, I bound the hoods in place with the brown plastic tape I kept in my desk. I stood back to view my handiwork. The tape around the bottom of the balaclavas had created the effect of rimless German World War II helmets while the floppy top halves looked like deflated busbies.

Mr Chin brought up another gift-wrapped brick and then climbed out of the projection room. With slow, deliberate movements, Jocelyn placed it on a neat stack of fourteen similar bricks. He then shuffled over to Mr Chin's Komfort King and flopped down with a long sigh. His hands twitched as Herb Alpert leaped on to his lap. Mr Chin shut the trap door and replaced the damp carpet. With a shove, he moved the desk back to its original position and rolled his chair with Jocelyn on it back into place.

He then removed several supermarket bags from an upturned cabinet. They were the durable plastic kind with reinforced handles. Into each of these, he placed two bricks.

I did not understand what was going on until I took a closer look at the bricks. The wrapping had torn off in places. I blinked and began making a calculation in my head.

How many dental crowns had gone into making such a stack of gold?

24

'So it *is* true,' I said. 'You do have a lot of gold.'

Mr Chin looked up as he placed the last bar into a shopping bag. His look was sharp and suspicious. 'Who tell you Chin have much gold?'

I realised my mistake too late. 'Mr Ding.'

'What! Chin precisely forbid talking with Ding!' His voice was dangerously high. His eyes flashed. 'You check on Chin!'

'Yes.'

'Spy! You talk other person?'

'Mr Lung.' I did not like the way Mr Chin's face had flushed but I was helpless under his penetrating gaze. 'And the Chinese Friendship Society.'

'Gamblers! Worst kind of gossip and fool.'

'They were not very friendly for a friendship society.'

Mr Chin whinnied. 'You not obey Chin. You sneak behind back. You spy and gossip.'

'*Mais, Monsieur Chin*, she did it for the best possible reasons.' Jocelyn had emptied the pencils out of Mr Chin's pencil jar and was filling it with plum liquor. 'You don't mind, do you?'

Mr Chin nodded absentmindedly, confused by Jocelyn's comment.

Jocelyn daintily put the jar to his lips and drained it. '*Prunus mume* with a hint of almond. *Délicieux.*'

'Hong Kong plum. Excellent and best in world.' Mr Chin pursed his lips in a proud way and then remembered to glare at Jocelyn. 'What you mean best reason?'

'Sherry was worried about you.' He refilled the jar. 'She saw a stranger in the office and witnessed a criminal driving your car.'

'But she defy order of boss.' Mr Chin looked from Jocelyn to me. 'What tricky Chinese that is Ding and Lung say?'

'They said you were a chicken.' I knew this would not please Mr Chin but I felt compelled to tell the truth. 'They also said you abandoned your brother in Macao to men carrying sticks and knives.'

'Wrong and incorrect! Chin not chicken!'

A thrill went through me. 'I did not believe them.'

'What you think gold for, foolish girl?'

'Chinese are very fond of it.' I did not bother reminding him that cash is king.

'Chin not Charlie Bronson. More smart and clever than so-called hero of American Hollywood. Only solution for stupid brother is buy debt. Gold for foolish and stupid brother.'

'You're very kind!'

Mr Chin looked pleased with my comment. 'Kind and generous every time.'

Jocelyn let out a contented sigh. He reclined the back of the Komfort King. His eyes closed.

'What lady man doing?' Mr Chin shook his head in a disappointed way. 'Job not finish.'

'Jocelyn has been violently assaulted twice in the past two days, which is quite a lot when you think about it. He needs to rest.'

'Crook attack Chin many time but Chin never rest.' He tapped his temple. 'English have problem up here. English have laziness for work.'

'I love work.'

'You strange and peculiar girl.'

Mr Chin pointed to two supermarket bags and gestured for me to pick them up. The gold bars had been covered with a page of the *Cockerel*. The paper was crumpled but I recognised a familiar classified advertisement: 'Put yourself in the hands of an expert. Will cure addictions, perversions and overeating.' I thought of the non-random principle and pictured the events of the past three days as a series of neon theatre scenes connected by an iridescent electrical cable.

I glanced over at Mr Tanderhill and then back to Mr Chin, who tapped his wrist in an impatient way.

Gold is a heavy precious metal, heavier than silver but not as heavy as platinum, a popular choice for wedding rings and cufflinks. I bent my knees to protect my back as I picked up the bags. Mr Chin had already handed me the car keys from Shanks's pocket. As he was doing up the money belt around his waist, he gave me strict instructions. I was to hide the bags in the back of the car and return for the others, two bags at a time. I had to do it as quickly and discreetly as possible.

'Why do you want to put the gold in the car? The police are coming.'

'So-call police and authority worst crook in Hong Kong. Wear uniform with big pocket. Stuff such pocket full of cash and money.' He made an impatient gesture. 'Hurry and fast before such person come.'

'It would be faster to form a relay and both take the bags to the car.'

'You understand nothing of English brain. Chinese with bag very suspicious.' Mr Chin narrowed his eyes. 'For English person, Chinese with bag carry dead cat or many piece of wife all chop up.'

I nodded but did not repeat what the chipman had said about Chinese and cats.

'No person notice or look at girl like you. Best safety.'

'Does that mean I'm normal now?' This was a question I had wanted to ask Mr Chin since my arrival but he had been gagged and under duress for most of the time.

'No!' Mr Chin gave me a sharp look. 'Certainly still abnormal.'

'But a moment ago you said I was strange and peculiar.'

'You abnormal, crazy and nuts.' He exhaled impatiently. 'Also strange and peculiar.'

'Oh.'

'Talking, talking too much now. Finish job then talk-talk with new so-call friend. Priority first.' He patted his lower abdomen. 'Most urgent. Crook forbid urination many hour. Painful and excruciating.'

I should have felt disappointed by Mr Chin's assessment after the efforts of the past three days, but strangely it did not seem to matter any more. Something far more important was dawning on me. Mr Chin trusted me. Never before had he allowed me to use one of his keys.

This new understanding spread through me like warm oil syringed into an ear canal as I sprang into action, dashing down and up the stairs and walking briskly to and from the car. It took less than five minutes to put all the gold in the Fiesta. When I had locked the car and returned from my final run, Mr Chin was removing the blindfold helmets from the captives, tearing the tape off their faces with relish and smiling as they cried out, blinking in fear at the light. The helmets were dismantled and the tape was stuffed in the pockets of Mr Chin's jacket. The balaclavas were placed on my desk like exhibits A and B but the ear tissues were thrown in a dustbin.

'Lady man do strange thing.' He pointed to Jocelyn. 'Make noise like kettle that is boiling.'

Jocelyn's head was tilted upwards. He was talking to the ceiling. 'Apparently the finest comes from Hong Kong,' he said. 'Native plum.'

'He's talking to his deceased mother.'

Mr Chin raised an eyebrow. I waited for him to scoff or criticise but instead, he nodded in approval. 'Make peace with ancestor best policy.'

The door at the bottom of the stairs clanged and someone began stomping up the stairs. The footsteps were solid and determined.

Big Trish appeared in the doorway and expelled a jet of air between her teeth. She gave Mr Chin a curt nod before looking around the room, taking in the jumble of furniture, cables and papers, the two bound men and Jocelyn reclined on Mr Chin's chair. She arrived at me last. Her eyes fixed on mine and narrowed.

'You want to get that light fixed on the stairs,' she said.

I nodded.

She glanced down at Shanks, nudging his bottom with the tip of her police boot. The moan she got in response seemed to satisfy her. She looked up at me with a smile. 'Looks like you've been busy.'

'Chin explain everything,' said Mr Chin, moving between us. He pointed to Mr Tanderhill and Shanks. 'Here I present crook one and two.'

'Two birds in the hand.' She looked at me over Mr Chin's shoulder.

'Chin agree fully.' He bowed graciously.

'We've been looking for these two in connection with a burglary.' She nodded at the chainsaw. 'The Hammer and Tongs hardware shop was done over.'

'Chin capture crook. Do police big favour.' Mr Chin slapped his chest to get her attention.

'I assume you're Mr Chin.' Big Trish removed a notebook from her breast pocket. 'Nigel Coote gave us a brief summary of the situation.'

'Augustus Randolph Chin is full and complete name on passport. Passport is genuine British foolproof.' Mr Chin pursed his lips into a point and nodded. 'Crook here tie up Chin for money in liquid cash. Beat and slap to inch of life. Chin say clear: "No money on premise. This telephone business not bank." But crook never believe. Crook take Chin to personal house, slap, slap, slap. Chin say again: "No money on premise. This normal house not bank." But never believe. Again, slap, slap, slap. How many beating Chin endure.'

'You look remarkably good, considering.'

'Chin always look good!' Mr Chin raised his eyebrows and flashed the policewoman a warning look. 'You look good, considering.'

'Thank you.' Big Trish looked pleasantly surprised. People with ginger hair are not often on the receiving end of compliments. 'Now, let me take your statements.'

She began with Mr Chin, who recounted the events of the past two days in a dramatic manner. I followed the description carefully, matching each turn of his story with my own experiences and taking mental notes for my OBSERVATIONS ring binder. Mr Chin explained that he had spent Friday night in the office and had been captured on Saturday when he tried to leave. The two men had been waiting for him on the stairs.

'You're in the habit of sleeping on the premises?' The policewoman frowned and surveyed the chaos.

'Friday, good and special occasion. Many plum wine for celebration. Too fiendish and painful for head. Chin must sleep many hour in luxury chair.' Mr Chin rubbed his forehead dramatically and then described how the men had tied him up and demanded money. 'Slap, slap, slap over face many time. Face skin red like arse of baboon. Chin tell them: "No liquid cash here." But they believe Chin? No and never!'

'You don't keep valuables on the premises?' Her eyes roamed around the office, pausing at Mr Chin's desk before returning to his face.

'No cash or valuable here, like Chin say.' Mr Chin shrugged his shoulders in an exaggerated way. 'Police free for search.'

'Don't worry.' Big Trish gave him a severe look. 'We'll be making a thorough investigation of the crime scene.'

'Best policy.' Mr Chin pursed his lips again before resuming his story. The assailants had then ransacked the office, turning to desperate measures when nothing of value was found. 'Small crook go out. Big crook do hurdy-gurdy with swinging necklace in face of Chin. Chin close eye. Crook get angry. Slap, slap, slap. Small crook come back. Very drunkish. Big crook attack small crook. Fighting then sleep. Then morning, more slap to Chin. Then drive to personal house. Wreck and loot. Slap, slap, slap over face many time. Then back here at office.'

'Don't tell me, then there were more slaps?'

'No!' Mr Chin gave the policewoman one of his looks. 'Slapping all finish now. Crook angry and mad. Take electric saw tool. Chop, chop, chop furniture and desk and so on.'

'That would be with one of the stolen Husqvarnas.'

'Then employee girl and lady man arrive. Chin think, "Very good and finally!" But no chance. Crook attack and tie up foolish two. Then little bastard arrive fast and suddenly. Small crook fall down too hard, hit head. Then girl do strange thing. Very tricky and wise.' Mr Chin glanced over at me and flattened his lips. 'She trick big crook. Suddenly damage knee of crook with drawer then kick in nuts that are testicles. Then so on and so on.'

'So you're the real hero here?' The policewoman moved Mr Chin aside to give me eye contact.

'No,' I said. 'It was just a series of fortuitous events.'

She shook her head in a final way. 'But a normal person wouldn't have done what you did.'

'Correct.'

'It takes courage to bring a criminal to his knees. That nut trick took some nerve.'

'Chin tell her many time. Rolly, rolly, rolly of drawer forbidden and not permitted. But she never listen.' Mr Chin was making a bid for attention but the policewoman ignored him. Her eyes remained focused on mine.

'She abnormal girl.' Mr Chin's voice was shrill.

'*Vive la différence.*' Big Trish raised an eyebrow and smiled at me. 'You're one brave lady.'

'Bravery! Ha!' Mr Chin coughed loudly. 'Try many slap over face! Sore and painful every time!'

The policewoman nodded to Mr Chin. 'Thank you for your statement, sir. Now, if you'll kindly let me get on with the others.'

Mr Chin flashed the whites of his eyes but did not say anything. I waited for him to move away before I spoke. I kept my statement brief and to the point, ending with Mr Chin subduing the men with bamboo. 'He showed no lack of courage. Mr Chin is definitely *not* a chicken.'

'But you'd already disabled the menace.' The policewoman stopped writing and looked at me approvingly. 'You were the author of the nut trick.'

'It's in the handbook on self-defence. I didn't write the handbook so I cannot say I'm the author.'

'You're not talking about the *Council Handbook on Women's Self-Defence*?'

'Yes, the 1973 edition.'

'Excellent tome. If I had it my way, we'd reprint it.' She bit her bottom lip and shook her head. 'I've read that handbook cover to cover multiple times and there's no mention of using a drawer as a weapon. As far as I'm concerned, you're not only a brave but also a very smart lady.'

The policewoman's praise made me uncomfortable, especially with Mr Chin hovering nearby. 'Is Nigel Coote in custody?'

'The boy's where he belongs.'

'With Chantal Corby?'

'That wench is in the slammer. Assault. Benefit fraud. Child abuse. We're going to throw the book at her.' Big Trish clearly took pride in putting people behind bars. 'Nigel's with his father.'

'His father was in prison.'

'The man made a mistake but he's paid for his crime. We believe he's on the straight and narrow.'

'*Quelle bonne nouvelle!*'

At the sound of Jocelyn's voice, Big Trish turned. 'You must be the gentleman Nigel mentioned.'

'*Enchanté.*' Jocelyn raised himself off the chair and gave a small bow. 'Jocelyn de Foiegras.'

'We know all about the incident in the gents.'

Jocelyn's smile froze.

'You'll be pleased to hear that Sidney Clapp's locked up. The desk sergeant would like him to shut up, too. Everyone's sick of hearing about a red Ferrari.' Big Trish shook her head. 'That scoundrel won't be beating or robbing innocent gentlemen again.'

A hesitant smile returned to Jocelyn's lips.

'We understand your reluctance to report the crime but we'd appreciate a call next time. Things are going to change around here. Warren Crumpet's promised a war on intolerance.'

'Warren Crumpet?' I asked.

'Mayor Crumpet.' Big Trish turned to me with a smile. 'The *Cockerel's* saying he won by a single vote.'

The Babylon was saved! I sought out Mr Chin's eyes but they were on Jocelyn, who was dabbing powder on his face. Jocelyn snapped the compact shut and smiled. It was the magnificent smile of a beauty queen or professional show host. It remained in place as he gave Big Trish his statement, congratulating her on the incarceration of Chantal Corby and Sidney Clapp. 'A very unpleasant pair. No manners or flair.' He smiled over at Mr Chin. 'Very slap-happy by all accounts.'

The policewoman flipped her notepad closed and rummaged in her large trouser pockets, handing business cards to Jocelyn and Mr Chin. 'If anything else comes to mind, give me a call.'

She then turned to me and held out a card. As I tried to take it from her hand, she held on, looking at me in a meaningful way. 'Give me a call,' she repeated.

'Chin tired now,' announced Mr Chin. He had moved to the doorway and was drumming his small, plump fingers on the door-frame. 'Now leaving. Chin drive employee and lady man home. Kind and generous every time.'

I smiled at Big Trish and tugged the card out of her hand. 'Thank you. I think you're a very good policewoman.'

She flushed, running her fingers over her utility belt in a self-conscious way.

'I noted your interest in tartan earlier today. I have some books on its history and the origins of the clan system. You can borrow them if you like.'

'That sounds like fascinating reading.'

'I have an affinity for the tartans of Scotland.'

'I'm a fan myself. I'm very partial to the Black Watch.'

'A handsome tartan.' I nodded to emphasise our shared admiration. 'I'll drop the books at the station.'

'Call first to make sure I'm there.'

'I will.' I held up the card. 'I would also like to ask you a few questions.'

Big Trish raised an eyebrow.

'I have a personal interest in the study of criminology. Crime is on the increase.'

'You're not wrong about that.'

'People are disgruntled and restless.'

'You've noticed.'

'I've trained myself to be observant.'

'An excellent skill.' She smiled and nodded in a satisfied way.

I caught up with Jocelyn halfway down the stairs and helped him to the bottom. Mr Chin was already in the car with the engine running. He waved and tooted impatiently as we came out from under the awning.

I was buckling up my seatbelt in the back when the car lurched out of the parking space. The dog barked and Jocelyn let out a surprised 'O-là-là' as he hastily closed the passenger door.

'First thing first,' said Mr Chin. 'Now must deposit valuable cargo.'

'I thought you were taking us home,' I replied.

'After first thing first.'

Mr Chin accelerated and released the clutch. The car shuddered and leaped forwards. I had never gone anywhere in the Fiesta but I had seen Mr Chin park it often enough to know that he was an impatient driver. He did not use indicators and had a habit of speeding up when he should have been slowing down. He did this as we neared the intersection with the high street. The lights were orange and Mr Chin was accelerating when they changed to red. He kept accelerating until we were a car length from the pedestrian crossing before slamming on the brakes and covering the distance in a skid. He cursed as the car stopped with its wheels over the white line. My seatbelt gripped and held me anchored in place but I heard a thud as Jocelyn threw his hands on the dashboard to prevent Herb Alpert from being crushed.

'If you don't mind,' he said, as he was thrown back into his seat, 'I might disembark here.'

Mr Chin twisted his head to glare at him. 'Why here now?'

'Look, over there!' Jocelyn pointed to man in a safari suit standing on the stage platform. 'It's Warren Crumpet.'

Mr Crumpet was much shorter than I had expected but held himself with poise as he spoke into a microphone. As Jocelyn got out of the car, I wound down my window hoping to catch what the new mayor was saying but his voice was drowned out by the cheers of the crowd gathered in the square below him. People were shouting and whistling and a group of revellers had formed a conga line and were cheering their way around the perimeter of the square.

Mr Chin revved the car engine as Jocelyn leaned in close to my window.

'Thank you for the adventure, my dear,' he said. 'I haven't had a whirl like that since my mother left me.'

'I'm sorry you were treated in such a brutal manner,' I said.

'It's been a while since I was manhandled.' He smiled and tucked his hair behind his ears. 'My last hurrah, I'm afraid. I'll be back on the wagon tomorrow. One thing this town does have is a vibrant AA social circle.'

This was good news. 'Your liver will be the better for it.'

Mr Chin crunched the gear stick into first and pressed his foot down hard on the Fiesta's accelerator.

'You must call on me again soon.'

I nodded but did not have a chance to reply because Mr Chin suddenly released the clutch. The car leaped forwards and flew across the intersection at high speed. As we tore past the council buildings, I saw a tall familiar figure emerge from the crowd. The Dutty looked at me and made the birdy with his hands. I rapidly put my hands together and mirrored his gesture as the car roared away.

Mr Chin kept his foot on the accelerator all the way to Val Doonican Terrace, where he skidded to a stop in front of number eight, running the wheels of the car up the kerb. I looked across the road but could see no sign of life at Roger Bottle's house. The curtains were drawn and the lights were off. The Globcom sign was gone from the gate.

Mr Chin was already unlocking his front door with two supermarket bags at his side when I got out of the car. I retrieved two more bags from the back of the car and followed him to the porch. Very soon I had ferried all the bags into the living room and placed them beside Mr Chin, who was squatting next to the large rocker-recliner chair.

Using his car key, he prised the vinyl-covered side panel off the chair to reveal a small metal door with a dial. He spun it several times. The door opened with a click. Inside were more gold bars, neatly stacked.

'Is this a safe place to keep your valuables?' I asked.

'Thief stupid and lazy,' he answered. 'Never look obvious place.'

It was true that Mr Tanderhill and Shanks had not examined the chair properly or discovered the trapdoor in the office. Mr Chin certainly understood the criminal mind. He finished stacking all the gold inside the safe and slammed its metal door shut with a satisfied sigh.

'Nice and safety.' He looked very pleased with himself as he replaced the chair's panel. 'Now Chin make special service. Driving to personal home.'

It was now or never. 'Mr Chin, should I come to the office tomorrow?'

He stood abruptly and frowned at me. 'What you mean?'

'Should I come to work tomorrow morning?'

'You think tomorrow holiday?'

'No!'

'You think you more brave than Chin? Deserve rest and relaxation and so on?'

'No!'

'Brave lady! Ha! Nut trick take no courage and nerve.' Mr Chin glared at me.

'Correct.'

'Of course, correct! Try many slap.'

'I experienced two today and that was enough.' I nodded for emphasis. There was no doubt he had endured great hardship but I needed to know where I stood. 'I want to know if I am still employed with you. I've enrolled in a part-time degree at the Open University. A job is crucial to my future career plans.'

'Why you not tell Chin before and already?' His glare turned into a scowl. He put his hands on his hips.

'I thought you might get angry.'

Mr Chin's face reddened on cue. 'Crazy and nuts!'

I waited for him to continue, afraid of what he would say next.

'Of course must do education! Education key and crucial for future. Best idea.' He took his hands off his hips.

'Are you saying that my job with you is secure?'

Mr Chin's gaze lingered on me for a moment. He sighed and, turning abruptly, led me out of the room and through the hall towards the front door. He stopped when he got to the shoes scattered over the floor to pick up a Secret Boot. Taking it by the heel, he gave it a shake. A key fell into his waiting hand. He held it out to me.

'For me?'

'Personal key for office.'

My fingers curled around the key. I felt warmth rise from my ankles to the crown of my head. 'Would you permit me to come to the office early?'

'Chin never pay overtime!'

'I would never presume.'

He nodded reluctantly and then opened the front door, ushering me out of the house. The sky had cleared and the sun was giving its last fiery blast of the day. I turned back to Mr Chin, expecting him to follow, but found him about to close the door.

'I thought you were driving me home?'

'Chin change mind. Tired now.' His face softened and he flashed a rare if not shrewd smile. 'Walking best exercise for health. Walk fast, arms up-down like soldier of Buckingham. Build up yang force. Best policy.'

ACKNOWLEDGMENTS

Heartfelt thanks to my publisher, the fabulous Patrick Janson-Smith of Blue Door, and my literary agent, the super Sophie Hicks of Ed Victor. Kindest thanks also to Laura Deacon of Blue Door and Morag O'Brien of Ed Victor. Special thanks to my writing pals Jennifer A. Donnelly and Laura Angela Bagnetto, and thanks to Gary McCreadie, Jonathan Sale, Roland Lloyd Parry and Nicholas Long. A tip of the hat to faithful friends Wayne Robinson, Tomoaki Murakami, Martin Breiter and Brian O'Donnell. To my loving brothers Robert, David and Bruce and to friends and family who kept the faith, thank you. Sincerest apologies to legitimate therapists and practitioners of genuine hocus pocus.